Seven Ghosts in Search

Fred Urquhart

Also by Fred Urquhart

Novels
TIME WILL KNIT
THE FERRET WAS ABRAHAM'S DAUGHTER*
JEZEBEL'S DUST*
PALACE OF GREEN DAYS

Short Stories
I FELL FOR A SAILOR*
THE CLOUDS ARE BIG WITH MERCY*
SELECTED STORIES
THE LAST G.I. BRIDE WORE TARTAN
THE YEAR OF THE SHORT CORN*
THE LAST SISTER
THE LAUNDRY GIRL AND THE POLE
THE DYING STALLION
THE PLOUGHING MATCH
PROUD LADY IN A CAGE
A DIVER IN CHINA SEAS
FULL SCORE (edited by Graeme Roberts)
A GOAL FOR MISS VALENTINO**

Edited Books
NO SCOTTISH TWILIGHT (with Maurice Lindsay)
W.S.C.: A CARTOON BIOGRAPHY
GREAT TRUE WAR ADVENTURES
MEN AT WAR
SCOTTISH SHORT STORIES
GREAT TRUE ESCAPE STORIES
THE CASSELL MISCELLANY, 1848-1958
MODERN SCOTTISH SHORT STORIES (with Giles Gordon)
THE BOOK OF HORSES

Other
SCOTLAND IN COLOUR (with Kenneth Scowen)
EVERYMAN'S DICTIONARY OF FICTIONAL CHARACTERS (with
William Freeman)

Reprinted with new introductions in this series by Kennedy & Boyd
** *First publication in THE FRED URQUHART COLLECTION.*

Seven Ghosts in Search

Fred Urquhart

WITH AN INTRODUCTION BY
OWEN DUDLEY EDWARDS

Kennedy & Boyd
an imprint of
Zeticula Ltd
The Roan
Kilkerran
KA19 8LS
Scotland.

http://www.kennedyandboyd.co.uk
admin@kennedyandboyd.co.uk

First published in 1983 in London by William Kimber
Text Copyright © Estate of Fred Urquhart 2014
Introduction Copyright © Owen Dudley Edwards 2014

Front cover image from *Ellen Terry* by Clement Scott
Back cover photograph from Fred Urquhart's own collection
Copyright © Colin Affleck 2014

ISBN-13 978-1-84921-129-1

To
MONICA
in memory of
JOHN PUDNEY
(1909-1977)

Author's Note

'Seven Ghosts in Search' was first published in *Blackwood's Magazine* in May 1980; 'The Saracen's Stick' in *The Twilight Book* edited by James Hale (Gollancz, 1981); 'Weep No More, My Lady' in *Queen*, August 1966; 'Witch's Kitten' in *The Midnight Ghost Book* edited by James Hale (Barrie & Jenkins, 1978); 'The Lady of Sweetheart Abbey in Denys Val Baker's anthology *Stories of the Night* (William Kimber, 1976); 'Cleopatra Had Nothing On' in my collection of stories *I Fell for a Sailor* (Duckworth, 1940); 'Water, Water Wallflower' in *The Fourth Ghost Book* edited by James Turner (Barrie & Rockcliff, 1965) and 'Proud Lady in a Cage' in Giles Gordon's collection of Scottish ghost stories *Prevailing Spirits* (Hamish Hamilton, 1976). 'What's a Few More Deaths Between Friends?' is published here for the first time as a novella, but two parts of it appeared first as short stories: 'The Ghostess with the Mostest' in James Turner's anthology *The Unlikely Ghosts* (Cassell, London, 1967) and 'He Took Me Among the Rhododendrons' in *Exclusive* magazine in December 1968.

FRED URQUHART

Introduction

I am a historian to trade, with a predatory eye to literature. Ghosts are a means to confront the past, whatever their authenticity. I was one of the occasional free-lancers used in BBC Scotland's Arts programmes in the 1980s. I wasn't usually presenter, but John Arnott, the Senior Producer, asked me to be so the week in November 1983 when Fred Urquhart was to be interviewed on his new collection of ghost stories, *Seven Ghosts in Search.* Urquhart and his partner, Peter Wyndham Allen, were still living in the wilds of Sussex at this point, but publishers produced telephone numbers and Urquhart intimated that he could get a lift to Brighton with a local farmer in order to mingle with voices broadcast from his native heath. His voice on the telephone had a strongly Scottish but slightly ladylike lilt, appropriate enough for an author frequently happier as a female narrator. For some reason I had a mental vision of Mrs Quiverful in Trollope's *Barchester Towers* travelling to Barchester courtesy of Farmer Subsoil's cart, to urge the claims of her husband to the Wardenship of Hiram's Hospital: perhaps Urquhart's fatherhood of *Seven Ghosts* inspired thoughts of the Quiverful children grimly asserted in the chapter-heading 'Fourteen Reasons in Favour of Mr Quiverful's Claims'. On the other hand, neither John Arnott nor I thought of ourselves as Mrs Proudie. We both looked forward to it. Farmer Subsoil, or whatever his name might be, seemed a welcome substitute as enabler in place of the swarms of literary agents, publishers' public relationships, or other leeches sprouted at book festivals more than broadcasts but sometimes suffered by studios which usually found them more interested in themselves than in their authors.

Fred Urquhart was of course well known by name to John Arnott, as a distinguished novelist and short-story writer but one seldom if ever in Scotland those days and hence less used by Radio Scotland. His name had been known to me since the late 1940s when I had seen it in the list of authors published in the Hour-Glass Library by Maurice Fridberg, a Dublin Jew of more generosity and imagination for Celtic authors than most of his Christian colleagues. I was young to see the list, but my mother had made me know and love 'First Confession' in the Frank O'Connor selection, and I remember being interested in the names by which the different lands were represented. Elizabeth Bowen was Ireland as well, but she was a Protestant, so this didn't count as Ireland as much as O'Connor did. Norah Hoult, a friend of Fred Urquhart's, was another Irish choice by Fridberg, but I didn't know that (she was of mixed-marriage parentage but the name Hoult, being from the Protestant parent, distanced her). But this Urquhart I was assured was Scottish. A Protestant too, I supposed. If I had managed to get hold of the Urquhart volume it might have held me almost as well as Frank O'Connor. I liked reading history stories about other small boys, notably in the Irish writers Eileen and Rhoda Power's *Boys and Girls of History*.

After I had come to Edinburgh to teach at the University, one of the most remarkable Scottish students I ever taught was Colin Affleck, who reawakened me to the claims of Urquhart, so Arnott's summons found me ready and eager. That Ellen Terry was one of the volume's ghosts – in 'Seven Ghosts in Search' – was an additional incentive. Wilde declared he would readily have married her, Shaw wrote her a passionate series of letters (the passion being mostly about theatrical performance, hers even more than his), so to meet her as a ghost (or ghosts) had all the charms of being haunted by a goddess of performance. Arnott and I were delighted by the credibility of her ghostly voice, and settled on that story to provide the appropriate extract for listeners' entertainment, intermingled with my interview of Urquhart courtesy of Farmer Subsoil (actually a wealthy, cultivated, retired formerly urban gentleman). We needed a voice in which to clothe the ghost of Ellen Terry, but Arnott had no doubts. Frank Forbes, the chief announcer, a fully licensed and unionised actor, would answer all our needs. He certainly did. His normal clear, bell-like accents vanished, and in their place purred an elderly, but magnificently resonant lady of cultivation, charm, and gracious humour. For our benefit alone Forbes settled his neck within imaginary furs as he created for radio life the greatest British Shakespearean actress of her generation. However regal its voice, Fred Urquhart could make the past live on the air no less than on the page.

Resurrecting Ellen Terry, or some other immortal, works within limits. You may bring it off, as Urquhart does here, but the more famous the ghost, the more restricted the space for the haunting you ordain. There is a great deal of information about Ellen Terry in performance, from Shaw's theatre reviews of her roles, to Wilde's sonnet in her honour, to innumerable photographs, and the Ellen Terry Museum (on which Urquhart sensibly focussed) – and then on the men in her life from her lovers to her offspring, and the playwrights, stage crews, fellow-performers, beyond them. Yet the enchantress at the remote edge of our visions with Wilde or Shaw in the foreground has the endurance and the unreality of the Pre-Raphaelite heroines alluring them whether via Ruskin (in Wilde's case) or William Morris (in Shaw's). Being Irish, they were less likely to admire Ellen Terry for her sheer Englishness, but this was precisely what the very English Max Beerbohm saw as her most obvious characteristic. Here he dissected it in the *Saturday Review* (26 March 1906):

> ... Miss Ellen Terry's sunniness seems to the English ... typically English. Exotic though this sunniness is, there is in the actual art with which Miss Terry conveys it a quality that really is native. Hers is a loose, irregular, instinctive art. It has something of the vagueness of the British Constitution, something of the vagueness of the British genius in all things – political, social, religious and artistic. ... it is just because her art is so spontaneous, so irreducible to formulae, that she has been and is so matchless in Shakespeare's comedies. She has just the quality of

exuberance that is right for those heroines. Without it, not all her sense of beauty would have helped her to be the perfect Beatrice, the perfect Portia, that she is.

The word 'British' of course means 'English' here, which is what is usually meant by English people wanting to be polite lest the poor Scots feel out of it (or even get out of it). The Irish of Ellen Terry's time (however fully in command of the English stage) were still too combative to appreciate the relaxed realities of Englishness. The Scots as always regarded Englishness as too remunerative to be left to the English, and thus the Scot Fred Urquhart knew precisely the materials whence to fashion an English ghost (including, perhaps, this Beerbohm essay, reprinted in 1970 in Beerbohm's *Last Theatres*), and thus the Scot Frank Forbes knew exactly the inflexions and intimacies with which he could make Ellen Terry's ghost haunt the airwaves from Fred Urquhart's script.

'The Saracen's Stick' as a story may reach greater heights of affection than Urquhart's tale of Terry, however much readers may turn back again and again just to see how well he captures her. The theme exists on many levels, especially dear to those who are or who were lonely children: the appearance of another child apparently befriending the solitary infant. Agatha Christie produced few short stories of the quality of her finest novels, but 'The Lamp', an early, brief ghost story, turns on a little boy dying happily having realised that by his death he will forever companion the hitherto weeping ghost of another boy who had starved to death long before. Urquhart may have known the tale (it's in Christie's somewhat neglected *The Hound of Death* [1933]): while not echoing 'The Lamp', 'The Saracen's Stick' seems to harmonise with it. Christie used without attribution lines from the first edition of Fitzgerald's version of the *Rubáiyát of Omar Khayyám*:

> Then to the rolling Heav'n itself I cried,
> Asking, 'What Lamp had Destiny to guide
>   'Her little Children stumbling in the Dark?'
> And – 'A blind Understanding!' Heaven replied.

The modern (and, as it proves, doomed) child is interpreted by his grandfather after quoting Omar:

> 'Geoffrey has that – a blind understanding. All children possess it. It is only as we grow older that we lose it, that we cast it away from us. Sometimes, when we are quite old, a faint gleam comes back to us, but the Lamp burns brightest in childhood. That is why I think Geoffrey may help.'
> 'I don't understand', murmured Mrs Lancaster feebly.
> 'No more do I. That – that child is in trouble and wants – to be set free. But how? I do not know, but – it's awful to think of it – sobbing its heart out – a child.'

This somewhat uneasily shows its cultural proximity to the Victorian era in its play with *Kindertotenlieder*, songs of dying children, to which Christie didn't return (she would have a child as very self-centred murderer many years later). But it resembles 'The Saracen's Stick' in the idea of ghost-boy and real boy strengthening one another. Urquhart makes a happier story of it for all parties except the remarkably sinister villain. But the Spirit Sinister does not have to confine its attentions to miscreants. Possibly the most frightening moment in J. K. Rowling's Harry Potter epic is in the second story, *Harry Potter and the Chamber of Secrets* (1998), when Harry finds a diary of a schoolboy of an earlier generation, Tom Riddle, who seems reassuringly and nomenclaturally akin to Tom Merry of St Jim's or Tom Redwing of Greyfriars developed over many years in the *Gem* and the *Magnet* by Charles Hamilton (aka Martin Clifford aka Frank Richards); but Riddle proves to be the cruel, treacherous schoolboy identity of the later arch-enemy of all, Lord Voldemort. It is as though Sherlock Holmes turned out to be Professor Moriarty. Was Rowling acquainted with 'The Saracen's Stick'? It exudes a faint flavour of the future Hogwarts.

But whatever its future influence, 'The Saracen's Stick' takes its strength from the past. The boy in the present may know how to cope – he certainly has the Lamp of blind Understanding – but for his thirteenth-century friend a firm if largely invisible historical grounding was essential. When I interviewed him Fred Urquhart was startled at my respect for his sense of history. 'The Saracen's Stick' is partly based on the Children's Crusade of 1212 and its myths. As it happens the subject has been transformed by my Edinburgh University colleague Gary Dickson's *The Children's Crusade* (2008), which works out its place in reality and in historical legend and the imprint of each on subsequent generations. Urquhart would die without seeing this invaluable resolution, but reputable works were available to him such as Sir Steven Runciman's *History of the Crusades* and the Powers' *Boys and Girls of History*, both of which took seriously the belief that countless French and German children turned nomads to free the Holy Land from the Saracens and were betrayed by profiteering merchants and enslaved by the Saracens. Urquhart in our interview admitted historical investigation but curiously stressed the inspiration of the detective novelist Gladys Mitchell, author of 66 mystery novels. As neither of us probably knew, Mitchell had once written a novel on the First Crusade, rejected by her publisher, which may have accounted for her bringing the idea of children trying to be detectives to *The Rising of the Moon* (1945) and to her fiftieth detective novel *Late, Late in the Evening* (1976), in which one chapter was indeed entitled 'The Children's Crusade'. Mitchell may have been all the stronger in Urquhart's mind when we talked as she had died only three or four months earlier. As he noted in this book, 'The Saracen's Stick' was its most recent item, evidently written close enough after *Late, Late in the Evening*. Urquhart in fact had forgotten its title when we spoke though remembering *The Rising of the Moon* (still in print and held in much higher esteem by Mitchell's admirers and critics in general). But it's noteworthy that both stories were admitted by Mitchell to have their child 'crusaders' based on herself and a beloved brother, and in the earlier book she made the self-portrait a boy. Urquhart might well have learned this – he came to know literary London gossip well in the later 1940s – but whether he knew it or deduced it (or neither), it harmonised well with his own methods of autobiographical gender-switching. Urquhart loved detective stories, but attempted little directly in their form: he made much use of his knowledge of their techniques in his own writing. Here he mixed them with ghosts, myths, and history, and the most chilling ingredient may be actual historical reality at back of the story.

The historian is more directly confronted by the author in 'Proud Lady in a Cage', the fruit of Urquhart's abiding fascination at his country's history throughout his near-half-century in England. In our interview he declared it based on 'straight' history (probably with an inward chuckle) by contrast with the uncertain myths revivifying themselves in 'The Saracen's Stick'. 'Proud Lady in a Cage' is from the same years of composition, but here Urquhart was required to inhabit a twentieth-century shopgirl who discovers herself to be inhabited by the ghost of an early fourteenth-century Scots noblewoman imprisoned in a cage by order of England's Edward I for crowning Robert Bruce King of Scotland. The challenge for the historian must always be how to make the reader know what happened, how it looked, how it sounded, how it smelled. The challenge for the novelist is how to make the reader believe that what is being read was true whether yesterday or seven centuries since. It is possible that other writers may be as successful as Fred Urquhart in making the fate of Isabella Countess of Buchan come to credible life, but I doubt it. The success derives in part from the austerity with which Urquhart discards his own book-learned knowledge of the Countess's fate and throws everything into the consciousness of an almost illiterate (though emphatically not innumerate) girl apparently imprisoned in the present as hopelessly as the Countess in her cage. And Urquhart leaves his audience as uncertain as his protagonist regarding what certain others know or knew of her condition. The method has been tried by other hands. M. R. James conjured up the plunging of a modern (i.e. Edwardian) lady into trial by Chief Justice Scroggs, one of the worst hanging judges in the era of the Popish plot, 1679-81, and this was horrible enough without the additional means of persecution across the centuries summoned up by Urquhart. Appropriately, James's biographer the late Michael Cox listed Urquhart as a significant contributor to the modernisation of the ghost story by reinterpreting conventions ('GHOST STORY' in *The Oxford Companion to Crime and Mystery Writing* [1999]) and even more appropriately remarked that any truly representative list would emphasise the 'continuing importance of women writers'. That would have drawn a proud smile from Fred Urquhart, on two grounds.

When I asked Urquhart about what he took to be important literary influences his first reaction was to name Americans, above all William Saroyan and Ernest Hemingway, Hemingway for directness of style, and forcing each word to count, presumably, and Saroyan probably from his ability to show tragedy from the absurd. Perhaps Saroyan's most important Irish heir in this regard was Flann O'Brien, in *At Swim-Two-*

Birds (1939) and *The Third Policeman* (posthumously rediscovered). The earliest story in *Seven Ghosts in Search*, 'Cleopatra Had Nothing On', might initially seem to turn on a titular confusion between the American usage declared at the end and the British-Irish usage of 1940 (now long ago dissolved of meaning by our Americanization but a simpering naughtiness then in keeping with viewing machines in which ladies' clothes fell off when you turned the handle). On the surface it is a harmless little lampoon of Hollywood crassness; more profoundly it pitilessly records the destruction of ancient pieties by the dictation of modern profiteers. Although none of the other stories are nearer this than a quarter-century's distance, we must remember that the 1940s established Urquhart as a mature artist of rare distinction. It is hard for us today to realise how unpopular aspects of his literary identity could make him: for instance, George Orwell was initially alienated by his homosexuality (and no doubt by his Scottishness, Orwell only losing Scotophobia after World War II). On 26 April 1940 Orwell wrote in *Tribune*:

> Mr Fred Urquhart is a short-story writer with vastly more life in him than the majority of the tribe. A striking thing about his stories is their great variation in subject-matter. They range from the sweat-shop to 'cultured' middle-class life, and from America to the slums of Glasgow. ... But I wish Mr Urquhart would keep off the subject of homosexuality, which he is apt to drag in not only when it has something to do with the story, but also when it hasn't.

xvii

But six years later Orwell was telling readers of the *Manchester Evening News* on 28 March 1946: 'few people now writing are able to handle dialogue more skilfully', and acknowledging 'One seems to hear the sharp Scottish voices rising and falling all the time as one reads' – alluding to female voices. Orwell was no mean conquest. (At that point he was reviewing the Hour-Glass Library series, and for all of his respect for the others he gave Urquhart pride of place in order of merit.) Convinced that 'sooner or later' Urquhart was 'liable to write a superlative novel', Orwell was reading his latest short stories in October 1949, four months before his own death. *Jezebel's Dust* (1951) seems to have been what he was waiting for, and may have anticipated from literary journalists' rumours, or from its precursor, *The Ferret Was Abraham's Daughter* (1949). By that stage he knew Urquhart as a fellow-worker in *Tribune*.

Urquhart did not return to the ghost story until 'Water Water Wallflower' in the mid-1960s, which looks as though it might have evolved from rhymes popular with children which suggest sinister origins. But it may in fact counterpoint the first of Somerville and Ross's 'Irish R.M.' stories, in which what servants know, and what the chimney-sweep discovers, are also pivotal, though with startlingly different results, the R.M. tale, 'Great-Uncle McCarthy', proving a mockery and swindle of the innocent narrator, while 'Water Water Wallflower' turns out to be the real thing for very ugly reasons. Urquhart cuts the solution surgically fine to throw the full context of the ghost's origin at the reader's imagination, to worry it well after the reading is over. Yet Somerville and Ross for all of their ridicule seem to have seriously believed in supernatural manifestations, to the extent that Edith Somerville insisted her cousin Violet Martin 'Ross' kept up the collaboration long after she died, whereas Fred Urquhart used ghosts with the same scientific objective dexterity with which he pigeon-holed women's cadences and concerns. If the ingredients of 'Great-Uncle McCarthy' were what brought Urquhart back to the ghost story, we may need to thank his lover, Peter Wyndham Allen, whose Irish Protestant cultural heritage would certainly have included the elegantly observant Victorian-Edwardian cousins. It is definitely known that Urquhart read and greatly admired their work; he would have found fellow-mastery in it, since for all of their landlord status (Edith Somerville was Master of her local fox-hunt), their ear for speech at all Irish social levels has never been equalled.

Somerville and Ross may also have influenced the development of Urquhart's awareness of female malevolence, their *The Real Charlotte* (1894) being a classic dissection of it. 'Witch's Kitten' unfalteringly claws the same effect in opening, where a cat's ghost eyes its own murderer while sitting on the coffin of its mistress whose death had meant the cat was promptly killed by the chief mourner. Urquhart clearly enjoyed being a cat, alive or dead. The story exploits the old belief (possibly quite true) that in the first hours after death the spirit (ghost if you prefer) clings around the immediate proximity of its body and/or its place of death. The economy of the cat's emotional responses is well judged: it can see the cruelty of heirs' indifference to the sentimental treasures of their deceased benefactor, it can indeed measure it, but it cannot suffer from it as the ghost of the former owner can. There is also an implication that cats are too independent to love humans (Urquhart knew Kipling's 'Cat That Walked by Itself' in *Just So Stories*) but that they respect and are moved by loyalty, and by revenge. The title carries its own quiet moral. The cat is not a familiar, nor its owner a witch: but the wrongs they suffer inspire their ghosts to think of themselves as such, and the implication is that over the course of history many persecuted women (and cats) may in the bitterness of ostracism and exploitation come to think of themselves as witches, or at least seek to terrify their persecutors by claiming witchly status, and hence suffer the final cruelty of being burnt alive. With their usual neglect of animals, historians don't tell us that cats were burnt alongside supposed witches who owned them, but sometimes they must have been. So much thirst for killing yearns for additional victims. The witch-theme here is worked out with care, in an impressively contrasting form to its usage in 'Proud Lady in a Cage'. But while 'Witch's Kitten' is farcical by contrast to the other's tragedy we have to be sensitive to the potential suffering behind Urquhart's laughter. It is not sadistic; often (as here) it is cold indictment even more than exultant vengeance; but the cat knows how to record cruelty. Readers are likely to treat cats with a more uneasy respect after reading 'Witch's Kitten'. It invites comparison with what surely influenced it, Saki's 'Tobermory', but that particular cat is a mental sadist with no sign of loyalty to owners. Urquhart's feline diagnosis certainly follows Saki's in one regard: if cats could talk, they would be inveterate gossips.

'The Lady of Sweetheart Abbey' opens up yet a further possibility of witchcraft, one making further use of multiple history to heighten the haunt. It works on the idea of the occasional possession of a modern by the spirit of an ancestor (Conan Doyle may have pioneered it in his 'Through the Veil', where a tourist couple visiting a ruined Roman fort discover his barbarian ancestor had killed her ancestor's fellow-Roman lover). But Urquhart's story moves from that to a different perturbation of history. Initially it seems preoccupied with the Wigtown martyrs, the famous case of the two Covenanter women drowned by Royal troops in the 1680s vividly recounted by Macaulay if slightly unconvincingly added to his indictment of Graham of Claverhouse, 'Bonnie Dundee'. The very existence of the martyrs has been called into question. Urquhart does not diminish the horror of the martyrdom, if any, but seems to have been inspired by the doubt to embroil the story with an earlier and subtler martyrdom, that of John Baliol, adjudged correctly nearest heir by male primogeniture to the dead Alexander III of Scotland but forced to defer to and depend upon the arbitrator Edward I of England, who ultimately repudiated him as thoroughly as did the Scottish people (if for different reasons). That the people ultimately rallied behind Baliol's cousin Robert Bruce explains why our rulers were subsequently called King or Queen (or even Emperor) of the Scots rather than 'of Scotland' with the right to rule ultimately coming from the community of the realm rather than the varieties of regal genealogy. (But he had to be crowned by the appropriate traditional noble ruler of Scone Castle whence the vengeance of Edward I on the Countess who thus legitimised the people's choice.)

Urquhart correctly diagnosed another tragedy in the usually despised Baliol, and zeroes in on his mother, Devorguila (all Gaelic names are spelled wrong in English). She was a claimant to the Scottish throne in her own right as the descendant of King David I (son of King Malcolm III Canmore and St Margaret). Urquhart seems to suggest she could enchant future Scottish history from her own time. We know that myths of the past are made by the future. What if the future, the present, or the more recent past, were (and are) all myths created by the remote past? In any case if the Kingship had been retained by the Baliols (or Balliols: Norman-French doesn't spell well in English either), Scotland would have settled into a Kingship subordinate to England and thus have been made a football during the Wars of the Roses in the fourteenth century, but unless the Baliols had died out in a hurry Robert Bruce's daughter's marriage to a Stewart would have been irrelevant and so the Stewart descendant Charles II would never have persecuted the Covenanters in or out of Wigtown (but someone else might have). Given the moronic obsessions of Royal Genealogy it seems only reasonable for Fred Urquhart to have put it to some worthwhile fictional and supernatural use.

The remaining stories are best read together, 'Weep No More, My Lady' being cited in 'What's a Few More Deaths Between Friends?' and both showing interesting signs of original contemplation as part of a novel (indeed, of a ghost soap opera). History is enhanced by several stories in this book (we are made to focus on the realities of rebellion and repression in Scotland's wars of independence, for instance), but in these two (what with our interval from original publication) we have perhaps the fullest documentation of the time of composition. The swinging '60s have arrived and our author is in more than one mind about them (not a bad condition in which to write ghost stories). Gay Liberation in the North Atlantic really began in 1971, but (as A. J. P. Taylor wrote in *English History 1914-1945* concerning the most famous four-letter word) gays by the 1960s had obtained 'literary but not conversational respectability'. In particular Angus Wilson's *Hemlock and After* (1951) had shown itself a novel of the first rank in which homosexuals were taken seriously, although no more immune to satire, ridicule or reproach than the rest of its vivid characters. As Orwell had rather petulantly complained, Urquhart's early work had indicated homosexual preoccupation, but in the 1940s this was more a use of the camouflage of wartime or a plea for covert acceptance than the sometimes brazen gay assertiveness in mid-1960s fiction. Urquhart in these later stories is obviously relishing the new right to speak of homosexuality as a fact of life, no worse than any other sexual expression and better than some. He was surely breaking new ground or at least new space in noting the disapproval of homosexual orgy by unwilling lady ghost spectators, though it was probably inspired by the moment in *Hemlock and After* when a bourgeoise opens a door on the oddest embrace during public building inauguration ceremonies.

But while it is agreeable to have one's way of life admitted if not accepted, liberation brought much that was less welcome. The honesty of the 1960s was one of the decade's greatest services to humanity, but it included honesty about Philistinism instead of previous deference to conventions secretly disliked. The 1950s and 1960s in particular brought devastation of architectural and environmental heritage on a scale which made the blitz of the 1940s seem almost decorous. Today most of us try to have a conscience about the conservation of our planet, and Urquhart in fact shows himself a pioneer in his disgust with contemporary profiteering vandalism. Ghosts are certainly an admirable vehicle through which to register anger at impiety to the past. But for all of the horror so frequently and even gracefully peeping out from beneath his comedy, Urquhart knew like Wilde and Shaw that laughter is a vital weapon for the crusader. Oliver Onions could use the mechanism of ghost assembly and authority for fun with the skill with which he terrified his readers, but while Urquhart admired his work he knew how to bring the discordant fear and fun to unison. He should also have been influenced by Caryl Brahms and S. J. Simon whose *No Nightingales* ends with the blitzing of the ancient house in Berkeley Square haunted by the protagonists, but his humour unlike theirs confronts the offstage brutality affecting the action. His confidence in assuming the ghostly skin of a black woman and attempting her speech carries him through to the firm assertion of the more hideous forms of white oppression under slavery. His ingenuity is endless, it seems, and his passionate love of horses eventuates 'What's a Few More Deaths' carrying on the work of Apuleius' *The Golden Ass* and Swift's fourth destination for Gulliver, where the horses are masters.

Urquhart and I didn't have time to go into all this (and much of it is necessarily a product of the thirty years since). But while he was unaccustomed to broadcasting (and his 71 years were by now weighing on him), the gallantry and *joie de vivre* were ably summoned forth. Moreover he responded to the spirit of John Arnott's decision to honour him in BBC Scotland. He began to think of returning, and when his beloved Peter Wyndham Allen died, he moved back to his native Scotland.

Owen Dudley Edwards
University of Edinburgh

Contents

I

Seven Ghosts in Search

Which ghostly part will I play today? Will I be Cordelia or Beatrice? Or will I be a Merry Wife being a bawd to shock some of our primmer visitors who remember that Ellen was a Dame Grand Cross of the British Empire?

It is the hottest afternoon of the hottest summer, and I am tired. Even though the heat cannot affect me physically any more – if someone like me can be called physical – I have not the heart to do much. I am getting so old. I was born in 1847, so what does that make me? My memory has got so bad, I need Marguerite Steen here to help me out, as she helped me that awful week in Manchester in – was it 1921? – I know it was the steamiest week of a very steamy July, several years before I became a ghost altogether. I was engaged to give Shakespeare reading between films at the Gaiety Theatre that had been turned into a cinema. Such a vulgar programme, but perhaps they hoped to make it less vulgar by having poor old Ellen Terry in it.

I would never have contemplated it, but Edy said we needed the money. After all, it was a hundred and fifty pounds for the week, and that seemed a great deal. Edy was to have come with me, but she was ill, and Marguerite took her place. Dear Marguerite, she was a godsend. She nursed me through the whole long wretched week, prompting me when I forgot my lines – which was oftener than I care to think. The manager was so pleased with her for propping old Ellen up that he gave her a cigarette case. Silver was it? Expensive I know. Where is that cigarette case now? Marguerite herself is haunting somewhere in Spain looking for the shades of her matador and Sir William Nicholson.

In Manchester, between the Pathé Gazette and a dreadful

comedy film – Chester Conklin or somebody – I did the 'mercy' speech. Shall I do it now for these two American tourists gazing at my stage costumes through the glass wall? What are the opening lines? Maybe if I did step into Portia's scarlet robes it will help me remember ... Something about mercy ... Ah! The quality of mercy is not strained.

'God have mercy on us! Hank! The dummy's moving! It has a woman's face, and she's smiling at me. Do you see her, Hank? It's a spook!'

Silly creature. What does she expect? If she visits Ellen Terry's house, even if it has been turned into a museum, does she not expect to see some ghosts?

Look at these people hurrying to find why that fool is making all the fuss. A pity they would not slip and fall on that uneven polished passageway, as I so often slipped until I got too old to hurry and crawled along holding onto the wall. But I am being uncharitable. They have paid their money and must be entertained. They are the audience and as long as they applaud, or seem to applaud, by appreciating my former possessions, I must appreciate them.

Will I give them another ghostly showing now that I have stepped out of Portia's legal robe? I wander among my other costumes displayed on the dummies. Will I be Ophelia? But no, let us leave that until I go outside, then I shall float on top of the scummy canal-like stream that runs beside the garden. Edy always called it 'the river' but it is not broad enough, not wild enough, not abandoned enough to be a real river.

Will I be Ellen playing Juliet? While the visitors look through the glass wall, and her husband tries to pacify that screaming woman – poor man, I feel so sorry for him – shall I step into Juliet's shoes and show them the magic of old Verona?

Or is it Lady Macbeth, the dark one, the forlorn one, the mad one, the visitors would like to see? Oh, my loves, which one of you shall I be? Where are all of you now, the parts I used to play? Not in these gossamer-thin stage costumes that would crumble at a touch stronger than that of ghostly old Nell.

I shall go downstairs and stroll in the garden.

There is a coachload of blue-rinsed ladies outside the gate.

Are they coming in? Is entrance to the Museum part of their conducted tour? They are gawking at the house and giggling to each other. Shall I show myself? Shall I play the part of Dame Ellen Terry receiving guests at her farmhouse at Smallhythe in Kent? Shall I make this the most memorable day of their limited suburban lives? What would they do if they saw old Ellen in her regency-striped pink and mauve dress rising from the sunny haze of the garden?

That was what I was wearing one day when a coach like this – only much smaller, what used to be called a charabanc – with a similar contingent of gossip-hungry women stopped at the gate. Even in those days this was a common enough occurrence. I always went inside and hid whenever a charabanc appeared. But that day I couldn't hide. Already I was sitting in the pony-trap with Edy beside me holding the reins. 'Bow to them, Mother,' she said. 'Bow!' And so I did what I was told, and Edy whipped up the pony and away we high-stepped to Tenterden to do the weekly shopping. I sat beside Edy on the green leather cushion with one hand clutching my large pink straw hat, the one with violets sewn all over the brim, though there was really no need to hold, for a mauve tulle motoring veil was keeping it firmly in place.

In Tenterden Edy drew up the pony with a flourish in the middle of the street, opposite the grocer's. You could do that in those days, there was so very little traffic. And she shouted: 'Ahoy there, Mr Sidebotham! Mr Sidebotham!' And she cracked the whip several times and little Mr Sidebotham came running. He had strands of dyed black hair glued across his brown bald skull, and he smoothed them down even more as he stood beside the trap, bowing and saying: 'Good afternoon, Miss Craig. Good afternoon, Miss Terry madam. And what can I do for you this fine afternoon, Miss Craig?'

After Edy had given the order she shouted for the butcher. He was waiting. He catapulted out as soon as she shouted: 'Ahoy there, butcher!' And once again we heard the chorus: 'Good afternoon, Miss Craig. Good afternoon, Miss Terry madam.' They always called me 'Miss Terry madam.' I found this rather irritating.

That was a few years before I was made a Dame. I wasn't made one until 1925 and so, seeing I died in 1928, I hadn't long to enjoy being called 'Dame Ellen'. I should have been made a Dame much earlier. I would have been if my friend Queen Alexandra had had anything to do with it. She was a nice woman and a real friend. But it wasn't politic then to make actresses Dames of the British Empire. Genevieve Ward was the first. In 1921. Who remembers Genevieve Ward now? I should have been made a Dame at the same time, but I was passed by although my name was a household word.

It grieved Edy much more than it grieved me. She was a curious girl, Edy. Always a strange one. The servants were more in awe of her than they ever were of me. Or of my dearest Ted, even though he must have appeared strange enough, for I once heard one of them say: 'Mr Gordon Craig's a proper coughdrop with 'is sombrero and 'is long black cloak.' But Edy – they never called her 'Miss Edy'. She was always given the benefit of the full 'Miss Edith'. I did not know she was a lesbian until after I died. How could I? People did not talk then about lesbianism, even the ones who knew about it. I knew Edy was odd, of course; I knew there was something fishy about the great friendship between her and that girl who called herself Christopher St John, the one who helped Edy to write *Ellen Terry's Memoirs*. I never really liked that girl St John. I didn't like the book either. She wasn't the girl I would have chosen to be my ghost. I preferred Marguerite Steen, and I told her: 'You must write all this after I'm dead. You must make a picture of all of us.' And that is what she did. She wrote a very good book about the whole family, *A Pride of Terrys*. Old Ben would have been proud of it and the raggle-taggle race he spawned.

Bugger it, I manifested too late! The blue-rinsed gapers have gone.

I learned that word from Ben, who had quite a flow of picturesque expressions. He used them along with his slipper when we were children and did not learn our lines or enunciate words properly. Ben disapproved of anything slipshod. He would have considered this manifesting too late to be very bad stage-management indeed.

A pity I was not on cue. There is nobody here now to see old Nell in her regency-stripe. So many motors are parked along our road that the coach has had to go as far as the bridge to find a parking place. I shall go there and be Ophelia madly dying. That will give the blue-rinsed ladies a treat. I say ladies rather than women, for they give such genteel comic ladylike squeaks when they look over the bridge and see me floating on the scummy green stream.

I wave up to them and cry: 'There's fennel for you, and columbines; there's rue for you; and here's some for me; we may call it herb of grace o' Sundays. O! you may wear your rue with a difference. Sweet ladies.'

Perhaps they already rue the cost of their coach tour? So that will make up for it. That will make them remember their visit to Ellen Terry's house. I wish Henry had been here to give them his gloomy Hamlet glower and declaim, while he held my head: 'That skull had a tongue in it, and could sing once.' The gapers would then have had their money's worth. Two stars for the price of one. Even though I was sometimes overshadowed by Henry at the Lyceum – only because his parts were longer and his lines more abundant – we were good partners. Dear Henry, I miss him.

In the dining-room there are only a few visitors. The one who attracts me most is a tall young man with shoulder-length golden hair, perfectly straight and shed in the middle, giving him an almost prissy look. He wears a very dark business suit, and his hands are clasped behind his back as he marches – there is no other word for his brisk military movements – from one exhibit to the next. He looks at them with an impassive face. He is looking now at the portrait of Sarah Bernhardt. I wonder who he is and what has brought him here. Is he an actor? Is he a BBC producer? I wish he had someone with him so that I might hear his voice. Voices mean so much to me. Has he come here as a Terry admirer? Or was he just passing and come in to spend an idle hour? Or is he hoping to pick up a girl? He looks lonely. I shall show myself to him.

As I was when I was sixteen. The tomboy Nelly with what Charles Reade used to call my 'harvest-coloured hair', my big hands and my big feet, and wearing the brown silk dress I wore when I married old George Frederick Watts. I still wonder what made me marry 'The Signor', as that malevolent woman Prinsep always called him. He thought about nothing but his painting, and Mrs Prinsep encouraged him. That nasty woman who was responsible for separating us. But I forgot Mrs Prinsep long ago – if I still don't forgive her. And I forgot Watts too. Let him stick to his old canvases and the drip at the end of his nose. All I want to remember is that everybody said then that Nelly Terry was a romp.

'Excuse me, sir, can I help you? You look lost. Perhaps I could guide you round the exhibition? I am very familiar with the place. I am Mrs G. F. Watts. I was billed as that before I was divorced from Watts – you may perhaps have seen the famous portrait he painted of me? I was furious because I meant no name to be as famous as that of Ellen Terry, but the management insisted.'

Whatever is the man saying? Gabble, gabble, gabble. Sounds like German or Russian. Double Dutch to me, anyway! He gives me a jerky bow, unclasps his hands and marches out of the door. Oh dear, you backed a loser that time, Nelly. Obviously the one man who does not think Nelly is great fun.

I shall go upstairs and see what response I get there. It is my duty to appear to my public. Somebody once said – was it Bernard Shaw? – that I was an actress who needed to be seen as well as heard. I am beginning to feel like one of Pirandello's six characters in search – of what? Satisfaction? Perfection? Or the real Nelly Terry?

A family is crowded against the glass wall of the costume room. The father is a big man, very broad, wearing a white shirt and tight fawn trousers. Rather a handsome man, distinguished-looking. The mother is a little wax doll nonentity, and her arm is clamped firmly into the man's while she gazes up at him. My costumes mean nothing to her. They have two daughters, big and fair and cowlike, aged maybe twelve and thirteen, wearing bathing costumes that hardly cover them decently. Also a boy of nine or ten, very slim and dark, quite unlike his sisters. He is good-looking and wears nothing but a pair of briefs. For a moment I think I have strayed onto Brighton beach. I can almost hear the cries of the hokey-pokey man and the deck-chair attendant. The girls are pressing so tightly against the glass that their noses are squashed, making them more pudding-faced than ever. They will grow up to be like their mother. The boy stands back, aloof and silent, but he is taking in everything.

One girl says: 'Dad, what're we lookin' at all them old dresses for? Dad, why did we come into this creepy old place? When're we gunner Camber Sands?'

'Yes, Dad, when're we gunner 'ave chips?'

The boy says nothing. He eases his briefs and lets them slap back against his moist brown skin.

Old Ben Terry, that purist of language, would have slipped these girls. I think of manifesting as Lady Macbeth sleep-walking to give them a fright. But they are not worth it. I content myself by slapping each girl on her bottom. They do not even move. As I pass him I caress the boy's back. He looks over his shoulder, but his aloofness does not waver.

There are only two people in the Library. Two middle-aged men who are not together and obviously don't want to know each other. It is extraordinary that the Library should be the least visited room in the house. Of course, few people read nowadays; they are too busy watching television. That would never have done for me. I loved to have books on the shelves, taking them out and looking at them. Not that anybody can do that here. The National Trust has fenced my books in behind immovable glass. A reasonable precaution, of course. Otherwise they would become tattered by mishandling and also perhaps get stolen.

I stand beside the man looking at the telegrams and letters in the glass case in the middle of the room. He is reading a letter inviting me to visit her little mountain home and ending 'Best love, and bless you, Nellie Melba'.

I materialise beside him wearing the lavendar muslin dress I wore at Melba's home that time I was on a lecture tour in Australia. Dear Melba, she was a marvellous woman, but a bit of a trial sometimes. I always appreciated her most when she was singing.

'Good afternoon,' I say.

He looks at me over his half-moon glasses and says: 'Didn't notice you coming in. Come by helicopter, ha? Might have. One minute nobody, the next you're here. Do I know you? Seems to me I've seen you before. Face is very familiar.'

'My face is all over this house, sir,' I say and vanish.

I hover in the Lyceum Room watching the ebb and flow of

visitors. Some examine everything closely, standing long before each exhibit. Some hurry through, glancing only briefly while talking all the time to their companions. I would like to sit down, but two old women are sitting on my day-bed, although a notice says it is not to be touched. Will I frighten them off? No. I will be charitable; they are dazed, like myself, by the heat.

My attention is diverted by a handsome young man looking at the poster advertising my 50th anniversary on the stage in 1906 in *Captain Brassbound's Conversion*. With James Carew as my leading man. Bold brash James with his face like a Red Indian's. Not indeed unlike this young man.

'Tell me, sir, are you interested in the work of Mr Shaw? Or are you interested in Ellen Terry? Have you seen any recent productions of Brassbound? If so, I should be interested to hear who played my part?'

The young man – he is much bigger than James Carew but as magnetic – backs away a step at the sight of Ellen, nearly sixty years old, in Lady Cicely Waynflete's black velvet gown. 'Ellen Terry,' he whispers. 'I never expected to meet your ghost.'

'And why not, sir? If you come to my house, you must expect to find me – in spirit, anyhow.'

'I am honoured, Dame Ellen. I'm so honoured that I can't believe it's true. I must be dreaming ... but oh, what a magnificent dream!'

'You're a sweet young man,' I say, and I touch his cheek with my lips before I drift through the wall into my bedroom.

Certainly a much sweeter young man than my third husband, James Carew, the Red Indian from Indiana. James and I didn't last long. When he kicked my dog it was a good excuse to get rid of him.

The afternoon is almost over. The visitors are thinning out. Yet there are more in my bedroom than I care for at nearly five o'clock. Here are big fair Dad and his wife and family. I thought they had gone long ago to Camber in search of chips. Little wifie and those two blonde hockey-players don't have as big a grip on Dad as they think. The dark good-looking boy moves silently behind them. Like Dad, he looks closely at the large paintings of my mother, Sarah, and Edy and Ted as children. He reads the telegrams from Queen Alexandra and George V. Then he moves to the school-desk where my children were taught their lessons. And he sits down.

What is he thinking of, this aloof boy with the brooding eyes? Is he thinking that he too will go on the boards? Does he see himself as a Laurence Olivier or a John Gielgud of the future? Who knows what is going on inside that dark head? I sit beside him and say: 'I was about your age – I was nine – when I made my debut as Mamillius in *The Winter's Tale* on the 28th April 1856. It was a fine occasion, not only for me but for the whole company, for we acted in the presence of Queen Victoria and Prince Albert. I should have been nervous but I wasn't. I wasn't at all nervous of the Queen, who smiled and waved at me from her box when I made my bow. I was much more nervous of Charles Kean and his wife Ellen Tree. Even though she was my namesake I was terrified of Mrs Kean. I was with the Kean Company for three years – years that were too often punctuated by Mr Kean ringing a handbell every time one of the actors did something that displeased him.'

'Where did that little gal come from, Hank? Oh my God! Don't tell me it's another spook!'

That stupid American woman again. I thought she had gone long ago. She is spoiling what is perhaps my most rewarding encounter of the day. This boy has imagination and will never forget our meeting. A pox on that woman! I stick out my tongue at her before I vanish, giving the dark boy a reassuring pat on the head. I know that he knows I have planted a seed that will flower.

I am tired; I have manifested seven times, and that is enough for one day. The audience is going. As the curator ushers out Dad and his family and Hank and his wife, the dark boy looks towards the corner where I am standing, unseen to all the rest, and he smiles.

I smile back to him, and I bow. 'Farewell, boy, may the gods be kind and let you do what you wish.' Then I look at the photograph of the young man on the wall beside me, the photgraph inscribed 'To Ellen Terry with love from Siegfried Sassoon'.

And so I settle on my bed to while away another night in the realm of the dead, and I will recite Siegfried's poem *Grandeur of Ghosts* if I can remember the lines:

> When I have heard small talk about great men
> I climb to bed; light my two candles; then
> Consider what was said ...
>
> How can they use such names and be not humble?
> The dead bequeathed them life; the dead have said
> What these can only memorise and mumble.*

* Reproduced by kind permission of George Sassoon.

II

The Saracen's Stick

Cameron was sitting, chin on knees, in an embrasure of one of the three remaining towers of the ruined castle, gazing out to sea, when he saw Mr Hikmet waddle through the great archway into the courtyard. Knowing that the fat Turk had not seen him yet, Cameron slipped down and crouched behind some fallen masonry.

A voice behind him whispered: 'Who are you hiding from?'

A boy of about his own age, eleven, was leaning against the green-tinged stone wall: a boy half-naked like himself, except that Cameron wore brief white shorts and this boy wore a kilted kind of saffron coloured loin cloth. Cameron stared. It was like looking at himself in a mirror – the same cap of short-cut curly scarlet hair, the same white face with an alabastrine sheen, the same height, the same arrogant poise of the head thrusting out from the same slim shoulders.

'Who are you hiding from?' the strange boy repeated.

'From him,' Cameron said. 'That man down there.'

The boy said: 'Why?'

'Because he keeps touching me with his sweaty hands and poking me with his stick,' Cameron said. 'I don't like him.'

'The Emir Sulieman, lord of all he surveys,' the boy said. 'Who could like the Saracen slug?'

'He's not an emir and he's not a Saracen,' Cameron said. 'His name is Hikmet and he's a Turkish millionaire.'

'He is the Emir Sulieman,' the boy said. 'I know him from olden days. I know him far too well, and I have an old score to settle. I'll get rid of him. As soon as I speak to him, run for your life and don't look back.'

Cameron said: 'Who are you?'

'I am a Christian boy called Simon,' he said and vanished.

The next instant he was in the courtyard walking towards the fat Turk. Cameron did not pause to wonder how Simon had reached the courtyard so quickly; he skirted round the masonry and, looking to make sure the Turk's back was to him, he darted down the stairs and into the archway. Once inside the shadow of its thick wall, his curiosity made him look back. He saw Simon dancing in front of the Turk and, walking backwards, lead the man towards the wide stone steps down to the black passages and underground caverns, all that remained of the old Saracen dungeons. The boy kept capering provocatively, and the Turk was waving his stick and laughing.

Cameron ran towards the village, the hotel and safety, wondering who the boy was and how he could have appeared like that out of the air.

*

Perhaps if Nanny Cruikshank had remained in the Lebanon Cameron might never have been pestered by the fat Turk or have visited the Saracen's castle. If Nanny had had her way Cameron would have spent the summer in Scotland with his parents. But Sir Ranald Locherbie did not want to interrupt a very delicate dilpomatic negotiation in Beirut by going home to Ardavalloch for even a short period. And so Cameron came to the Lebanon instead. Sir Ranald had arranged that one of his prep school teachers would take Cameron to the airport and a stewardess would look after him on the plane. But Sir Ranald had reckoned without Nanny Cruikshank, who had been ruining his plans since he was a boy and whom he thought safely ensconced now, out of reach, as chatelaine of Ardavalloch. Nanny said it was a fair scandal that the poor bairn should be expected to travel all that distance alone into the wilds with only a label round his neck, so to speak. It was a perfect disgrace to the Family, and although she loathed setting foot in a plane she would bring the dear lamb to Beirut herself.

If Sir Ranald had reckoned without Nanny, she had reckoned without the Lebanon heat. 'However do you thole it, Miss Ollie?' she said to Lady Locherbie. 'It's like being in a steaming hot bath-tub. All my undies are sticking to me.'

'You shouldn't wear so many, Nan dear,' Olive said. 'Be like me and wear practically none.'

'Och, I wouldn't feel decent. Just think if I got knocked down and what they'd say at the hospital when they found I hadn't a stitch on except my jumper and skirt. I'd never live it down. And neither, I'm sure, would you nor Sir Ranald either.'

'Well, you'll just have to keep your weather eye open and see you don't get knocked down,' Lady Locherbie said.

Nanny's stay was not long enough, however, for her to keep her weather eye on anything; for she had been only two days in Beirut when Dr Mitchell at Ardavalloch phoned and told her to return to Scotland at the toot because her sister Libby, who had been left to uphold the family name and keep the other estate retainers on their toes, had broken her hip. And so, protesting loudly at the inconvenience and about leaving the Family to cope without her, Nanny set off, in grey twin set, thick grey flannel skirt, thick ankles overlapping stout sensible black lacing shoes, her apple cheeks wrinkled and her small mouth puckered with self-righteous Scottish disapproval of Middle Eastern dirt and degradation.

Cameron was delighted to see the back of Nanny. So was his father. 'I'm so chuffed to get rid of the old girl, I'm over the moon,' Sir Ranald said. Ranald had endured Nanny's domination ever since his mother had died when he was two years old. Even marriage to Olive had not lessened the domination, for Nanny had taken on a mother-in-law role. Olive, heiress of the neighbouring estate, was an orphan too, and Nanny had taken her under her wing. At Ardavalloch the Locherbies were also under the domineering eye of Libby Cruikshank, who had been the fork to her sister's knife from the time they were born within sixteen months of each other in the head gardener's cottage. 'Sometimes I wonder why some of the other peasants don't do Nanny and Libby in,' Ranald said to his wife when he returned from seeing Nanny off at the airport. 'I could lay a bet on it that some joker is responsible for our Lib's broken hip. What odds'll you give that she wasn't up a ladder keeking into the kitchen maid's bedroom?'

'There are no kitchen maids at Ardavalloch nowadays,

darling,' Olive said.

'Well, I mean the equivalent,' he said. 'You know that every girl on the estate, whether she's a groom or an *au pair*, is pure dirt in the gimlet eyes of the Cruikshank lassies.'

Nanny left Beirut before her gimlet eyes and the lady herself told her that Olive was pregnant again. Olive had had a few miscarriages and two children who'd died in infancy, but she and Ranald still hoped for another boy so that Cameron need not bear alone the burden of family tradition.

*

Soon after Nanny Cruikshank left, Sir Ranald took his wife and son to a large seaside hotel several miles from Tripoli. Their Egyptian *au pair*, Faerida, came with them to keep Cameron company while his mother was resting and his father was away to Beirut for diplomatic meetings. Faerida, a rather overblown sixteen, quickly became acquainted with a soldier at the barracks outside the village, so she and Cameron came to an understanding: as long as Cameron did not tell his parents, Faerida would leave the boy alone to do what he liked.

Cameron spent a lot of time exploring the ruins of the Saracen's castle on the cliff a mile from the hotel. And it was on the castle battlements that he first encountered Mr Sulieman Hikmet.

Cameron had witnessed Mr Hikmet's arrival at the hotel. It had impressed him. It was an arrival embellished by much scurrying of Arab page-boys carrying Mr Hikmet's pile of expensive luggage while Mr Hikmet stood in the centre of the foyer waving a long thin gold-topped cane, shouting instructions and once, to Cameron's horror, striking one of the pages on the bottom with his cane.

Cameron remembered this when he came face to face with Mr Hikmet at the top of the castle that afternoon. Mr Hikmet still carried his cane, though it was so slender and delicate it could not have been any help to him in his climb to the battlements. He was a large stout man who seemed old to Cameron. The boy had heard his father telling his mother: 'The fellow's a bit of a git by the look of him, millionaire or no millionaire. He's over-weight and over-oily. He waddles like a dirty old duck, m'dear. About my own age, I'd think.'

Cameron knew his father was forty. He could not believe that Mr Hikmet with his large pockmarked nose, thick lips and skull of close-cropped grey hair was anywhere near as young as his jolly, effervescent good-looking and boyish Dad, always game for a lark.

'The little English boy!' Mr Hikmet greeted Cameron on that first afternoon. 'I see you in hotel. *Bon jour*, English boy. How are you?'

'*Je suis* smashing, monsieur,' Cameron said. 'And please, monsieur, I am not English. I am Scottish.'

'English! Scottish! What does it matter, eh? You go school in England?'

Cameron said: '*Oui, monsieur.*'

'You go Rugby?'

Cameron said nothing. He was watching the sweat glisten on the Turk's wobbling jowls, and the beads of moisture sliding out of the huge pores on his bulbous nose.

'Dr Arnold! Cold baths! Beatings!' The Turk sniggered. Cameron turned his head and looked down at the waves dashing against the rocks far below.

The Turk placed a plump hand on the boy's head and pressed it down. Cameron's scalp crawled with distaste. 'Pretty English boy,' Mr Hikmet lisped. 'Your master beat you?'

'Scottish,' Cameron said. 'And he doesn't.'

Mr Hikmet giggled. He flicked Cameron's bottom with his cane, then he let it slide caressingly down the boy's thighs. Cameron shivered as the cold wood touched his bare skin.

'Don't do that,' he said.

The fat Turk giggled. 'Say please!'

Cameron glared at him. 'Excuse me,' he said, moving past the man, 'My parents are waiting for me.'

And he ran down the worn old slabs of stair and did not slacked his pace until he was well beyond the castle's archway.

*

That evening when Cameron and his parents and Faerida

were waiting for the elevator to take them to the restaurant on the hotel roof, Mr Hikmet joined them. 'Aha, my little English friend!' he said, putting his hand on Cameron's shoulder. 'You must introduce me to Mama and Papa. And this beautiful young lady. She is your sister?'

He was carrying his cane. In the crowded elevator he stood behind Cameron and pushed its gold top into the base of the boy's spine, grinding it like a chemist grinding a pestle in a mortar. When Cameron jerked forward, Mr Hikmet pulled him back and held the boy firmly against him.

'I can't stand that man,' Olive Locherbie said when they were seated at their own table, having resisted Mr Hikmet's attempts to stay with them.

'Don't be so ridiculously Auld Kirk, Ollie,' Sir Ranald said, 'You're as bad as Nanny. There's nothing wrong with the fellow, except he's too fat and laughs too much. And why does he carry that grotty cane? All right if he was on a horse, but no bloody good for walking. Got no body in it. What the fellow needs is a stick as stout as himself. But why bring it to the dining-room? He's not lame.'

'He's a *poseur*,' Olive said. 'He keeps wanting to draw attention to himself. There's something slimy about him that I can't bear. He gives me the grue. Don't have anything to do with him, Cameron. I heard him inviting you to go for a walk with him tomorrow. Well, don't.'

'I won't, Mummy. I told him I couldn't.'

'Cassandra of the League for Presbyterian Purity!' Ranald said, laughing. 'Honestly, dear, you take the bloody biscuit. Stop behaving like Jenny Geddes throwing her stool at the poor old Archbishop. You and Nan! What a mercy she's not here. She'd have been after poor old Hikmet with bell, book and candle.'

'I wouldn't blame her,' Olive said. 'There's something evil … something dreadfully uncanny about the man … "

*

Cameron dodged Mr Hikmet successfully for several days. The only times he allowed the Turk to speak to him were when he was in the foyer or with his parents or Faerida. It was difficult, though, to avoid him outside the hotel, for Mr Hikmet was always walking on the mile of beach between the hotel and the castle. So, unless he went on the terrace, which usually was crowded with other visitors, Cameron stayed in the foyer close to Leo, the tall smiling young Nigerian at the reception desk. There were no children of Cameron's age in the hotel, but he and Leo were attracted to each other, and Cameron felt safe when he was within his big black friend's orbit. Leo was an archaeological student at the French university in Beirut, and he had taken this hotel job for the summer.

It was Leo who took Cameron in the first place to the Saracen's castle on the cliff. The castle had been a stronghold in the days of the Crusades, and many of its old battlements and defences still remained. Leo told Cameron a great deal about the original layout and the customs of the Moslems who had lived there, and the boy was so fascinated by the pinkish-beige ruins with their subterranean passages and strange nooks that he visited them alone several times without anything out of the ordinary happening. The ruins were always deserted except for sea birds and lizards and small scurrying animals. But after Mr Hikmet's arrival, although still drawn towards the castle, Cameron did not dare approach it in case he met the Turkish millionaire either on the beach or on the rough track leading past the garrison and through the sand dunes. If he met Mr Hikmet among the high lonely sand dunes it would be almost impossible to escape from him.

Three days after the fat Turk's arrival, Leo managed to get some free time, and he again took Cameron to the castle. They explored the dungeons beneath the ruins: parts of which Cameron had been afraid to enter when alone. Some of the dungeons were still in much the same condition as they had been in centuries ago, but the walls of others had collapsed, leaving only great black holes that reeked of rotten vegetation, from the depth of which the bright eyes of rodents appeared like miniature searchlights.

Cameron kept close to Leo as they scrambled over the piles of fallen stones and wormed their way from one dark cavern to the next. Their torch-beams picked out bits of rusty iron chains still hanging from the walls, and in one dark corner the remains of a great bench studded with barbaric iron brackets and spikes.

'I certainly don't take to this place, Cameron boy,' Leo said. 'It's got a voodoo. There's something real evil about it. It doesn't bear to think about what men did to other men in these dark holes. C'mon, let's get out of here quick-quick before we start meeting spooks.'

Cameron shivered and clung to Leo's warm comforting waist. They climbed to the top of the battlements to get welcome sea-fresh air. Leaning against a broken turret, they watched Mr Hikmet walking on the beach far below. He was wearing a dark reddish suit, and he resembled a large undecided crab as he kept pausing uncertainly and poking in the sand with his thin stick. Leo grinned at Cameron, then he bent over the parapet and spat in Mr Hikmet's direction. He made some esoteric signs with his hands.

'My people's way of warding off evil spirits, Cameron boy,' he said. 'But I wouldn't advise you to copy it. If ever you see anything bad, boy, you run away from it. Quick-quick. You listen to Leo and do that. Quick-quick.'

*

Next day, emboldened by his visit with Leo, Cameron went alone again to the castle. And it was then he encountered both Mr Sulieman Hikmet and the scarlet-haired boy who came out of thin air.

He ran as fast as he could to the hotel. He spoke to Leo for a few minutes but said nothing about Mr Hikmet and the strange boy. He knew his mother was resting, and he guessed his father would be writing letters or on the telephone to Beirut; so he went to his room and started to read C. S. Lewis's *The Horse and His Boy*, which Leo had given to him. But he could not concentrate. Even though he realised there was a similarity between his own detestation of Mr Hikmet and the boy Shasta's fear of becoming the slave of the Tarkaan lord who owned the talking horse Bree, he could not give the story his full attention for wondering about the boy with the scarlet hair. Where had he come from? Had he been hiding somewhere? Cameron had been in the castle for an hour before Mr Hikmet arrived. He had been alone in the ruins. Where had the boy been hiding? How had Cameron not seen him approaching the castle's gateway, which he had had under observation all the time? Had the boy Simon really come out of thin air as he had appeared to do? Was he one of the spooks in the dungeons that Leo had spoken about?

That evening, after dinner, Leo came to the Locherbies' sitting-room to play cards with Cameron and Faerida. He told them with amusement that Mr Hikmet's man-servant had been worried all afternoon because the millionaire had not returned from his after-lunch walk, and there had been a great commotion a short time ago when the Turk had arrived with his garments in a filthy state, his feet and legs wet, and behaving in a hysterical fashion. 'He says that you shut him in a dark hole in the old Saracen castle, Cameron, and then ran away and left him to die,' Leo said.

'*Quel menteur!*' Faerida cried. 'I was wis Cameron all day and we never see one tiny speck of that horrid Turkish man.'

'Of course, he's a liar,' Leo said, and he winked at Faerida; he knew she had spent most of the afternoon with her boyfriend at the garrison. 'He says Cameron pushed him into the old dungeon and then rolled a great boulder in front of it so he couldn't get out for hours.'

'I never heard such bloody nonsense,' Sir Ranald said, looking up from the diplomatic papers he was supposed to be reading. 'I'm not denying that Sunshine here is a pretty good strong boy for his age, but I'm damned if I can see him doing this to a man of that fat git's weight. I'll have a word with the fellow.'

'What a shit the man is,' Lady Locherbie said. 'But what else can you expect from a man with his background? They say he was a rag and bone man before he became a millionaire.'

'The fellow's just a jumped-up git,' Ranald said. 'He's got no breeding. He'll be more hysterical by the time I'm through with him.'

'Y'know, there's something terribly old, something terribly evil about him.' Olive Locherbie shivered. 'I can't bear the sight of him. Those oily chops ... "

'Mr Hikmet has lost his stick,' Leo said, shuffling the cards.

'No harm,' Sir Ranald said. 'Grotty stupid thing – like the grotty stupid clot himself. I say!' He grinned at them all. 'Do excuse me for using such an outdated jargon word. I don't particularly care for it, but it seems to suit the fellow.'

'He is a super clot, sir,' Leo said.

'Super clot or not, we should all steer clear of him,' Olive Locherbie said. 'And you, Cameron, steer clear of that old ruin as well. It bodes no good.'

*

Despite his mother's warning, Cameron set off early next morning for the Saracen's castle. Leo had told him that Mr Hikmet was still in bed, suffering from shock, and was likely to remain there for a time.

There was something so menacing about the ruins high above the great piercing spray-splashed rocks that Cameron was tempted to stay on the sandy beach, heed his mother's warning, call it a day and retrace his steps. But he was determined to find the scarlet-haired boy, Simon, so he climbed towards the archway leading into the ruins, every nerve alert.

There was no sign of a living soul anywhere. Cameron went up the worn stone steps to his favourite seat in the embrasure of one of the towers. At the top of the steps was Mr Hikmet's gold-topped cane. Cameron kicked it aside and went to the embrasure. He sat down with his back to the sea, so that he could see anyone approach the gateway from all sides. He had been sitting for ten minutes when a voice said:

'So you have come back, *mon cher*, to release my ghost from bondage?'

The Christian boy called Simon stood beside him.

'I willed you to come back,' Simon said. 'I knew you'd come because of the ties of blood. For only someone of my own blood can free me from bondage.'

Cameron said: 'Are you truly a ghost?'

'I am truly a ghost.' Simon sat beside him and put a hand on Cameron's knee. Although it was cold, it felt like any other boy's hand, and the shoulder pressing against Cameron's was solid enough.

'I am one of your ancestors,' Simon said. 'In truth, I am not one of your forebears, for I died in the year 1213 when I was eleven years old. But my father was Sir Uchtred de Locherbie, and I presume you are descended from the child my lady mother was carrying when I set off on the Crusade.'

'There are several Uchtreds in our family tree,' Cameron said.

'And many Simons?'

'The eldest son is always christened Simon,' Cameron said. 'It has been a custom for hundreds of years, though he has several other names attached and often is called by one of these. I was christened Simon Alexander Uchtred Cameron, and my father is Simon Ranald Uchtred.'

'My ghost may be allowed to return to Scotland if you will help me,' Simon said. 'I have longed for over seven hundred years to leave this Moslem castle and go home.'

'But how can I help you?' Cameron said.

'By killing the Emir Sulieman.'

Cameron stared at the boy who might have been his twin: examining the features he saw every time he looked in a mirror. Simon smiled and said: 'I was one of the boys who went on the Children's Crusade, and I was sold into slavery. Can you think what that meant? Can you imagine how I felt to be handled and caressed and whipped, depending on the mood of a fat sweaty old Moslem emir? Our family is of Norman blood, and you know how proud we are.'

Simon had a thin gold chain round his neck. A huge gold Islamic crescent dangled from it. Seeing the movement of Cameron's eyes, the ghost-boy touched it and said: 'The Saracens hung these on their horses' bridles and on their foreheads. They also hung them on their slaves. They are said to ward off the evil eye.'

'And did it?' Cameron said.

Simon laughed. '*Au contraire, mon cher*, I think it encouraged it. My master's eye was more evil than Satan's.'

'Why did you go on the Children's Crusade?'

'Because my father told me to join and give honour to our

house.' Simon shaded his eyes and looked along the beach. 'The Emir is coming,' he said. 'There is just time to tell you about my short life before he arrives – to meet retribution at your hands.'

'But I can't kill Mr Hikmet,' Cameron said. 'He hasn't really done me any harm. My mother thinks he's evil, and I think he is, but he hasn't actually *done* anything to me.'

'He has sullied the honour of our house,' Simon said. 'He must perish. Only when he perishes – and your Mr Hikmet *is* the Emir Sulieman in human guise – will my spirit be free to go home.

*

'Though where my home is I cannot truly say,' Simon said. 'Is it Scotland? Or is it France? I was born at Ardavalloch, but I spent more than half my eleven years in France. My father was a friend of our king, William the Lion, and I was brought up with the king's son Alexander. He was four years my elder and I was supposed to be his page. I had a serf of my own, Donald, a boy from the north, my own age. When Alexander adopted too princely a manner, Donald and I united against him. The only time we were not able to overpower him was when he refused to go on the Children's Crusade. We were in France then, on one of the great estates King William had inherited from his mother. The king wished Prince Alexander to become a good Frank, so he put my sire, who was more a Frank than a Scot, in charge of the Prince's household, to act *in loco parentis* when he himself was in Scotland. In the year 1212 we went to the Abbey of Saint-Denis to attend the French court. And there, alas, Alexander and Donald and I listened to the ravings of Stephen, a shepherd boy, who said he had a letter from the Lord Jesus Christ telling him to preach a new Crusade. Stephen was an unlearned peasant, but he had imagination and such a gift of oratory that thousands of children – girls as well as boys – flocked around him and swore they'd follow him to the Holy Land. One of Stephen's prophecies was that the Mediterranean would open wide – as the Red Sea had opened to the Israelites – and he and all his followers would be able to march on dry ground all the way to Outremer.'

'Outremer?' Cameron said. 'I thought you said the crusade was going to the Holy Land?'

'Outremer is what this part of the world was called then,' Simon said. 'The Holy Land is only a small part of Outremer. My sire also listened to some of Stephen's ravings. Sir Uchtred thought it fitting that Prince Alexander should join the crusade and lead it instead of the half-daft peasant boy. He invited Alexander to volunteer, but His Highness wouldn't. His Highness was now fifteen and looked on himself as a full-fledged knight. Sir Uchtred was so angry at his pupil's disobedience that forthwith he ordered me and Donald to join the crusade, hoping that Prince Alexander would be ashamed and follow our example. But Alexander did not, so, urged on by my sire, Donald and I rode off alone to Vendome and joined the thousands of children gathered around Stephen. It was my sire's wish that, since Alexander would not lead the crusade, I should take his place. If he had not pictured me leading the young crusaders to glory, I believe Sir Uchtred would not have sent his only son on such a mission. But Stephen would not listen to my argument that I was by birth and breeding the rightful leader; he said rudely he was God's appointed, and as he was a year my senior and very strong I had perforce to submit. We even had to submit to our ponies being taken from us and sold to buy food for our fellow pilgrims. And so it was in no great state of grace or happiness that we arrived in the port of Marseilles. By this time many of our young fellow crusaders had died or turned homewards. Donald argued that our journey seemed futile and we should return to Varenne, but I did not wish to stir up my father's ire.

'I still do not know whether, like Stephen, we expected the waters of the Mediterranean to open wide and display a dry path, but if we did we were deceived. The Mediterranean remained deep and dark and blue in front of us. And then two kind-hearted merchants, Hugh and William said they would give us seven ships and would take us free of charge in them to the Holy Birthplace. These kind gentlemen wanted no recompense. All they required was that we should recite their names in our prayers when eventually we reached Jerusalem.'

'And did you?' Cameron said.

'You are ignorant, aren't you?' Simon said. 'I would have hoped for a Locherbie to show more historical knowledge than – shall we say – a peasant like Stephen in his stinking shepherd's clothes.'

'I'm sorry,' Cameron said.

'You should be, but I forgive you,' Simon looked down into the ruins of the bailey. 'The Emir approaches. It will still, however, be a few minutes before he reaches this place of destiny.'

He continued: 'We had been at sea only a few days when our ships were seized by pirates in the pay of William and Hugh. We were all taken to the North African coast and sold. Donald and I were sold in the slave market at Alexandria. I don't know what happened to Donald after that. I was bought by fat Emir Sulieman and brought to this castle. Sulieman was – he still is – a wicked man, and I will not tell you how badly he treated me. He used to take me to his bed and make me do disgusting things. When I wouldn't, he whipped me and had me chained in a dungeon. Sometimes he was slobbering over with lust; at other times he was like a glacier in his indifference to mercy. Often he threatened to sell me to the Bedouins. I knew that when I grew bigger and he lost interest in me he would send me to the galleys. The Emir tried to make me become a Moslem, but I refused. All his slaves and soldiers hated me because I was a Christian. The only one who was kind was Amar, a big Numidian eunuch. He often brought me sweetmeats when I was in the dungeon, and he would take me in his arms and comfort me for hours and make the darkness less frightening and keep the rats away. I loved Amar. One night Amar told me that he and I would escape together and flee far from the Emir, and he promised to free me from the chains next day.'

Cameron said: 'And did he?'

The ghost-boy sighed: 'No. Next morning the Emir himself came and had the chains taken off. Then he drove me in front of him with his stick into the castle's bailey. And what I saw there made me scream. Amar, my big warm-hearted Amar, was strung up on a gibbet. He was not dead, and some Saracen soldiers were doing unspeakable things to his naked body. I knew I could do nothing to help him, so I ran towards the gateway. The Emir ran after me shouting: "Wait, Christian boy, and watch your friend die slowly, ·slowly!" Soldiers headed me off, and I ran up the stairs to the battlements. The Emir followed close, striking me with his stick. I leapt on that battlement there and ran along the top, and then ... The Emir kept poking me with his stick, and I slipped and fell on to the rocks below.'

*

'Good morning, English boy,' Mr Hikmet said.

Cameron rose from his seat in the embrasure and watched the fat Turk climb wheezily up the stone stairs. He put out his hand to clasp Simon's but felt only empty air. Yet he knew Simon was still there, so putting on a bold face he walked towards the Turk.

Mr Hikmet leered and said: 'I have come to punish you, English boy, for what happen yesterday. You are a wicked boy.'

'I am a Scottish boy,' Cameron said. 'How often must I tell you this? Please let me pass.'

'No, no! *Un moment!*' Mr Hikmet's foot kicked his stick. His eyes glistened and he pounced, a plump bird of prey. 'So you have the instrument of punishment in readiness! Thank you, thank you, Scottish boy, it will give me great pleasure.' He put out his hand to hold Cameron's arm. 'You kiss my stick, Scottish boy, and you say: "I am sorry, master. I kneel before you, master." '

'Fuck off,' Cameron said.

And he pushed past the Turk, giving his protruding stomach a violent jab with his elbow. The Turk tried to grab Cameron's shoulder but the jab had upset his balance and he fell against the boy instead. Cameron was sent spinning. The Turk raised his stick and screamed.

'Run, Cameron,' Simon said, appearing out of the air.

The Turk stared at the ghost-boy with amazement. 'Two boys! Twins!' he cried. 'You play no more tricks on me. I beat you both. And I complain to Papa who will beat you again.'

It was impossible for Cameron to get near the steps, so he

ran towards the battlements. Simon followed, running backwards before Mr Hikmet, who kept yelling and waving his stick. Cameron leaped on top of the thick stone parapet and started to walk to the ruined tower growing out of it; he could climb the wall at the end of the parapet and so elude Mr Hikmet, that stout crab incapable of tackling anything so high. But before he could reach the wall, he discovered that Mr Hikmet had managed to scramble on top of the parapet and was close behind him. 'Cameron, don't go any further,' Simon called. 'Wait!'

And he danced on the parapet between Cameron and the Turk. Mr Hikmet came forward cautiously and poked his stick at Simon. 'Aha! I got both boys now! You not escape from Sulieman the Magnificent!'

He pushed his stick at Simon and it went through the ghost and touched Cameron on the chest. 'Seize it!' Simon shouted.

Cameron grabbed the thin end and tried to push it away, but it was so supple that it bent towards the empty air above the sea, and it brought Mr Hikmet almost on top of him. Simon had dissolved. In a frenzy of fear, Cameron flung out the arm grasping the stick. The movement upset Mr Hikmet's balance again. He staggered unsteadily, gave a great scream and fell over the parapet.

It was several seconds before Cameron could stop trembling. He had his hands clapped over his ears to drown the screams. He opened his eyes. There was no sign of Simon. Cameron cautiously climbed off the parapet, then he leaned over and looked down. Mr Hikmet lay on the rocks below, white waves already splashing over his insignificant body. Cameron wiped the cold sweat off his face, and he looked again for Simon. There was still no sign, but from high above the nearest tower his voice called: '*Bien merci, mon frère.*'

The tall black figure of Leo was leaning against the tower wall. Cameron started to cry with relief as he ran towards him. Leo clasped the boy in his arms.

'I saw it all,' he said. 'It was his own fault. He chased you onto the parapet. I will tell everybody what a wicked man he was, and how he deserved to die.'

Cameron snuggled into the warmth of Leo's big body, and they walked towards the steps. Suddenly there was the sound of wings flapping. They looked up at a great sea bird with a scarlet crest poised on top of the tallest tower. It hovered for a moment, then they watched it circle slowly over them, the sun shining on its crest, before it flew off towards the north-west.

III

Weep No More, My Lady

They returned home to 11 Abercrombie Terrace as dawn was breaking. For the two hundredth time young Mr Fitzmaurice helped Lady Kate out of the carriage and escorted her through the gate and up the steps. Mercy Milligan clambered stiffly off the box beside the coachman, opened her reticule and took out the key. While Mr Fitzmaurice was kissing Lady Kate's hand with a flourish, Mercy opened the door. She was sunk in a dour state of apathy. Lady Kate, so tired that she was almost hysterical, stood and waved until the carriage was out of sight, then she and Mercy entered the dark hall to meet their fate.

As always, Hamish MacAlpine of Fintravoch was waiting for them. Without saying a word he raised his pistol and shot Lady Kate. 'And you take that, you two-faced limmer!' he shouted, firing at Mercy. 'It's a just reward for taking my siller and pretending to help me court your mistress, while all the time you were taking more from that fool Fitzmaurice.' A few minutes later there was a clatter of hooves as Hamish MacAlpine galloped out of the Terrace on his way north to Scotland.

'Well, thank God that's over for another year,' Lady Kate said peevishly.

'Ay, thank God indeed, my lady,' Mercy said, wiping the blood off her bodice. 'A body gets right fed up with doin' the same thing ower and ower again. I whiles think if I could write I'd write to the N.U.B.G. to complain.'

'Mercy Milligan! How often have I told you about this new-fangled way of using initials instead of proper words? I won't have it in my house. If you *must* refer to them, you must aye say the National Union of British Ghosts, otherwise you can pack your kist and leave my service.'

'Och, it's such a mouthful. Anyway, this hasnie been your house for twa hunnert years. And besides, ye cannie get rid o' me. Dinnie forget that, my lady. It's like the Bible says, Whither thou goest, I goest. We're tied thegither like.'

'Except that death can't part us,' Lady Kate said bitterly.

'It might be easier if there was a Scottish National Union of Ghosts,' Mercy said. 'What a pity we hadnie gotten killed at Kilcheviot Castle. We'd ha'e been a lot happier in our ain fresh Hielan' air.'

'And have Hamish MacAlpine for a next door neighbour and see him nearly every day? No thank you. Once a year is sufficient for that big red brosey face and those big red knees and short kilt. Anyway, I could never bide in Kilcheviot with all those big empty rooms and long draughty corridors. I'd get my death of cold.'

'Ye havenie fared ony better doon here in London, my lady. This has never been a comfortable hoose, and it's been unliveable in since it was bombed.'

'I doubt you'll have to thole it, my woman, for we're here for eternity.'

'I cannie help that.' Mercy said. 'I ken I have to bear it, but I miss Kilcheviot and I miss my friends.'

'Mercy Milligan, you ken fine that you have no friends left,' Lady Kate said. 'You ken fine that none of the poor creatures ever reached the status of being a ghost. Only the Chosen Few live on. If every poor glaikit Tommy and Lizzie became ghosts there'd be no room in the world for us all. It's a good thing that the Union of Ghosts made that rule. Not that I hold with Unions, but this is one time when I see eye to eye with them.'

'I dinnie hold wi' Unions either, my lady. But I just wish there was a Scottish one. I'd feel more at hame like, if I could talk to a Scottish union official.'

'Most of the heads of the National Union of British Ghosts *are* Scottish,' Lady Kate said grandly. 'They're the only ones with brains. If you'll remember, it was a Mr Cameron I saw when I got the special dispensation for us not to go through the farce with Hamish MacAlpine more than once a year instead of, like some poor souls, having to act out our drama every time a mortal glimpses them. And it was Mr Cameron and another Scottish childe, whose name I forget, who gave us the bonus of being able to go back into the world as living beings for a week once a year, so long as we behaved ourselves as haunts.'

'They can keep their bonus as far as I'm concerned, I'm sure,' Mercy said huffily. 'I never enjoy that week. It's nae fun to be jostled about and elbowed in the street by strange folk all rushin' helter-skelter as if their lives depended on it. Why most o' them cannie walk quiet-like and decently is beyond ma comprehension. I mind last year I got such a push goin' doon the escalator in the Oxford Street tube that I nearly fell and broke ma neck.'

'Enough! Enough!' cried Lady Kate. 'We're both tired, so stop ronnying. We must rest.'

The ghosts dissolved. Lady Kate went upstairs to the bedroom she had used for over two hundred years, a room that had been slept in by generations of uneasy people since her murder, but which since 1940 was no more than a piece of floorboarding about three feet wide clinging in a corner to the crumbling walls. Mercy's spirit remained in what had been the drawing-room and brooded dourly. The drawing-room was the only room in Number Eleven that still had four walls and was recognizable as a place that once had been lived in, even though weeds grew through holes in the sagging wooden floor and ivy and other creepers had come through the spaces that had been windows, creeping over the inner walls. Apart from the drawing-room and a piece of the old staircase the house was a shell. But almost all the former mansions in Abercrombie Terrace were shells, and they had been shells for a long time. All that remained of Alfriston Lodge, the house opposite Number Eleven, was a hole surrounded by heaps of bricks and stones in its weed and shubbery filled garden. A few houses at the other end of the Terrace had escaped the bombing, and for the past twenty years they had been broken up into flats and occupied by people who came and went. But some time ago the flats had emptied, and now, except for a few passing cars, the Terrace had sunk into a seedy bombed-out backwater.

Shortly after seven o'clock Mercy was aroused by the roaring of a motor car. It stopped in front of Alfriston Lodge and two young men got out, and leaned against all that was left of the garden wall. They had long hair and wore windcheaters and jeans. A few minutes later another car, a flashy saloon, drove up and stopped behind the first one. Three youths got out. One wore a short suede coat lined with sheepskin, the others had on duffel-coats. All had long hair and jeans. Within the next ten minutes ten cars were parked outside Alfriston Lodge and Number Eleven, and about thirty young men were lounging against the garden walls. Then a couple of lorries arrived, laden with planks and tools. While some of the young men were half-heartedly unloading these, a bulldozer came thundering along the Terrace.

'God ha'e mercy on us!' Mercy cried. 'What's happenin' here?'

For the next hour there was sporadic activity. Some young men moved leisurely about the garden of Alfriston Lodge with planks and ladders; others lounged and smoked. The bulldozer crashed through the garden wall, ploughed up some weeds and shrubs, and then shuddered to a halt. A huge notice-board was erected behind the wall. Mercy still could not read, although she could have taken advantage of the National Union of British Ghosts' excellent evening classes, and Lady Kate, who was shortsighted, could make out only LUXURY FLATS FOR SALE.

After a time two youths crossed the street and started to put up another sign in the garden of Number Eleven. About nine o'clock all the young men at Alfriston Lodge piled into the cars and went off with yells and roaring of exhausts. The two at Number Eleven stopped tinkering with the notice-board and came into the house. Their jeans were so tight that they walked stiffly and slightly bow-legged like cowboys. Each had a sullen, deadpan face. Their eyes were cold, their jaws like rat-traps. They carried transistor radios. From one transistor came the painful pullulations of a pop singer; from the other a pseudo-cultured B.B.C. voice talked about sport. The youths laid the transistors on the floor, put packets of sandwiches beside them, took out combs and rearranged their long glossy hair.

After an earnest conversation about pop groups, they put away their combs, sat down and began to eat their sandwiches.

'If ya don't buy records whadja do with yer lolly?'

'Savin' for a new car,' the blond boy said.

'Ya just gotta new car.'

'Yeah, but I wan' one of them new Jags. By the time I trade this one it'll cost another coupla hundred. Besides I gotta save up for m'oliday, and I gotta give the old lady 'er whack.'

'Much you give yer mum?'

'Coupla quid a week.'

'Cor, you're soft. I only give me old lady thirty bob. She's bloody lucky to get that. Fund money for 'er. I'm never at 'ome to eat a meal 'cept on Sundays.'

The blond grunted.

'Much you got saved for yer 'oliday?' the dark youth said, tossing his empty sandwich paper through a hole in the wall.

' 'Bout ninety quid.' The blond took a roll of notes out of the inside pocket of his windcheater and began to count them slowly, mouthing and muttering. The other watched with lack-lustre eyes, his face expressionless.

At last the blond came to the end of his counting and stowed the notes back into his pocket. 'Ninety two,' he said. 'Need another ninety or so, then I'm all set for a week in Majorca. Reckon I should save that in the next six weeks on this job.'

'I've 'ad Majorca,' the dark youth said. 'Gonna try Austria this year.' He lay down on the floor and curled up, his head in his arms. 'Might as well 'ave a kip.'

The blond grunted. He lit a cigarette and stretched out, looking up at the sky. After a while he put out his cigarette, put the end carefully in his breast pocket, turned on his stomach and slept.

An hour passed. Several other programmes groaned and screamed their way out of the transistors. Then the cars belted again along the Terrace, stopping with a grinding of brakes, and the rest of the young men drifted back into the garden opposite. The dark youth woke, stretched, yawned and said: 'Better get back on the job, mate.'

The blond grunted.

The dark one lit a cigarette, picked up his radio, and swaggered out. The fair-haired one yawned, got up slowly, stretched and farted. He lit the butt of his cigarette, picked up his transistor, stood for a moment, then put it down again. He unbuckled his belt, walked to the corner of the room, let down his jeans and squatted.

'You filthy peasant,' Lady Kate said.

'In our own drawing-room, my lady!' Mercy cried. 'I never thought I'd live to see the day!'

The ghosts materialized.

The fair-haired youth's face changed expression only slightly for a second. Then he rose, gave a sceptical laugh, pulled up his jeans, lifted his transistor and walked out with stiff legs, saying 'Ta ta, girls.'

As he crossed the street his swagger returned, intensifying to such an extent that his buttocks jiggled from side to side. He joined his dark friend and said: 'I just seen a coupla ghosts, mate.'

The dark one grunted.

'Straight, two darlings appeared,' said the blond. 'Outa thin air like. One minute they wasn't there, the next minute they was. One o' them wasn't a bad lookin' bird, either. The other one was a sour-faced old cow about fifty with red 'air. Jeez, you shoulda seen them, mate. Proper darlings. They looked as if they was in one of them plays on telly about history. All trailin' skirts, and long black cloaks.'

'I thought ghosts was white.'

'Nah.'

'Whadja do?'

'Zipped up and came away. What else?'

During the next six months the ghosts became almost deranged. Their existence was disorganized. The bulldozer levelled the ruins of Alfriston Lodge and the houses on that side of the Terrace to the ground; great steel scaffoldings were erected, piles of new bricks were unloaded from lorries; cement mixers whirred; window and door frames appeared, and gradually the skeleton of an enormous building grew up, towering far above Number Eleven and its companion ruins. From morning until night cars and lorries roared through the Terrace. Young men went up ladders with hods of bricks; they shouted to each other and they whistled to every girl who passed along the Terrace. Great hammers clanged. Cranes were in action all the time. Transistor wirelesses screamed ceaselessly. The noise was intense, deafening and never ending.

'It's demoralizing,' Lady Kate said. 'My head birls with it all. Even those aspirins you stole from Woolworths won't work. Can we not have some peace?'

'Oh for the guid auld days when this was a quiet street!' sighed Mercy. 'But I doot we've had it, my lady. We're for the high jump.'

'Mercy Milligan! Where do you pick up these weird expressions? I won't have it. If you must haunt that new institution called the supermarket, pray don't bring any of their *parvenu* jargon back here.' Lady Kate swept her cloak around her and soared up to her boudoir with the parting shot: 'Otherwise I'll get in touch with Mr Cameron and ask him to have you removed to Kilcheviot.'

'It might not be a bad idea,' Mercy shouted. 'But what would happen to you, my lady, if ye hadnie me here to look after ye? How would ye manage on yer lone with all thae awful-like young men runnin' about half-naked on your doorstep?'

And she gazed dourly across the street as a group of workmen who, stripped to their waists, were sunbathing while they shouted rude remarks to their fellows, most of them also half bare, who were still making a pretence of working.

Before the skeleton of the giant building had reached fourteen storeys Number Eleven and the rest of the ruins on that side were knocked flat by the bulldozer. 'God save us all,' Lady Kate exclaimed, drawing her cloak over her mouth and nostrils as she and Mercy hovered in the air high above the clouds of dust. 'We're finished now. We haven't got a place left to rest our weary heads.' And she burst into tears.

'Dinnie greet, my lady,' Mercy murmured soothingly. 'Dinnie greet, my wee hen, my bairn. Ye've still got auld Mercy Milligan wi' ye. We'll be all right as soon as the dust settles. They cannie shift us. Not even their devilish contraptions can move our spirits awa' from here. We were here before them, and we'll be here a long time after them. As Dame May Whitty once said about some young actress.'

But in the weeks that followed, Mercy and her mistress

often wondered how they could manage to survive. Concrete foundations were laid on the site of their ancient home, joining it to its former companions. Steel scaffoldings were thrust up, fresh loads of bricks were brought, and another giant block started to take shape. The two forlorn ghosts spent their days hovering high above the thundering activities, and every night they found it more and more difficult to find the rooms they had inhabited, for each day box-like apartments, identical in shape and size, appeared among the intricacies of the steel and brick skeleton.

The time came for their annual materialization into human form for one week. Usually Mercy did not look forward to this; although she was fond of crowds she preferred to mingle with them in spirit form, not caring to be jostled by human flesh. But this year she could hardly wait for the time to come when she would don a navy blue costume and a hideous po-shaped blue plush hat stolen from a shop in Bayswater.

'Where'll we go?' Lady Kate said.

'Need ye ask, my lady!' Mercy exclaimed. 'Lindenford, of course. Where else? It'll be a relief to get awa' frae this hell for a while.'

Lindenford Manor in Sussex was one of the former estates of Lady Kate's father. Neither she nor Mercy had liked the place when they were alive, but since their deaths they had visited it occasionally. The last time they had been there, staying in the Maypole in the village of Lindenford, it had rained almost the whole time, and Mercy had never been able to get much farther than the public bar of the 17th century inn. She had wearied of the repetitious mumblings of the three old men, its main customers, and had sworn that she'd never go back. 'It was aye a dead and alive hole,' she'd said, 'and it hasnie changed much in twa hunnert years. Fancy not even havin' a telly in the pub, and havin' to go four miles to the nearest picture hoose! I'm glad that Hamish MacAlpine didnie shoot us here. If he had I'd ha'e gi'en up the ghost a long long time ago.' But now Lindenford seemed a paradise, and even the thought of old Uncle Will Curd's tale about his dog and Mrs Jenner's chickens, which she knew by heart, was preferable to Abercrombie Terrace. And so Lady Kate wrote to Mrs Jenner, the landlady of the Maypole, to book rooms.

'How nice to have you back with us, Lady Kate,' gushed Mrs Jenner. 'Imagine, it's five years since you and Miss Milligan were here, and if I may say so neither of you look a day older.'

'It's our easy consciences, Mrs Jenner,' Lady Kate said sweetly, wondering why the events of the past nine months were not showing their ravages.

'You'll see some changes in the village, I reckon,' Mrs Jenner said. 'We've had quite a few nice council houses put up since you were here. A very good thing, too. They add quite a bit of life to the village. A lot of them insanitary old cottages were condemned, and not before time, I says. They're just starting to build another twelve in old Gaffer Dann's field. The old skinflint made a hell of a row about it. Wouldn't sell the land, though he was offered ever such a good price by a private firm, so then the Council stepped in and requisitioned the field and he 'ad to take what they gave 'im. Quite a few thousands less than what this private builder had offered. Serve him jolly well right, too, I says. Tryin' to keep decent hard-working people from having a nice home.'

Gaffer Dann's field was opposite the pub. Next morning they were awakened by the roaring of cars and the crashing of a bulldozer, and when they looked out they saw a gang of workmen moving about the field. 'My God, it's just like bein' at hame!' Mercy cried, watching a blond youth in jeans stroll slowly from a car, carrying a bucket in one hand and a transistor wireless in the other.

'But isn't that the one who ... ?' Lady Kate exclaimed. 'Surely he can't have followed us down here?'

'God knows,' Mercy said. 'They all make themselves look as near like baboons as they can, so it's hard to tell one frae the t'other.'

After breakfast the ghosts went for a walk, but they couldn't escape from the sounds of the bulldozer, lorries revving, radios whining and young men shouting at each other. The village was built around a green some distance from the main road. They hurried past the hideous new council houses: red brick boxes on the far side of the green, with doors painted in the individual shades selected by their occupants, heliotrope, lemon and ice blue mostly, contrasting sadly with the mellowed timber and weatherboarding of the dwellings that lay nearest the old pub. But instead of the noise decreasing when they reached the main road, it intensified. And in an instant they realized why. A stream of cars was tearing along, most of them going in the same direction, towards the coast. The ghosts walked along the verge of the road, as close to the hedge as possible, but the swishing of cars passing them, some cars almost touching their skirts, made walking nearly impossible. Petrol fumes filled their nostrils, dust puffed and clouded around them. At last Lady Kate said: 'We must turn back. I'm nearly demented. In London, at least one has the pavement to feel reasonably safe on.'

They returned to the pub, to sit in the saloon bar and sip ginger wine. But even there they could not find peace. Besides the noise from Gaffer Dann's field, a juke box in the public bar was blaring at highest pitch, fed with shillings by two teenage youths who leaned on the counter, staring into vacancy while they drank double rums and blackcurrant. 'We had to get it to move with the times,' Mrs Jenner said. 'All our young customers demanded it.'

'What about the three old men – I forget their names – who sit in there?' Lady Kate said. 'Don't they object?'

'They can't. Two of them's dead, and Uncle Will Curd ain't able to walk this length no more. Not that it would make any difference if they were still here, They'd have to go before the juke box did. They wasn't worth much. Only about nine pints of mild a day between 'em. But the juke box crowd drinks nothin' but shorts. We do a rare old line in brandy with 'em.'

At that moment there was the clatter of a horse's hooves. Lady Kate and Mercy moved expectantly to the window; this was something they knew and were in sympathy with. A handsome bucolic young man astride a big chestnut hunter was pulling in close to the public bar window. Lady Kate, who had always had an eye for handsome males, raised her eyebrows in admiration. Despite his modern attire of black velvet hunting cap, black coat and white breeches, he reminded her of an old flame, the dashing young Duke of Inverness. 'This must be the new Squire at the Manor,' she said to Mercy.

He banged on the window with his riding crop and shouted: 'Give us a brown, Miz Jenner, and make it snappy. I must rush. I got to be at Nobbin's Wood to meet the rest of the 'unt in ten minutes.'

'Not working today, Freddie love?' asked Mrs Jenner, handing the glass through the window.

'Nah. Took a day off. Soon make it up with overtime.' He dashed down his brown ale, handed back the glass, shouted 'Ta, Miz Jenner! Square with you after,' gave his horse a wallop and galloped off.

'That was Freddie Curd, old Uncle Will's grandson,' Mrs Jenner said. 'Do you remember him, Lady Kate? Used to come and collect 'is grandfather at closing time sometimes.'

Lady Kate dimly recollected a boy of fourteen or fifteen hanging around the public bar door. And she recalled that a scullerymaid at the Manor in her father's time had been called Curd; there had been Curds in the village for generations.

'Freddie and his Mum and Dad are goin' to have one of the new council houses,' Mrs Jenner said. 'He's ever such a nice boy and doin' well for 'imself. Works in the building trade like most of the boys in the village, but takes a day off to go 'unting when he feels like it. He paid three hundred for that horse. Stables it with old Gaffer Dann. He's got a car, too. One of them new Mercedes. A lovely job.'

That night Lady Kate and Mercy retired early. They could not stand the noise of the juke box and the screaming teenagers who filled the public bar. But they could get no rest because of cars arriving in the pub's car park every few minutes, driven by more young villagers. It was long after the official closing time that the last car drove away.

Next day Lady Kate stayed in bed with ear-plugs to shut out the noise from Dann's field. Mercy walked to Lindenford Manor to try to find quietness in its great park. She returned before lunch with eyes popping in a scarlet face.

'Oh, my lady!' she cried. 'That we should have lived to see the day! The Manor's been turned into a home for pregnant women, and most of them's blacks.'

'Nonsense,' said Lady Kate. 'You're exaggerating, Milligan. No blackamoor has ever been allowed to set foot in Lindenford. The Earl wouldn't have it. Do you not remember the fuss he made when I wanted a little blackamoor page?'

'Well, I'm tellin' you what I saw wi' my own two eyes,' Mercy said. 'If ye dinnie believe it, come and look for yersel', my lady.'

Lady Kate looked, but still she couldn't believe it. Several large Negresses were sitting in deck chairs on the lawn in front of the mansion. There were also several large white women, but a rapid count showed that the Negresses were in the majority. 'Oh, my poor papa!' Lady Kate wailed. 'He'd turn in his grave.'

'Ay, it's a good job that his lordship never rose to the status o' a ghost,' Mercy said. 'What a to-do there'd ha'e been if he'd seen them. He'd have licked their arses with his stick.'

'No need to be coarse,' Lady Kate said. 'If we're condemned to be ghosts in a socialistic age we must put up with its discomforts. But I doubt we can't put up with Lindenford any longer. Let's go back to London.'

Haughtily Lady Kate told Mrs Jenner that they were leaving immediately. Handing her the full week's payment for both of them, she said: 'That'll help you to buy another of these fiendish juke boxes, my good woman, and you can rest assured that we'll never darken your doors again.'

With that, she and Mercy dissolved into thin air. High above the pub Mercy pulled off her po-shaped blue plush hat and threw it into Gaffer Dann's field.

The day came round again for Lady Kate and Mercy to play out their drama with young Mr Fitzmaurice and Hamish MacAlpine of Fintravoch. By this time many of the flats in the huge new blocks were occupied. Radios blared out of them from morning until night. Cars of every shape, colour and variety roared continually along Abercrombie Terrace. Day after day Lady Kate and Mercy cowered in the corner that once had been theirs, trying to escape contact with wealthy company directors, their brassy wives and brassier mistresses, millionaire pop singers and their dirty-looking jeans-encased girl and boy friends. Only in the small hours of the morning could they find peace from what Lady Kate termed 'the caterwauling of cretins with no foreheads and earnings of several thousand pounds a week,' and even then an all-night party in one of the flats usually set their nerves on edge and their teeth gritting.

It was with great relief that they heard the noise of Fitzmaurice's carriage horses. Disregarding custom, they went out to meet him. 'Otherwise it might have been difficult for you to find us in this jungle,' Lady Kate said, settling back against the cushions while the carriage bowled along in the direction of Kew and the dowager Duchess of Inverness's ball.

They returned home to what had been 11 Abercrombie Terrace as dawn was breaking. For the two hundred and first time young Mr Fitzmaurice helped Lady Kate out of the carriage and escorted her to the former front door. Mercy Milligan clambered stiffly off the box beside the coachman, opened her reticule and took out the key. While Mr Fitzmaurice was kissing Lady Kate's hand with a flourish, Mercy opened the door. She was sunk in a dour state of apathy. Lady Kate, so tired that she was almost hysterical, stood and waved until the carriage was out of sight, then she and Mercy entered what was no longer a dark hall but a tycoons' neon-lighted lounge to meet their fate.

But Hamish MacAlpine of Fintravoch was not waiting for them, as usual. He arrived ten minutes late, his red face bursting with indignation. 'God love us, Kate!' he cried, raising his pistol. 'What's been going on here? I couldn't find the damned place. I've been in dozens of rooms in this rabbit-warren looking for you.'

'This can't go on,' Lady Kate said. 'None of us are fit for it. We'll never be able to stand the wear and tear. Tomorrow I must go to my friend Mr Cameron and ask for a special dispensation for us to spend the rest of our days at Kilcheviot Castle.'

'And not before time, my lady,' Mercy said as Hamish MacAlpine fired the fatal shot at her and she began mechanically to wipe the blood from her bodice. 'No decent ghost would put up with this riff-raff.'

'Ay, it'll save me a long dreich journey,' Hamish said, dashing out to leap on his horse. The women listened, but the wailing of a pop singer drowned out the sound of the horse's hooves as he galloped out of the Terrace on his way north to Scotland.

Two days later, Lady Kate and Mercy Milligan followed him there. Mr Cameron and the other officials of the National Union of British Ghosts had granted them a special dispensation without much fuss; the only proviso they made was that the yearly drama must be played out at Abercrombie Terrace no matter how many youths caterwauled or how many petting and cocktail parties were being given by company directors, wives and mistresses.

'I fear that Hamish 'll no' be pleased,' Mercy said. 'And it means we'll likely ha'e to travel doon wi' him to do our bit o' play actin'. Still, what does it matter, we'll be able to enjoy the peace and quiet of Kilcheviot for all the rest of the year.'

'Dear Kilcheviot,' Lady Kate murmured as they came in sight of the ruined castle on top of the grassy slopes that stretched down to the clear waters of the loch. 'There's not much of it left, but these old grey stones have more love and peace in them than what we've left. They're enough to house us for the rest of eternity.' And she burst into tears.

'Weep no more, my lady,' Mercy said. 'Dinnie weep, my bairnie. All our troubles are over. We're hame! Hame!'

The ghosts glided down towards the ruin, their eyes straining to take in all the old familiar landmarks. They were so busy cooing and exclaiming to each other with joy and thankfulness that neither noticed a week-old newspaper that had been left by some picnicker on the grass. Glaring headlines announced that the land on which Kilcheviot Castle stood was to be turned into a new satellite town to house the workers on the new hydro-electric scheme that would be supplied by the waters of Loch Kilcheviot.

IV

Witch's Kitten

Cyn and I sat on top of her coffin and watched the mourners enter the kirk. Muriel Brunton and Nurse Abernethy sat in a back pew. In a wee while Bessie Dodds crept in and sidled down beside them. I had never seen Mrs Dodds wearing a hat before. She had worn the same green and red headscarf over her curlers all the years I'd known her. Two women from the village that I knew only by sight had a confabulation just inside the door, then they chose a pew about the middle of the aisle where they could miss nothing. Old Mr Nisbet who used to do the garden before he had to give up with his rheumatics, hirpled down near the front on his stick. He sat with his head down, biting his straggly smoke-browned moustache. A couple of middle-aged women I didn't know sat behind him and studied their hymn books.

'They were great pals of Kathy's,' Cyn said. 'I can't see why they've come – except from curiosity. They're women I never liked.'

I could not resist a merry mew when Mrs Drummond and Mrs Jarvis-Waddell, two great galleons full of importance, sailed slowly down the aisle to the front pew as chief mourners. Nan Drummond, all solicitude, hovered over her friend like a mother hen, holding her elbow and settling her as she'd set precious porcelain. I mewed again hysterically, knowing the Jarvis-Waddell woman needed no help, knowing only too well to what lengths of devilment she would go.

'Wheesht!' Cyn hissed.

'They cannie hear me,' I said.

'How do you know?' she said. 'You haven't been dead long enough yet to know what they can hear and what they can't.'

I was a few months short of eleven when Cyn died. The vet

did me in, at Mrs Jarvis-Waddell's command, the same day. So I missed becoming seventy years and seven, which I would have attained if he'd left me alone. I knew how old I was because often in the last year I had heard Cyn say: 'Anne of Austria is seventy. She has reached her allotted three score years and ten.' And always I'd heard her give a sad wee cackle after that, implying that it wouldn't be long now before the fairies got me. She never seemed to remember that she herself had long since passed the same life-mark. It is true that she'd said from time to time, on her 85th, her 88th and her 89th birthdays: 'I'll not see another birthday.' But a year ago, on her 90th, I'd noticed she hadn't repeated this.

I looked around the kirk with interest while we waited for the minister. I had never been in a kirk before. Cyn had not set foot in a kirk for many years either, and this was the Drummonds' way of getting their own back on her instead of having the funeral service at the graveside like other decent Presbyterian bodies.

'Not a bad turn out,' Cyn said. 'Ten mourners. Better than I expected. Though I'm surprised the lawyer-mannie isn't here to grace the festive board.'

'Surely you don't want him?' I said.

'Why not? I'd like him to see the damage he's done. It would be something to nag at his conscience for the rest of his days.'

'I doubt he's got a conscience,' I said.

'You should have more faith in human nature, Annie,' she said.

'How can I? I'm only a poor wee cat that's been ill done by.'

I could not help giving another skirling mew when Miss Beanie Gilmour garred the organ give an extra loud peal, and the Reverend Snotty Drummond came sweeping in from the vestry wearing his long black gownie with its purple and white accessories. I had never seen him in his Sunday togs before. I looked close to see if he had the usual snotter at the end of his neb, the reason for Cyn christening him this. She thought the nickname was a secret between her and me, but one day, in excitement, she let it out to Bessie Dodds, and it hadn't been long before the whole village knew and the minister got it back. It did not endear Cyn any more to him and nosey Nan.

'Wheesht!' Cyn cried again. 'Be quiet and you may learn something that'll be of advantage to you in the after-life.'

*

Cyn's name was Miss Cynthia Isobel Mackenzie, and she was a poet. It was because she was a poet and didn't give two hoots for them that Nan and Snotty Drummond disliked her. She never tried to hide her contempt and anger for their manipulation of Miss Kathy and their responsibility for her dreadful Will. The Drummonds came religiously once a week to visit her after/Miss Kathy died, and Cyn always received them with icy politeness, but they never dared call her anything but Miss Mackenzie. Only a few folk close to her called her Cyn. They were all lady-bodies of her own generation, and most were dead now, too. Some folk called her Miss Mac. She didn't like this, saying she was Miss Mackenzie to the *hoi polloi* or nothing.

So Miss Mackenzie she'd been to everybody for years. Except to Mrs Bessie Dodds, the cleaning-lady whose husband drove a tractor at the Barns of Dalbogie. Mrs Dodds called her Miss Mac behind her back, and often to her face. It was a kind of running battle between them. When first she came to be the daily at Seven Yewtrees, Mrs Dodds, a sonsy young farm-wifie, had been what Cyn called over-familiar and had kept calling her 'Miss Mac, hen,' and 'Miss Mac, m'dear' every half dozen words until Cyn had put her foot down. 'My name, Mrs Dodds,' she said in that loud upper-class voice of hers that could have filled a drill-hall, 'is Mackenzie. M.A.C.K.E.N.Z.I.E. Miss Mackenzie to you, if you please. And if you don't please, you can ask Miss Brunton for your wages and depart in peace. But if you do please, you must mind not to say "Miss Mackenzie" ower often. There's nothing worse than having one's name continually deeved in one's lugs.'

'Okay, Miss Mac hen,' Mrs Dodds said, fell affronted. And she tossed her head with such abandon that the curlers she always wore ablow her headscarf rattled. Mrs Dodds was a great head-tosser, and when she was having her mid-morning cup of coffee and biscuits in the kitchen with Miss Brunton and Nurse Abernethy her curlers clattered about so much you'd have thought she was conducting an orchestra. And they always rattled waur than usual after she and Miss Cynthia Mackenzie had a bit tiff about names.

Years long syne Cyn had been in love with a sailor called 'Sin', short for Sinbad. They had called themselves 'The Two Sins' and said it was the film they were starring in. They were introduced by an admiral, for Sin was a high ranking officer, and so they'd had their great love story. But it was a story that turned out badly for Cyn Mackenzie. Sin was drowned at Jutland. I never heard what his real name was.

I got mine when I was a month old. I used to be a twin. My sister and I were called Penny and Twopence by the village wifie whose black cat had kittened us. Miss Mackenzie bought us when she heard we'd been born in May. 'In olden days,' she said to the scandalised village wifie, 'witches would never have any but May kittens. They vowed they made the best familiars. They're stronger and more cunning than most cats. I hope these two will help to keep my broomstick in control when we're flying in a high wind.'

Cyn's sister, Miss Kathy, was still alive then. She was as scandalised as the village wifie when Cyn, a keen student of history, rechristened us Anne of Austria and Caroline of Naples. 'It's more in keeping with your new status as gentry,' Cyn told us.

'Havers,' said Miss Kathy, a bossy body who kept laying down the law. 'Carrie and Annie they'll be from henceforth. And I'll have you know, Cynthia Mackenzie, that your royal ladies will have to be a lot cleaner in their habits if they're to remain in my house.'

Miss Kathy always called Seven Yewtrees 'my' house. She would never have dreamed of saying 'our', although truthfully it was as much Miss Cyn's as hers. Seven Yewtrees was built in the early 18th century to house a large family, and it had stood in the middle of an estate of several hundred acres. But the acreage had dwindled like the family fortunes, and by the time Miss Cyn and Miss Kathy were born it was standing in a garden of three acres and a paddock. It was occupied then by the girls' parents, General 'Buffy' and Mrs Mackenzie and a staff of five indoor servants, a nanny and a coachman. By the time I came to it as a kitten the paddock had been sold; the house was well weatherbeaten and needed repairs; most of the garden was just rough grass; and only the two old sisters and their housekeeper, Miss Muriel Brunton, lived in a few rooms, the rest of the house being dust-sheeted and deserted.

When the General died at the age of ninety-four he hadn't mentioned the house in his Will. Miss Kathy had been Buffy's favourite, for he couldn't abide Miss Cynthia and her poetry and what he called her whimsy-whamsies; so he left seven thousand pounds to Miss Kathy, and the remainder of his possessions to be divided equally between her and Miss Cyn. But Miss Kathy always chose to forget that Seven Yewtrees and everything in it belonged to both of them. Since she was ten years younger than Cyn – there had been a wheen miscarriages and two babies that died in between – Miss Kathy fully expected to live long after Cyn, who was delicate and had a bad heart. Cyn was encouraged, therefore, to spend her money by paying all the household bills. Kathy hung onto her own.

Miss Kathy was seventy when Carrie and I came to bide in 'her' house: the age I am now, the age I suppose I'll be for all eternity. She was seventy-three when she died, so I had plenty of opportunities to watch her in action; I ken how true it was that Cyn did all the paying-out while Miss Katherine, as she insisted on being called by Mrs Bessie Dodds and others of the lower orders, sat back jocose and watched her own bank balance rise higher and higher. Miss Katherine, who deemed herself appointed by God to manage her older sister's affairs, was absolutely certain that Cyn would die long, long before her. Cyn would not be able to take her money with her, and nearly all of what she left would be taken by a rapacious government; so it was only sensible, right and proper that Cyn should pay the household bills, the gardener's wages, Miss Brunton's wages, the charwoman's wages, and the rates and taxes and insurance, forby the income tax, so that Kathy could hang onto her own money, and it would be there, in readiness, when the time came and she was left to cope on her lonesome.

Not that she would be on her lonesome. She would have her dear cousin, Willie Jarvis-Waddell, to be her staff and prop for the rest of her days. Willie Jarvis-Waddell was a third cousin of the Mackenzie sister's mother. He was a big bug in the

Foreign Office and had a mansion in Yorkshire and a house in Belgravia, which Cyn told me is a fashionable part of London. The Mackenzies' money had dwindled through the decades, but the Jarvis-Waddells had kept an iron grip on theirs. They were what Cyn called stinking rich.

Willie visited Seven Yewtrees twice or thrice when he was a bairn; then they didn't see him until Buffy's funeral. He was a good looking young man of twenty then, and Miss Kathy, aged fifty-four, a repressed spinster though she would never have admitted it, fell in love with him. For the rest of her life Cousin Willie was her god. Even when he married, it didn't make any difference to Kathy's great pash. She kept inviting him and his wife Bertha for holidays, which were paid for, of course, by Cyn. Nothing was too good for Cousin Willie and Dear Bertha. Crates of champagne were stocked. Expensive foodstuffs were sent up from Harrods and Fortnum and Mason. All on the account of Miss Cynthia Mackenzie, who had to hide it from Kathy if she was rash enough to buy a book that wasn't a paperback. A lot of the wines and foodstuffs got wasted, for Willie and Bertha never stayed for the full term that Miss Kathy had invited and expected them for; they always had some excuse and, after a couple of days, would hasten away farther north into the Highlands so that Willie could do a little fishing and shooting on some great estate. Yet, no matter how they abused her hospitality and invitations, Kathy always gushed about, 'My cousin Willie in the FO – such a brilliant administrator who's always travelling abroad with the Foreign Secretary.' If Cyn spoke about him she only said he was a distant cousin – 'a very distant one, and the more distance there is between him and me the better I'll like it.' Cyn called him and his wife 'Waddling Willie' and 'Bitchy-faced Bertha'. They did not like Cyn either.

I heard all this from Cyn in the long hours she used to lie in her bed with nobody to talk to. And over and over again she told me about the time Willie and Bertha came for a week and stayed only one night because Willie had to dash – he said – to Balmoral to confab with the Queen. This was a memorable night in Cyn's life, the night all the evil and damage was done.

That night Miss Kathy had invited the Rev. Snotty and Mrs

Drummond to dinner to meet her famous cousin. The Drummonds had just come to the village, and a great all-absorbing friendship had sprung up between Nan Drummond and Miss Mackenzie of Seven Yewtrees. Nan Drummond was a big stout body with a big damp face that always had beads of sweat on the temples and upper lip. Her large protruding eyes had great bags under them; the irises were so pale a grey and the whites were so unhealthily yellow, they looked like cold poached eggs that had got stale from lying in the pantry. Nan Drummond fair oozed sympathy and affection for those she thought in want of it. Kathy Mackenzie was a natural target.

When she wasn't directing Miss Kathy's life, Nan Drummond was tripping over with good works. In olden times she'd have been able to use up all her energy in saving village girls in trouble, poking her nose in where it wasn't wanted when they had bastard weans; but in our day the village girls wouldn't admit to belonging to the village at all, and they were all on the pill and too cute to get caught. So Nan Drummond would have had a very lean time in our parish if it hadn't been for Miss Katherine Mackenzie.

It was she who egged on Kathy to make yon Wicked Will.

This was after she met Waddling Willie and Bitchy-faced Bertha. Mrs Drummond was tremendously impressed by Willie, who hadn't started to run to fat yet. Like her buddy, Kathy, she fell for his diplomatic palavers. And when he was called to the phone in the middle of dinner and came back to say Lillibet wanted him to go to Balmoral the first thing next morning to help her and Tinker sort out a crisis in the Middle East, she was that overwhelmed by joy and pride at sitting next a man who was on such intimate terms with Her Majesty and the Foreign Secretary that she never once thought of the inconvenience and the waste and the cost caused by Willie's shortened visit. Nor did Miss Kathy.

She beamed at her cousin and said: 'We'll be so glad to look after Bertha while you're away, dear. Rest assured she'll be safe with us.'

'Bertha is coming with me,' Willie said. 'Lillibet insisted on it.'

Only Miss Cyn failed to be impressed. She neither believed

that Willie had been summoned to Balmoral nor that he was on Christian name terms with the Queen. 'I jaloused that he and Bitchy-Face were going to a hotel in Aberdeen or Strathpeffer or to the home of whatever man Willie had got to phone him,' she told me. 'They couldn't bear biding at Seven Yewtrees for any longer than I could bear having them in the house.'

Like Kathy, Nan Drummond was so unsuspicious of Waddling Willie's deceit that he and Bertha could scarcely have reached whatever haven they'd chosen before she started to agitate for Kathy to make her Will in Willie's favour. The whiff of Willie's presence, the powerful scent of a man who could speak so nonchalantly about his Sovereign Lady, was like gunpowder in a charger's nostrils to Nan Drummond. She saw herself becoming one of Willie's bosom pals. If she could be so chief with Willie's cousin, then she could be as chief with Willie himself – *and* his wife. Already Mrs Drummond saw that when Miss Kathy joined her ancestors – Miss Cyn would be away long before that, needless to say – she would become the greatest pal of the Jarvis-Waddells when they settled down in Seven Yewtrees, and – who knew? – she might become intimate with the Queen too.

Until Nan Drummond broached the subject, Kathy Mackenzie had not thought about her Will since the time thirty years ago when Buffy, straight-backed and bristly-moustached, had ordered his lawyer to make Wills in which each daughter made the other her sole heir and executor. Now, with Nan breathing so vehemently in her lug, pointing out that Cynthia couldn't last much longer with her weak heart, Miss Kathy was only too ready to summon the family lawyer.

The lawyer who'd drawn up their own and Buffy's Wills was dead. His place had been taken over by his son, Mr Ronald Glossop-Macleod, a smart young man who took a fancy to Cyn, but with Nan oozing advice at Kathy's elbow he was conned into drawing up what Miss Cyn always called the Wickedest Will in the World.

In this Will Kathy left Seven Yewtrees (forgetting half of it belonged to Cyn) and her jewels and all her money – except for two thousand pounds to her dear friend Mrs Nan Drummond – to her beloved cousin William Eric Jarvis-Waddell, appointing him her sole executor. Then Mr Ronald Glossop-Macleod said that *maybe* she had better make the Will a little longer than this. 'All of us are at risk, Miss Mackenzie,' he said (these were his exact words, Cyn told me, for she'd sat there in the drawing-room and heard it all from A to Z). 'It isn't at all likely, but there is always the possibility, of course, that Miss Cynthia *might* outlive you,' and he gave Cyn a wink and a special heart-warming smile, like a melting marshmallow – 'so I suggest that in case this happens you leave your property and money to her in trust for her lifetime, allowing her the income from your funds but not allowing her to touch the capital, until such a time as she, in turn, will hand them over – and her own funds too, I trust – to Mr William Jarvis-Waddell.'

Cyn protested that she had no intention of leaving Waddling Willie a halfpenny, but she was ignored. Miss Katherine said she agreed wholeheartedly with Glossop-Macleod, and she thought that maybe as her sister's own capital would be depleted should Cyn outlive her (and here she shook her head affectionately at Cyn to signify that, naturally, she didn't believe this) she would make it a condition of Cyn being allowed to stay on at Seven Yewtrees and to utilise the income from her own estate if Cyn would leave certain sums to charities in which she (Kathy) was interested. And she gave Master Ronald a list of these charities, saying she would have left them the money out of her own estate, except that she wanted as much as possible to go to her dearest cousin Willie.

Ronald most reluctantly put this conditional clause in Miss Katherine's Will and she signed it, despite all Cyn's protestations. 'I can't see why you're making all the fuss, Cynthia,' she said. 'You'll be dead long before me, so it doesn't need to worry you. Willie will see that the charities get their legacies from what money you've left to me.'

Nobody knew how really wicked the Will was until Miss Katherine Mackenzie kicked the bucket a great many years before it was expected. Cyn knew right away how dire it was when Willie and Bertha came to Kathy's funeral, and Bertha collected all the jewels. The sisters had some very precious ones that had belonged to their grandmother, who had bequeathed them equally to both sisters, though Kathy always claimed the lot. Bertha put the jewel case under her oxter, saying: 'Legally I shouldn't take them till you die. Cynthia, but I know you'll never want to wear them – it's hardly likely in the short time you've got left – so I might as well have them now. Jewels improve with wearing.'

Miss Cyn never stopped talking about these jewels and the Will for the next seven years. Day after day, night after night, when she couldn't sleep, she went over the Will and what it was doing to herself and her dependents. 'And that's means you, Annie,' she would say. 'You're my chief dependent now that your poor sister like my own sister is away.' For my twin, so grandly called after Queen Caroline of Naples, had been killed when she was only a year old by an Alsatian dog belonging to one of the village brats. 'You and Muriel Brunton and Bessie and Nurse Biscuits, you're all my dependents and I want to provide for you all after the fairies take me away. You can rest assured that Waddling Willie won't provide for you.'

The only thing that gave Cyn any joy over Miss Katherine's Will was the fact that Waddling Willie and his avaricious wife couldn't lay hands on Seven Yewtrees and the rest of his legacy until she died. 'It's what keeps me alive, Annie,' she said. 'Just to spite Willie I've told the fairies I won't be ready to go with them for a long time yet. Though, mind you, I'd fain often be away to join my dearest Sin, it's the thought of doing Willie down that keeps me here.'

She talked like this not only to me but to Miss Brunton and Mrs Bessie Dodds and Nurse Abernethy, the district nurse who, in the last years of Cyn's life, came in every morning to attend to her. There was always a tussle when 'Biscuits' gave Miss Cyn a blanket bath. Cyn hated anybody washing her face, and poor Abernethy had to keep saying: 'Now be a guid lassie, Miss Mackenzie, and let me give your phisog a wee dicht. Surely ye don't want to look like a smoked-out tinker when the doctor comes?' 'I don't care what I look like,' Cyn would say. 'The doctor'll just have to thole it. Better folk than

him have seen me with a smut on my nose. I remember once
when the Countess of Dalwhinnan came to call on my
mother ... '

When she wasn't talking about the Wicked Will and how
little siller she had left in the Bank and how it would be
depleted even more when yon charities got what by rights
should come out of Kathy's or Waddling Willie's money, Miss
Cyn recited poetry. She would recite her own poems, and she
would recite screeds and screeds by a man called Browning.
But her favourite poets were Emily Dickinson and Alice
Meynell. Hardly anything ever happened without giving
occasion for her to remember some apposite quotation from
one or the other.

A morning came when she was talking about Sin, her sailor
laddie, and the good times he and she had had, and she said:
'Maybe Emily Dickinson kent more about sailors than any of
us when she wrote: "Can the sailor understand / the divine
intoxication / of the first league out from land?" '

And then she sighed and said: 'Now, let's be quiet for a wee
while, Annie. I'm going to sleep.'

I went to sleep too. When I woke, Miss Cyn was still
sleeping, so I slipped through the open window and foraged in
the garden. When I returned, she was lying on her back, very
straight and stretched out, and there was a hankie over her
face. I sprang up on the bed, but I didn't curl up beside her. I
was debating whether I'd have another wee nap or whether
I'd go and see if Bessie Dodds had a tit-bit for me when Miss
Cyn said:'Annie! Now that I'm away, I want you to be a good
wee cattie until your own time comes. And I want you to give
Waddling Willie's fat legs a real good scratching when he
comes to the funeral. But mind he doesn't kick you!'

I looked round and there was Miss Mackenzie standing in
her nightgown behind me. She was that thin and worn-away I
could see right through her. I looked from her to the Miss
Mackenzie on the bed, and I cried: 'Guidsakes, mistress,
what's ado?'

'A stupid question, Annie,' she said. 'You ken fine what's
happened to me. You ken that I'm a ghost just as well as I ken
that you can speak like this when you feel like it.'

It was then that voices made me notice that the door, which

was always open, was now shut. Nurse Abernethy and Dr. Duncan came in. Dr. Duncan walked through Miss Cyn and bent over Cyn on the bed. 'I'm glad she went so quietly,' he said. 'Her old ticker just conked out.'

'I'll old ticker him!' Cyn said to me. 'When I think of all the heart pills that gowk's garred me swallow in my time!'

After the undertaker and his men had carried out Miss-Mackenzie-on-the-bed in a funny-looking purple blanket-box affair, Cyn and I joined Miss Brunton and Bessie Dodds and Nurse Biscuits in the kitchen. Miss Brunton and Bessie were still snivelling, putting their hankies to their eyes, and Abernethy kept trying to jolly them. She cracked a wee joke, and after a while Mrs Dodds tucked her hankie into her apron-pocket saying: 'Ah well, it has to come to us all. Puir Miss Mac, rather her than me, though. I'm no' ready yet.'

Biscuits cracked another wee joke, and they were laughing when the phone rang. Miss Brunton answered it. Cyn and I could hear every word that Bitchy Bertha said at the other end. 'Mrs Drummond has just phoned to tell me that Miss Mackenzie died last night,' she said. 'Why was I not informed earlier?'

'Miss Mackenzie died only two hours ago,' Miss Brunton said. 'I phoned Mrs Drummond at once, and she came to look at Miss Mackenzie before the undertaker took her away to the mortuary.'

'Who are you?' Bertha demanded.

'You know perfectly well who I am. If you had deigned to visit Miss Mackenzie even once in the seven years since her sister died you'd perhaps have know me better. I'm Miss Muriel Brunton, the housekeeper.'

'Why haven't you left? You've no right to be in the house now that the body's gone. I asked Mrs Drummond to give you notice. You will lock up the house at once and give Mrs Drummond the keys.'

'I'm staying until Sunday to look after the cat.'

'Have the cat destroyed,' the voice said. 'Immediately.'

'Miss Mackenzie wanted the cat to go to a good home,' Muriel said. 'We're going to find one for her, and I don't leave this house until we do. We haven't decided which day the funeral is to be yet, but no doubt your friend Mrs Drummond will keep you well informed.'

And she banged down the phone. She and Bessie and Nurse Abernethy started to discuss me. Mrs Dodds said she'd be more than glad to have me, but there were some collies at the Barns and she didn't think I'd take kindly to them.

'I'd have her,' Biscuits said. 'But a district nurse's house is no place for a cat. There are always interfering folk who'd complain about it being insanitary.'

They were still arguing back and forth when the phone rang again. 'If it's that woman,' Muriel Brunton said, 'tell her I've left for Hong Kong.'

'Hello,' Biscuits shouted into the mouthpiece.

'This is Mr Glossop Macleod. I'm so sorry to hear about Miss Mackenzie's death. Who are you? I've just had Mrs Jarvis-Waddell on the blower – all the way from Yorkshire. She says there are strangers trespassing in her husband's house, and she orders you all to be gone before this evening. Will you kindly hand the keys to Mrs Drummond? Mrs Jarvis-Waddell also told me to inform you that she has a complete inventory of all the furniture and valuables in the house and she will check this with the contents as soon as she arrives for the funeral.'

'She's feared we nick something,' Biscuits said. 'I've aye had my eye on yon picture of the wifie in the red cloak in the hall, but I doubt, I doubt ... '

'It's in the inventory,' Miss Brunton said. 'I went round with the agent at the time, and I remember him taking notice of it. It's not worth anything, but it's better not to take any chances with that woman.'

Mrs Dodds said: 'I'd have liked a wee memento. Could I no' take yon wee blue jug that's ahint Buffy's photy on the drawing-room mantelpiece? It would never be missed. I deserve somethin' after workin' here for donkey's years.'

'That jug's lapis lazuli,' Muriel Brunton said. 'It's one of the first things she'd spot. Anyway, you've been left a good few hundreds in Cynthia's Will.'

'Ay, if Waddlin' Willie lets me have it,' Bessie said. 'I bet he'll try to stop us all gettin' what Miss Mac put in the Will she made last year.'

Biscuits said: 'He can't do that. She was in her right mind, and what money's left of her own has nothing whatever to do with him.'

They were having lunch when Alick Buchanan, the vet, arrived and said a strange wifie had phoned from England and told him the cat was to be put to sleep. 'Instanter,' he said, lifting me and giving me a cuddle. 'It'll be all right, Annie my wee doo, one prick and Bob's your uncle.'

The three women set up a great hue and cry, but Alick was adamant. 'It breaks my heart,' he said. 'But orders is orders. I not only had the strange wifie. I had Mrs Drummond on the blower forby, telling me to get on with it.'

*

The vet didn't come to the funeral, but the lawyer did. He arrived as the coffin was being carried out of the kirk. Ronald Glossop Macleod was carrying a wreath. He held it behind his back, not knowing what else to do with it, when they all gathered round the open grave and Snotty said a long prayer. I had a keek at the wreath, and it said 'To Cynthia with deep affection from Ronald'. She had never called the man 'Ronald' in all her life. She had called him a lot of names, but never Ronald.

The undertaker began to dish out the cords so that the coffin could get lowered. He handed the first cord, with a bow, to Mrs Jarvis-Waddell; then he handed the second to Mrs Drummond. The third went to Mr Glossop Macleod. Then the undertaker hesitated, looking about to see which other mourner seemed most worthy to get the fourth, and after a pause he handed it to Mrs Bessie Dodds. But he didn't bother to bow to her. He was busy looking at his men to give them the signal to let the big ropes drop, which they did in a fell hurry, and so Cyn's coffin tumbled down into its last resting-place.

'I'm sorry Waddling Willie wasn't able to come because he's in some Bongo-Bongoland with the Foreign Secretary,' Cyn said. 'I'd have liked fine to put a cold hand on the nape of his neck when he was kneeling in the front pew.'

'Never mind,' I said. 'Maybe the Blacks'll pop him in a pot.'

'No such luck,' she said.

'Would you like me to rub against Bertha's legs and make her topple into the grave?' I asked. 'I'd fain like some revenge.'

'No, no, Annie,' she said. 'We must think of something better than that. Something more lasting.'

*

For the next two days Cyn and I watched Bitchy-faced Bertha and Nan Drummond rake through Cynthia's and the family's papers, screwing them up and throwing them into cartons that they carried out and emptied in a heap on the lawn. Drawer after drawer, cupboard after cupboard were emptied and the contents carried out. All the family photographs, their birth certificates and wedding licences, photographs of friends, letters that went away back to Cyn's great-grandparents – for the Mackenzies had been great hoarders – were picked up, glanced at and thrown onto the scrap heap. All the manuscripts of Cyn's poems and the letters Sin had sent her were laughed at and torn into smithereens. And while they destroyed several generations of family love and pride, the two women talked and talked. Bertha kept telling Nan Drummond about all the grand times they would have when she and Waddling Willie took residence in Seven Yewtrees, but Cyn and I, who could see right into her evil mind now that we were ghosts, knew this was just a ruse to keep Nan sweet in the meantime, for Bertha planned to sell the house and all its antique furniture and pictures as soon as she could make the arrangements with a big firm of London auctioneers.

By the second evening the two women were exhausted by their rummaging and destruction, and an enormous bonfire of papers, letters, birthday and Christmas cards, old clothes, children's broken toys, photographs, postcards, all kinds of cherished keepsakes, everything that had gone into the creation of three or four generations of Mackenzies, was standing six or seven feet high on the rough grass that once had been a well-kept lawn. And as the sun was almost setting over the Grampians, Bertha went to the scullery and brought out a can of paraffin oil. She sprinkled about half of it over the wreckage. Then both women struck matches and threw them onto the pyre. The bonfire flared up and was soon going merrily.

Bertha said: 'Well, that's a good day's work done.'

'It is that,' Nan said. 'Now, dear, let's go home to supper

and a nice wee drinkie to celebrate your inheritance.'

Cyn stood by the bonfire, moaning and wringing her hands. 'The years of love,' she cried, 'the years of joy that are going up in smoke!' I spat venemously in the direction of the manse, and went to find something to eat. I hadn't known ghosts got hungry. I was enjoying the remains of some fish when I noticed the half-empty oil-can left on the back-door step. The stopper wasn't screwed on properly.

I don't know where the idea came from. But I acted at once. I leaned against the can and knocked it off the step. In a jiffy I had got off the cap with my paws and teeth; then I started to roll the can towards the bonfire. The paraffin spurted out every time the can rolled over.

Cyn stopped moaning and watched my efforts to trundle the can. At first she watched with sad amusement; then she watched with irritation. 'You'll hurt yourself, you silly wee pussy,' she said. 'Aren't we in enough trouble without you doing that?' And then, suddenly, the purpose of my activity dawned on her.

'Oh, what a wonderful idea!' She clapped her hands and laughed. 'What a smashing idea, as your friend and my friend, Mrs Elizabeth Dodds, would say. "Right smashin' guid, eh, Miss Mac hen?" I do wish our good friend was here to shout encouragement from the side-lines. And maybe to help kick the can!'

Cyn shot out her foot, newly rejuvenated by death, and sent the oil-can two feet nearer the bonfire. I dunted it with my head and pushed with my forepaws, sending it another inch towards its destination. Cyn gave a wild screech of laughter and gave it another kick.

'It breaks my heart,' she said. 'Poor old Seven Yewtrees! I feel like the Vandals and the Visigoths sacking Rome.'

In a few seconds the fire rushed along the oily tracks I'd left and licked the back door. It was not long before the flames were thrusting into the house. The sun went down as the kitchen became one big fiery oven. Before it had been dark for an hour Seven Yewtrees was a blazing mass.

Cyn and I flew up and sat on the roof. I was nervous of the flames licking up towards us, but Cyn said: 'Don't be a fearedy-gowk. You must remember you're a ghostie now and you can't be harmed by fire, water, heat, snow, any of the elements you like to name. You're invincible and invisible.'

Still, I was nervous, and so I pranced about, thinking I could feel the heat seeping through my paws. It was all very well being a witch's kitten, but I didn't care for fire. At first Cyn said: 'Stop dug-dancing about.' Then she began to get excited, too, when the flames got higher and folk from the village started to arrive. Some of them stood and watched the blaze, standing like stookies and doing nothing. Others rushed away to get the police and the fire brigade and pails of water that they flung on the fire – as if their paltry contributions could help quench such a gigantic furnace.

By the time three fire brigades came Cyn and I were dancing sky-high above what was left of the roof, gurgling with glee at the sight of Bitchy-faced Bertha and Nan Drummond holding onto each other and wailing in the front of a crowd of villagers, which, by this time had swelled to well over a hundred. Cyn took higher and higher leaps in the air, and she shouted down to them: 'An eye for an eye, and a tooth for a tooth! Greet awa', my bonnie dearies. I aye knew I'd have the last laugh on you.'

They couldn't hear her, of course. But that didn't make her revenge any less sweet. 'Even if they do get the insurance to cough up,' she said, 'it'll not be as much as the property was worth. And I'm not sure that the insurance will pay. The insurance folk may say it's arson, for there's that oil-can in the middle of the bonfire. I wonder if their fingerprints are still on it? Wouldn't it be fun if Bitchy-faced Bertha and Nosey Nan were stood up in the dock and sentenced to twelve months hard! It would serve Nan right for wanting so much to be a guest of Her Majesty.'

Cyn gave a few skirls and a few leaps, then she cried: 'I feel just like Anton Dolin! What a pity it is that you never saw the ballet, Annie. You'd have loved it. You'd have loved Dolin in *Hymn to the Sun*. But what am I havering about? It's not Dolin I feel like. It's Nijinsky! I'll never forget him in *The Fire Bird* ... '

V

What's A Few More Deaths Between Friends?

A Black Supernatural Extravaganza

1

The Ghostess With The Mostest

The black ghost chuckled venomously and vanished. It was shortly after dawn. The gardener who had come into the kitchen, carrying two trugs of vegetables, had stared when he saw the large fat black woman in the old-fashioned clothes. And when she stuck out her tongue, chuckled and dissolved, he had let out a yell, dropped the trugs and fled.

'A pox on you, Lilywhite,' the Countess said. 'You've scared the poor fool out of his wits, you black cow.'

'He got no wits to scare, missy.'

Lilywhite clucked irritably as she examined the scattered vegetables. 'This cabbage full of slugs. This marrow not fit for pigs. I'd whip that gardener's bum good and hard.'

'I see no reason why you needed to manifest,' the Countess said.

'Just felt like it, missy. Lilywhite don' see why she shoulden manifest if she want to. It's a free country.'

'Too free. Like your tongue,' the Countess said. 'You need your own bum whipped.'

'Don' forget, missy, what happen the last time you try that caper,' Lilywhite said, glowering.

*

At the beginning of the 18th Century the Countess of Torryburn was the mistress of huge estates in her native Scotland as well as in the Midlands and Sussex. In London she was one of the great hostesses and, being an intimate friend of Sarah Churchill, Duchess of Marlborough, she was often at the court of Queen Anne. But she really preferred the country, and her favourite home was Ardmore Manor in Sussex. Usually she stayed there from May until September, and during these months hardly a week passed without her giving a large dinner party or a ball. No sooner had her servants cleared up after one party than they were ordered to make preparations for another. The Lady Margaret Campbell, Countess of Torryburn, a widow for ten years, had no children and she had nothing else to take up her attention.

Although there were many servants at Ardmore, this constant entertaining irked the ones who found they always had to do most of the work. There were constant dark murmurs and occasional flarings up of temper, especially among the kitchen staff, the grooms who baulked at having to look after the horses of the guests, and the gardeners who resented their fine vegetables being eaten by silly Sassenachs and their flowers used for floral decorations that were thrown out next day. Whenever there was a flare-up of temper, the Countess always outdid it with a flare-up of her own. She would scream and swish her riding-crop and threaten to whip whoever dared complain. To the men she always cried: 'Drop your breeks, you insolent rogue, and bend over,' and to the women: 'Put your skirts over your head, you brazen besom, and kneel down.' But her threats were never allowed to go beyond words. The maids would counter-threaten to leave, the grooms would grin and the boldest would seize the whip and boast that he'd use it on herself first, and the gardeners, most of them old men from her Highland estate, would say: 'Dinna you threaten me, my lady. Many's the time I've skelped yer ain doup when ye were a bairn, and I'm ower auld now to be bothered wi' yer tantrums. If ye want to use yer bit whip, why no' try it on that impudent nigger wench o' yours?'

The nigger wench was Lilywhite, who had been given to the Lady Margaret as a wedding present by her husband. Lilywhite, six years older than the Countess, had been brought to England when she was a baby. Ever since she was twenty-two she had been at Margaret's beck and call, looking after her clothes, listening to her complaints and cajoleries, cooking special dishes to tempt her delicate appetite, and ministering to every capricious whim. But although often threatened with the lash, Lilywhite had her own methods of quelling her mistress's temper, and she never felt it until the Baron Charles de Riveaux came to Ardmore Manor.

After the battle of Blenheim in August 1704, a number of important French prisoners were brought to England and lodged in honourable captivity in various country houses. The Countess of Torryburn was asked by Sarah Churchill to be the gaolor of Baron de Riveaux, a handsome young cavalry captain. De Riveaux arrived at Ardmore with his arm in a sling but with his sexual blandishments unimpaired. He was twenty-five, twelve years younger than Margaret Torryburn, but the discrepancy in ages was as unimportant to her as last year's ball gown or last week's dinner menus, and it made little difference to him whether he rode an old mare or a young one so long as she was mettlesome. When he swaggered out of the coach at the Countess's front door and saw her red hair and the dark, hungry eyes in her thin face, he knew that here was a frisky filly who'd canter at his slightest touch; and as he bent his blonde head over her hand and kissed it, Margaret's heart dropped as low as her curtsey.

He came to her bedroom that night. Margaret could not do enough for her lover, and in the following weeks she entertained even more lavishly than ever, if that were possible, to help amuse him and to make him forget each fresh piece of news of Marlborough's victorious campaign. At the end of September she usually went to London for the winter season, but this year she put off her journey to the middle of October. This caused great mutterings among the servants; those who came from London wanted to get back there before the cold Sussex winter started, and those who always enjoyed a peaceful winter at Ardmore wanted to get rid of her, her lover, the other servants and the constant entertaining. And when the chosen day of departure came and she announced that she'd decided to remain for another month and give a great dinner and ball for the opening of the hunting season, because the Baron wished to hunt with the local foxhounds, there was such an uproar in the kitchen quarters that Lilywhite said: 'White slaveys say they goin' to walk out, missy, if you have this ball.'

'What insolence!' the Countess screamed. 'I'll soon settle their hash. I'll have them all sent to the treadmill.'

'You be quiet, missy,' Lilywhite said. 'Slaveys is mutinous. No knowin' what they might do.'

'How dare you talk to your mistress like that,' said the Baron. '*Cette bête noire* needs a whipping, *madame*. I will do it for you with pleasure.'

'As much pleasure you got when you try to pull me in your bed, eh?' Lilywhite cried. 'This bad man, missy. He chase white maids too.'

'Enough! Enough!' screamed the Countess. 'You hold her, Charles. I'll whip the slut myself.'

Lilywhite was almost as tall as the Baron and almost as hefty, but she was much older and less supple; he reached down, grasped her skirts and pulled them over her head, using them to restrain her flaying arms and to throw her to the floor, where he sat on her head and shoulders while the Countess thrashed her naked bottom with her riding-crop.

The whipping of Lilywhite frightened the other servants and, although they muttered among themselves, they began to prepare for the Hunt dinner and ball. For days Lilywhite went about with a sullen face, speaking to nobody. The Countess had regretted her impulsive action almost before it was finished, mainly because she suspected that what Lilywhite had said was true, and now she did her best by cajoleries and small gifts to win back the allegiance of the sulky slave. But Lilywhite was unresponsive. She did everything asked of her, she accepted the gifts, but she did not respond to her mistress's smiles and shows of affection.

The day before the ball the Countess said: 'Lilywhite, will you be a love and make that delicious dish of mushrooms and trout that only you know the secret of, for tomorrow's dinner. The Baron dotes on it, and so do I, and I'm sure our guests will too. I know it means a deal of extra work for you, so I'm going to give you that blue brocaded gown you've always fancied. You'll like that, won't you?'

'Yes, missy,' Lilywhite said.

'Now don't be sulky, you black bitch,' the Countess said. 'After all, I didn't whip you too hard, did I?'

'No, missy.'

'And most slaves get whipped nearly every day,' the Countess said. 'So you're lucky. And the Baron's sorry about it, too. He told me to give you this gold piece. So now you've got that and the gown. What more can you ask for?'

Early next morning Lilywhite went into the great park to pick the mushrooms. She had refused the Countess's offer to send some other maids with her since many times the quantity she usually needed for a dish for two people would have to be picked. 'I manage by my own self, missy,' she said. 'White slaveys be better to prepare the trouts. Lilywhite don' like making her hands fishy.'

Amidst a clump of trees there grew a virulently poisonous variety of toadstools, and she picked them all; then she filled the rest of her huge basket with mushrooms. She prepared the dish in a small scullery off the kitchen and got rid of any maids who showed desire to help her. Not that many did, for they all kept running outside to watch the progress of the hunt and to shout 'Tallyho!' whenever they thought they saw a fox. Most of the toadstools went into a large dish, which Lilywhite had earmarked for her mistress and the Baron, and among them, for good measure, she put a quantity of deadly nightshade chopped up among herbs. The rest of the toadstools were distributed among the bulk of the mushrooms for the dishes that would be offered to the guests; there were not enough toadstools among them to do more than make the eaters ill. Lilywhite did not want to have too many deaths on her conscience.

There were twenty people at the dinner table. Lilywhite, dressed in her mistress's discarded blue brocaded gown, carried in the deadly dish and placed it in front of the Countess while the footmen and the white maids placed the other dishes in front of the guests. Then Lilywhite stood back, her arms folded across her great bosom, behind her mistress's chair, and watched every bite that she and her lover took.

As soon as the Countess began to moan and to clutch her stomach Lilywhite knew that the poison was taking effect, and when the Baron also went greenish-white and made gurgling noises, Lilywhite screamed: 'Oh, my pore missy, she ill! Get the physician man!' And she rushed out, so that she would be well away when the Countess died, for she'd heard a footman shout, 'The mushrooms!' And she knew by the look he gave her that she could expect no help or sympathy from her fellow servants. She hid outside one of the long windows and watched the confusion, and she grinned when she saw footmen lift the Countess and her lover and carry them out. But she became alarmed when old Squire Huggett, who had been sitting at the Countess's other hand, went into convulsions and died. A few seconds later, old Lady Carstairs, who had not uttered a groan but remained patrician to the last, sagged in her chair.

Suddenly she realised what would happen if she remained; she clutched her throat, seeing herself being hoisted onto the platform of death by the hangman. And she ran madly across the park and threw herself into the river.

On the day after the funerals of the Countess of Torryburn and the Baron Charles de Riveaux, the drowned body of the black woman was taken from the river. It was driven in a cart to the village green, and there it was stripped naked by the hangman from the nearest town. It was then dragged at the cart's tail to the gibbet outside the village and hanged ceremoniously. The body mouldered on the gibbet for many weeks before somebody with a strong stomach took it down one night and buried it in a hole beside the river bank.

*

For over two hundred and fifty years the ghosts of Lilywhite, the Countess and the Baron had haunted Ardmore Manor. Although they also had died at Ardmore, the ghosts of Lady Carstairs and Squire Huggett were allowed by what was then the Council of Ghosts to stay at their own homes; and now Lady Carstairs spent all her time in the tower of ruined Carstairs Castle working endlessly on the tapestry the dish of toadstools had interrupted, while Squire Huggett lived in the church where once he'd been chief worshipper, making nightly forays into the churchyard to lift the mini-skirts of village maidens who had strayed into its dark corners with their boy friends. But once a year, on the anniversary of the dinner party and the ball that had never started, they and the ghosts of the other guests, most of whom had died peacefully enough in their beds, had to return to Ardmore and re-enact the fatal dinner party.

Throughout the centuries the trio at Ardmore had found plenty to interest and amuse themselves. Descendants of a branch of the Countess's family lived in the Manor for generations without worrying about the presence of ghosts. Indeed, they were proud of them and always did their utmost to get them to emanate for the entertainment of guests. During the 1914-18 War, when it was turned into a hospital for officers, and again in the 1939-45 War, when it was a secret SOE headquarters for training special agents, Lilywhite had a wonderful time moaning and rolling her large white eyeballs beside the beds of light sleepers. But those good times finished after the estate was sold in 1947 to pay heavy death duties, and it was broken up into building plots for bungalows and pseudo-Tudor cottages. Only the house and the ground immediately surrounding it was left untouched. The house was occupied at different times by branches of the civil service, local government departments and other peculiar administrative bodies. None of these officials and their clerks and typists were in the building at night, so the trio had nobody to frighten, and they grew lonely and had to fall back on each other for company. They tried to relieve the tedium of their ghosthood by materialising at odd moments in daylight, but the little officials and their satellites were so wrapped up in their own petty importance that they never even noticed them. 'You're wasting your energy, you silly black cow,' the Countess said after Lilywhite had spent a whole morning groaning and waving her arms at a typist, who had stared through her and gone on chain-smoking and lacquering her nails. 'They have no imagination whatsoever, and you'll just make yourself a nervous wreck if you keep on at them.'

But in 1961, when they received a special dispensation from what was now called the National Union of British Welfare State Ghosts to travel within a radius of fifty miles, the ghostly life began to brighten for them again. Every night, with secret glee and without telling Lilywhite where they were going, the Countess and the Baron galloped off on horseback, for there were still several ghostly horses in the ruined stables. Lilywhite was left alone to wander through the deserted mansion. At first she amused herself by mixing up the papers in the office files and shuffling through the ones in the trays on the desks, but as this never caused the expected commotion, she got tired and joined a course of evening classes to learn reading and writing at the Brighton Ghosts' Technical Institute. She had always been afraid of horses, so every night she stole a motor scooter from a shed beside one of the bungalows and drove at full speed to the Prince Regent's favourite town. It was always a black night for her if she did not manage to cause at least one accident on the way. She learned quickly to write C.A.T. and D.O.G. but after she had graduated to four-letter words she became bored and dodged the classes. Instead, she took to gallivanting along the beach, frightening the lovers lying in dark corners by flashing her teeth and eyeballs at them. She even went as far as Hove, but one night after she'd made an old queen, who was teaching the facts of life to a delinquent youth, die of heart failure in the act, she never went back. Nor did she return to the evening classes.

'That ole nance tell me he tear my skeleton into little pieces if he ever catch me, missy,' she told the Countess. 'Though how he goin' to see my skeleton I don' know. It's black as the ace of spades. It's all nonsense that poem that they teach us in the evening class about the black man saying "But oh my soul is white." My soul is black and so's my bones.'

'Thank heavens, mine isn't,' Margaret Torryburn said.

'Don' boast, missy. Your soul is as black as mine. It only your bones that's white.'

The Countess said: 'Never mind. Charles and I'll take you with us to London tonight and then we'll see if your black skeleton frightens the blackamoors in Brixton and Notting Hill Gate as much as they frighten us.'

While Lilywhite had been enjoying her innocent pleasures in Brighton and Hove, the Countess and her paramour had been waging a campaign against the West Indians who had come to London in thousands, gone on National Assistance and brought up most of the old mansions that had housed the Victorian bourgeoisie, turning them into gambling clubs and brothels or partitioning the rooms and letting out the cubicles at huge rents to other immigrants who had followed them into the paradise of the whites' Welfare State.

That night when the Countess and the Baron were chalking

'Niggers Go Home' on doors and walls and pavements in Brixton, Lilywhite rolled her eyes and flashed her teeth in the houses, but so many other black people were rolling their eyes and flashing their teeth that hers were not noticed, and when she moaned and screamed they could not hear her for the noise of their calypsos. Disgusted, she went back into the streets and watched the Baron chalking on the pavement. 'What for you do this, Charlie boy?' she asked. 'What them black people done to you?'

'It is not what they have done, it is what they will do,' the Baron said. 'Wait until the blacks rule the world and make the whites their slaves. The sjambok will swish again.' He wrote 'Angleterre Needs Apartheid' and said: 'I am enchanted I am dead and will never need to call a nigger "master".'

Lilywhite began to chalk four-letter words beneath the slogans written by her fellow spirits.

'Don' count your chickens, Charlie boy,' she muttered. 'You might get borned again next century. I hopes I see you jumpin' when yo' master crack the whip.'

When dawn came and they prepared to gallop off to Ardmore, Lilywhite grinned malevolently at the Baron's back and, before she leapt on her scooter, she chalked: 'Frenchy Go Hoem.'

For the next few months the ghosts went to London every night, and their slogans caused a number of race riots, many innocent people being blamed for racial discrimination and incitement because of them. The trio enjoyed themselves enormously. Lilywhite chalked her slogans with the greatest enthusiasm. 'All them niggers should go home, missy, and leave more room for you and me,' she said. 'All foreigners should go home and leave the world to the English.'

'But I'm Scottish,' the Countess said proudly.

'That's what I mean, missy.'

And so not only the walls and pavements of Notting Hill Gate and Brixton but those in many other districts of London were treated to a deluge of slogans as Lilywhite raced around on her scooter, chalking 'Scots Go Hoem,' 'Yankees Go Hoem,' 'Jews Go Hoem,' and 'Poles Go Hoem.' But when she got a tin of red paint and splashed M PEES PIS OF HOEM on the Houses of Parliament, the Countess became alarmed at

Lilywhite's scholastic progress.

At that moment – luckily or unluckily, Margaret Torryburn could not make up her mind which it was – Lilywhite's attention was diverted by a new development at Ardmore. The Civil servants left; their files and papers were taken away. Gangs of workmen invaded the mansion and its remaining grounds. They tore down the old stables and erected a strange building in their place. The Baron, who affected to be knowledgeable about such things, said it was a Sauna Baths. Bulldozers dug a great crater in the park and a bathing pool was built. There was so much activity that the ghosts stopped their trips to London. Many of the workmen were Irish labourers, so Lilywhite plagued them by chalking 'Irish Go Hoem' all over the place.

While this was going on, painters and decorators transformed the mansion. The walls, drab olive and brown for many years, were repainted in garish colours, and every room was fitted with thick expensive carpets to match them. Electricians installed weird lights and heating appliances. Then rich silk curtains were draped at every window, and vanloads of peculiarly shaped Swedish furniture were carried in and arranged under the supervision of a chain-smoking woman with pink hair and a hard white face. And, at last, Ardmore began to resume a little of its former glory.

'Though it's different, of course,' the Countess said. 'It's in deplorable taste, and you couldn't say that about the place in my time.'

'It must have been bought by some important man, missy,' Lilywhite said. 'A Duke maybe? Or some Prince?'

'A film star, I should say. Whoever it is must be immensely rich.'

The Countess became so excited that she preened herself in front of all the new mirrors, wondering if by some wonderful means she could manage to persuade the National Union of British Ghosts to give her a special dispensation to renew her corporeal form for a period. She deserved it. She had put up with Charles for over two hundred and fifty years, so she was entitled to a bonus. After all, Madame Du Barry had been allowed to be reincarnated as Mata Hari in the days long before the Council of Ghosts had become a Welfare State

Union with much greater powers. Of course, poor silly Du Barry had made the same mistakes as she'd made in her previous existence and had died unpleasantly a second time. But Margaret Torryburn was determined that she wouldn't give cause for any complaint. Perhaps that nice Mr Cameron, the head of the Union and a fellow Scot, might be wheedled into seeing reason ...

But the Countess's dreams and hopes were shattered when she saw an announcement in a copy of the local newspaper that a workman had thrown down. Ardmore was to be opened the following week as a Motel for Underprivileged Youth. It was a new scheme sponsored by many people who believed that 'the products of poor overcrowded homes should have a chance to expand their horizons by sampling gracious living in glorious surroundings'. These 'deprived underlings' were to be given this opportunity at Ardmore at a price – 'since modern youth is independent and believes in paying its fair whack.' The newspaper reported that charges for a week's stay would be twenty-five to fifty guineas, though suites consisting of a bedroom, private bathroom and sitting-room would cost more.

*

The Ardmore Motel had been going now for nearly a year. It was efficiently run by the pink-haired woman, Mrs Courage, the Lady Supervisor, sycophantly addressed as 'Madam' by the staff, most of whom, male or female, looked as though they either had been or should be warders in prisons. The Countess often said: 'Seeing what they have to cope with, they need to be tough. They should have barbed wire whips to control their charges.' For, even yet, she and her fellow ghosts could not stop being suprised at the behaviour of the underprivileged visitors, whom everybody kow-towed to and respectfully called 'teenagers' as if they were a race apart.

Most of these teenagers spent their days sitting in front of the television sets, and their nights in racing around the countryside in fast cars or in smoking pot. Almost all were drug addicts of some sort. The more naive took amphetamines and barbiturates, the more advanced got high on heroin. Some who came with Purple Hearts in their zip-bags had graduated to LSD and cannabis by the time they left. Their favourite word was 'psychedelic'. One of them, Jeff Gayheart, who had occupied the most expensive suite for months and now looked as though he'd become a fixture, tried everything from marijuana to hashish. When Jeff came to Ardmore Lilywhite had taken a fancy to him; he was a pretty youth with a fine pair of legs. But after a few days Lilywhite's infatuation was flattened.

'You never guess what I see last night, missy,' she said. 'He in bed with two other boys, and you woulden believe the things they got up to.'

'Och, you're havering, woman,' the Countess said.

'It is the Gospel truth. Cut my throat and hope to die if I tellin' lies. He what they call a pop singer, missy.'

'Ah, a strolling player,' the Countess said. 'With the manners of a barnyard rooster.'

'He a cockalorum all right,' Lilywhite giggled. 'I don' know about his heart bein' gay, but somethin' else sure is. You should see what they was doin'. They a lot better than the telly.'

Lilywhite loved the television. There was a set in every room, even in the lavatories. Some of the swinging young would sit for hours on toilet seats, staring vacantly at the screen until Lilywhite either pinched their bottoms or switched the television to another channel. When she was at a loss for other diversions she rushed from room to room, playing havoc with the sets. Her pranks caused endless consternation, and the TV engineers were kept busy searching for faults on the sets and aerials. The Baron got his chief entertainment from watching the more athletic of the long-haired youths and girls being beaten by birch twigs in the Sauna Baths. But Margaret Torryburn, who loathed television and never had a bath if she could help it, had nothing to amuse her.

'Why'n't you frighten the knickers offen Ole Mother Courage, missy?' Lilywhite suggested.

'She doesn't wear any. I've tried my damnedest to scare her, but nothing'll shake her. She's got nerves like steel.'

The Countess had only the young to take up her attention, and by this time she was heartily tired of their antics and attitudes. 'They're such bores,' she said. 'I could forgive them for being almost anything but that. They never say anything worthwhile – a lot of them can hardly utter, they just grunt – and they keep doing the same stupid things day after day. They think they're trend-setters, but everything they do and say has been done and said a thousand times before – only much better. What's original about taking dope? My father smoked opium every night of his life. He kept ten mistresses at the same time and kept them all satisfied, but he didn't go around boasting about it and saying the world had never been so wonderful. There's nothing wonderful about it. It's dreary. Damned dreary.'

'They don' think that, missy,' the black ghost said. 'They say, like that ole Prime Minister, yo' fellow countryman, that we never had it so good.'

'I'm sick of them,' the Countess said. 'They must leave my house. We must get rid of them. *Canaille!*'

'Easier said than done, missy. And don' let them hear you usin' that nasty French word. Some of them not so stupid as they look. They got low cunning.'

'They must leave my house,' the Countess said. 'Immediately.'

A few days later she said: 'I've got a plan. I've put an idea into Old Mother Courage's thick skull. It was a job, but I managed at last to get my thought-waves to connect with hers. She has decided to have a fancy dress ball on our Anniversary Night.'

'So what?' Lilywhite picked her nose as she watched an art student kneeling on the lawn, throwing bits of mud and grass at the canvas he had streaked with red and yellow paint.

'That night we'll all meet as usual. We spirits will have our ghostly dinner party while the peasants amuse themselves in their own way. But instead of preparing your usual dish of toadstools, you will prepare one three or four times the size and put it where the mortals will eat it. And eat it they shall. I'm determined about that, even if I have to shove it down their throats. Nobody who once enters my house must leave it unnourished.'

'You nev' forget the times you was the hostess with the mostes', do you, missy? But you not that any longer, remember. You just the same as pore Lilywhite. A ghostie without two pennies to jingle on your tombstone.'

'Well, at least I've got a tombstone, and you haven't,' the Countess said.

'Don' boast, missy. You as bad as them teenagers – only you not so young and you got less excuse.'

Lilywhite stared again at the kneeling artist; then she leaned forward and kicked his bottom, making him fall on his face among the wet paint.

'I not goin' to do it,' she said. 'Lilywhite don' want any more deaths on her conscience.'

'You'll do what I tell you, ye black besom,' the Countess cried.

'I won', you white besom. You only callin' the kettle black, missy.'

'If you won't do it, I'll send you back to Africa.'

'Lilywhite never been to Africa.'

'Well, I'll send you there anyway, to join the rest of your black brothers.'

'I got no brothers, missy. Lilywhite was borned in Constantinople and brung here when she was a babby. She as English as you.'

'You'll do what I tell you. Or to Africa you'll go. The Ghost Control Commission will fix it. I have influence with them.'

'I won' do it. I got no bone to pick with them trendies, except they make a lot of noise and take funny drugs.'

"Well, it's Africa and *Uhuru* for you – and see how you'll like that!'

'*Uhuru*? What that mean?'

'Freedom, you daft cow.'

'I still not do it, missy. You can ask till you as black in the face as me.'

Margaret Torryburn threatened, wept, pleaded and wheedled, but Lilywhite was adamant. Even when the Countess and the Baron wrote 'NIGGER GO HOME' all over Ardmore, she refused to budge. 'If you don' like them teenagers in their funny clothes, missy, and if you can't stand their music and racket, why don' you go back to Scotland? You got plenty of big houses there,' she said. 'You could have a fine time scarin' the kilts off the Highlandsmens.'

'My houses are all in ruins,' the Countess said, 'and the Highlanders don't wear the kilt any longer. Anyway, I died here, and here I'm going to stay.'

'I died here too, missy. I not goin' leave it either. Lilywhite like it here.'

Day after day went past and the Anniversary Dinner got nearer, and at last Margaret sent for her friend, Mr Cameron. He tried to bribe Lilywhite with a free trip to Constantinople, but she still refused. 'Lilywhite not goin' kill any more people,' she said. 'Plenty of ghosties in the world already.'

'Well, well, this is a bonnie kettle o' fish, is it no'?' Mr Cameron said. 'I doubt, my guid woman, that there's nothin' for it but to send ye back to Africy, like my lady says. I'm thrang to do it, ye understan', but I doubt I'll have to take off the velvet glove. One word from me and the Immigration folk'll be on yer track. Ye've no right to be in this country.'

'Immigrations can't touch Lilywhite. She been here all her life.'

'Can ye prove that, my bonnie hen? Whaur's yer papers?'

'What papers? Lilywhite never have no papers. She got nothin' but this ole frock she die in.'

'Oho, so ye havenie got a passport, my wee black doo? If ye havenie, ye must have made illegal entry into this country.'

'Lilywhite came here as a babby.'

'Ah, so ye were smuggled in? This looks bad for ye. I doubt there's nothin' for it but to get the Immigration authorities to deport ye as an undesirable alien – unless, of course, ye change yer mind and give thae folk the poisoned toadstools like her ladyship says.'

'Lilywhite don' want to kill anybody.'

'Ah well, ye'll just have to take the consequences. We'll have to get the Immigration folk to deport ye on the night o' yer anniversary. I'm sorry aboot this, but the law must be upheld.'

And Mr Cameron disappeared back to his London office with a whiff of brimstone.

It was only a week to the anniversary dinner and ball. The Baron gave up his amusements in the Sauna Baths to taunt Lilywhite with tales of prisons and concentration camps in Ghana and other parts of Africa. 'You know, of course,' he said, 'that under the Deportation Act you will resume your corporeal form as soon as you are taken into custody? So, after ten o'clock on Friday night, *ma belle sauvage*, you will not be able to get up to any more ghostly high-jinks. You will become a poor human again until you are lucky enough to die another time. I hope you'll have a very long and unhappy second existence. I wonder which part of Africa they'll send you to? South Africa perhaps? The Boers will have a lot of fun with you. You won't be able to write any of your filthy slogans there. But probably they'll send you to the Congo. *Ma foi*, I would not be in your shoes. I hear they have the best witch doctors in the world there. You will not be able to queen it among them and the ju-ju boys. They won't put up with any of your silly nonsense. Instead of you frightening them, they will frighten you. Some of the witch doctors are more ghoulish than any ghost. And I hear they have cannibals. I expect you'll end up in some pot and your black bones will be used as chopsticks by a witch doctor. But I hope it will be a long, long time before I can say with the playwright, "That was in another country, and besides the wench is dead".'

The Baron gloated over Lilywhite so much that even the Countess thought he went beyond the score. 'Och, leave the poor wretch alone,' she cried. 'How would you like it if I got Mr Cameron to deport you to Devil's Island?' And she said to Lilywhite: 'Why don't you change your mind, you thrawn bitch? After all, what's a few more deaths between friends?'

Lilywhite said nothing. She went about in a sullen state, impervious both to the Baron's taunts and the Countess's wheedlings. She did not even try to lighten her last days of freedom at Ardmore by terrorising the staff and the visitors.

But three days before she was due to be deported she rushed to the Countess, her eyeballs rolling with agitation, and screeched: 'Oh, missy, that ole nance here!'

'What old nance?'

'That ole queen I scared the living daylights out of on the beach at Hove. He've come to Ardmore.'

'However did he find out where you were?' the Countess said. 'Don't tell me there are snoopers in the Brighton Ghosts' Technical Institute?'

'No, he sees one of Jeff Gayheart's boy friends swaggering

as Mister Muscles on the beach and he take a fancy to him and follow him here. Now he in Jeff's room watchin' him and his boys playing at being Roman slaves.'

'So what?' the Countess said.

'I happen to go into the room and he get a shock.' Lilywhite wrung her hands with agitation. 'He pleased to see me, missy. He *delighted* to find pore Lilywhite. Such a pleasant surprise, he say, I been lookin' everywhere for you. Revenge is sweet, he say. And he say he follow me to Africa and haunt me for ever and ever.'

'We'll soon settle his hash,' the Countess said.

She thought a minute. 'We'd better give up this African idea,' she said. 'I'll go and see Mr Cameron at once and tell him to get the Immigration authorities to deport this old queen instead of you. He can spend the rest of eternity playing at being a white slave in Africa. But if I do this for you, you'll have to do something in return for me.'

'Anything you say, missy. Only don' let me be haunted by that ole nance.'

'You can get rid of the trend-setters and Old Mother Courage and her brood.'

'Okay,' Lilywhite said.

*

On the day of the Anniversary Dinner and Ball there was great activity at Ardmore. The young visitors started to dope themselves early so that they'd get into the proper 'groove' for the evening. Transistor sets banged out pop music; the trendies rushed from room to room, showing each other their fancy dresses; and Mrs Courage and her staff drank quantities of gin and whisky to get themselves as high as their charges. By mid-afternoon there was such pandemonium that the Countess, arraying herself in her ghostly finery, thought the ball had already started. 'Ah well,' she said, placing a beauty patch under her left eye, 'it'll all soon be over and Ardmore 'll go back to its former peace and quietness. I must arrange with Mr Cameron to get Mother Courage and these trendies all sent back to their native places. We can't have their ghosts here to disturb our peace and quiet any longer.'

Early in the morning, as was customary, Lilywhite had

gone out into what was left of the great park to gather the toadstools. By mid-afternoon there was no sign of her, but the Countess thought she was probably in the kitchen preparing the fatal dish.

About six o'clock the first of the pantheon of ghosts, Lady Carstairs and Squire Huggett, arrived. Lady Carstairs was horrified when she saw the television sets and the crowd of teenagers. 'My dearest Margaret!' she cried. 'How can you possibly put up with the noise? I never realised it was as awful as this. I thought it was bad at the Castle when trippers come on Sundays and climb the ruins and yell and throw their sandwich papers around and spit into the moat, but it's nothing like this *bedlam*.'

'We won't have to thole it much longer,' the Countess said. 'Lilywhite is busy now, preparing to put an end to it all.'

'Hark! What's that?' Lady Carstairs cried.

'Sounds like the hunt,' Squire Huggett said. 'Here they come! Tallyho! Tallyho! They're after the fox.'

But it was not the fox. It was the ghost of the old queen screaming with terror as he was pursued by the Immigration authorities. They watched them disappear among the new bungalows and houses. 'I hope they get him on the plane for Lagos without too much trouble,' the Countess said. 'I told Mr Cameron to get them to give him a sedative before they grabbed him, but they don't seem to have managed.'

Some more ghosts arrived to watch the hunt when the old queen doubled back across the park, dodging here and there in frenzy as the Immigration men tried to lassoo him. 'I wonder what has happened to Lilywhite?' the Countess said. 'She should have been here by this time to help me with my ballgown – though there's little she can really do, the gown's got so tattered with all the wear and tear through the years.'

She went to the kitchen, but she found only the chef and Mrs Courage arguing about how much sherry he should put in a trifle while they toasted each other with champagne. 'This is most mysterious,' the Countess said, going back to her guests. 'I hope those stupid Immigration folk haven't grabbed her too. They're quite liable to make a mistake.'

'It is pleasant to think of Lilywhite and that depraved old man flying together in an aeroplane to Africa at this moment,' the Baron said, taking a pinch of snuff.

'For you, perhaps,' Margaret said acidly. 'But not for me. I must get rid of this *canaille*.'

More ghosts arrived, and by half past seven, the time when they should have been preparing to enter the dining-room for the fatal meal, they had all congregated except Lilywhite. The Countess was frantic. The human beings had already started their fancy dress dance. Many of them were standing in the ballroom, twisting themselves into quaint shapes, facing each other but scarcely ever touching. Others were staring, with drugged looks, at the television sets. A famous pop group with long hair, moronic faces, electric guitars and obscene gestures were posturing around a girl singer who was clutching a microphone and moaning strange, uncouth gibberish. Upstairs in his suite Jeff Gayheart and his boy friends, doped into unconsciousness, were lying in abandoned states of nakedness. The staff had already started to eat the buffet supper, knowing none of the teenagers would want to eat. The pantheon of ghosts stood helplessly among the gyrating and comatose humans; they were behind schedule, and each was wondering whether the National Union of British Ghosts would blame them for the delay and exact some dire penalty.

At that moment Lilywhite whirled into the dining-room, screaming: 'Missy! Missy! What we goin' to do, missy? There no toadstools left. I been hunting all over the great park. I been for miles, but all the toadstools gone. They been poisoned and killed by that new artificial manure they putting down everywhere. Lord have mercy on us all! What we goin' to do now, missy?'

2

Every Woman Her Own Ghost

When Lilywhite heard there was to be a Happening, she said to the Countess: 'What that, missy?'

'It's one of those do-it-yourself things, you daft black cow,' the other ghost said. 'It's like those books – Every Man His Own Lawyer, Every Man His Own Doctor, Every Man His

Own Carpenter – you know, you do it yourself and trust to luck.'

'Lilywhite don' know, but she willin' to learn.' She chuckled maliciously. 'She willin' to have a bit of fun, too.'

'Aren't we all?' said the Countess. 'Like Frederick Lonsdale.'

'Who he, missy?'

'Don't pretend to be stupider than you are,' the Countess said. 'We all know you never graduated farther than writing four-letter words, but you're not as daft as you sometimes let on. You must have seen one of Lonsdale's plays revived on the telly.'

Lilywhite giggled and said: '*Touché.*'

In the past two hundred and sixty years she had learnt some French from the Baron.

She had just returned from Brighton. She had gone there on the stolen motor scooter to play pranks on the holiday-makers on the beach and to see if she could learn any new tricks from them. Ever since Ardmore Manor had been turned into a Motel for Under-Privileged Youth, Lilywhite and the Countess of Torryburn and the Baron Charles de Riveaux, had been attempting to get rid of the long-haired, drug-taking teenagers who arrived continually in expensive high-powered cars. But so far they had not managed to frighten them away. Some of these labourers who wanted to be artists, factory hands who thought they were film stars, electrician's mates who were trying to write novels, girls who aspired to be models and actresses, and layabouts whose key word was 'pot' stayed for a night; but some stayed for a week and some for a fortnight, according to how long they could afford to pay the motel's high prices. The staff, headed by pink-haired Mrs Courage, was permanent; and so, apparently, was Jeff Gayheart, the pop singer, who had lived now for a year in the most expensive suite. He left it only occasionally to make recordings of songs or personal appearances at London airport before flying to Paris, Tangier or Rome to collect new boy friends. Jeff's boys changed so often that Lilywhite had lost count of them, even though she could count up to a hundred, with difficulty.

When she'd come home, jubilant because she had held a

beautiful but obnoxious muscle-man, who played with little girls, under the water for ten minutes and drowned him, the Countess told her that a new batch of guests had arrived. They were art students. They had booked for a fortnight and were going to stage a Happening in the middle of it.

'We must make their stay as unpleasant as possible,' the Countess said. 'Unwashed *canaille* that they are! They're from swinging London, but some of them obviously haven't swung their legs over a bath for six months.'

After having a look at the new arrivals, Lilywhite went up on the roof to think. It was a dark night; there was no moon, and the sky was filled with heavy rain clouds. She was gliding up and down in the corridor dividing the roofs between the east and west towers when suddenly there was an agonising pain in her arm. Lilywhite screamed:

'Stop that, nigger!'

She plucked the grinning black skull from her arm and held it aloft. 'What you bite me for, boy?' she demanded.

The skull grinned even wider. 'Give you a surprise, huh?'

'You shoulden do things like that to ole ladies,' Lilywhite grumbled, placing the skull in a raised part of the roof and sitting beside it.

'Old? You not old, sweetie pie,' the skull said.

'Over three hundred years,' Lilywhite said proudly. 'Was forty-three when I was drownded in 1704 after the big battle of Blenheim. How old you, boy?'

'Don' know,' the skull said.

'Why you not got a body, mate?' she said.

'It buried somewhere in Africa, sweetie pie,' the skull said. 'Some ole explorer brought ma head here and give it to the medicine men in a big college, and then they give it to some arty students who draws it. Them students bring me here for somethin' call a Happenin'.'

'I knows about that,' she said. 'We ghosties goin' have some fun with them hippies, eh?'

She placed the skull on her shoulder. 'See, boy! We be one black skeleton with two heads. We frighten the piss outen them arty students, eh?'

'Whatever you say, sweetie pie. I game for all kinds of larks.'

'Don' call me that,' she said. 'Lilywhite nobody's sweetie pie. She not sweet and she not a pie. I poison lots of folkses before I drowns myself. I poison my missy and her boy friend, Charlie. They been here with me ever since.'

'All ghosty pals together, eh?' The skull grinned so widely it nearly split in two.

'Charlie and me not pals,' Lilywhite said. 'He get on Lilywhite's tits. Lilywhite wish he'd go home and get lost.'

She put her elbows on her knees and stared into the darkness. 'All poor ghosties should go home and be at peace,' she said, brooding. 'Where you from, boy?'

'Where you from?' the skull said.

'Don' be cheeky, nigger. This my home. I not from Africa like you. I was borned in Constantinople and brung here as a babby. Lilywhite English through and through. She not poor black African trash like you.'

Lilywhite gazed at the skull as it hovered several feet above her, even blacker than the drifting clouds. 'What they call you, mate?'

'Me used to be called "you slave" by my master that was big sheikh in the desert. He the one that cut off ma head because I sleep with one of his lil Arab girls. Cut everythin' else too, before that. Arty students calls me Black Mamba now.'

'C'mon, Mamba,' Lilywhite said. 'Let's go talk to my missy and Misyew lee Baron about what we do to scare the jeans offen them fun kids.'

*

It was the night of the Happening. Lilywhite had decided to materialise and wear a mini skirt for the occasion. 'Jus' for a little while at the beginning,' she said. 'I go back to being a ghostie after that, and then me and Mamba create merry hell like we plan. So many people here, all colours, nobody know who I am.'

'But your legs, Lilywhite!' the Countess cried. 'Your big hams! And those great muckle calves of yours! You'll look as if you're bursting through a potato sack.'

'Can't look worse than some of them London dollies. They got legs like pillar boxes. See, I pinched this nice white mini skirt from that little bird in Room 16. Her they calls the Sex

Symbol. She think she Pola Negri, Jean Harlow and Marilyn Monroe rolled into one. Poor stupid cow, she never make the headlines. She not got a face like Gloria Swanson say they had in her day. 'S a bit tight, but Mamba think I look smashin' in it.'

'Do what you like, you crazy black besom,' the Countess said. 'But if your big backside bursts the seams don't blame me.'

'Lilywhite never blame anybody,' she said with dignity. 'What you goin' wear, missy?'

'Nothing,' the Countess said. 'I have no intention of taking part in the early revels. I won't materialise until the time comes, and then that phosphorescent paint should be enough.'

And so Lilywhite dressed in the stolen mini skirt, a white sweater that was so tight it hurt her breasts, and a wig of orange hair that reached her shoulders. She painted her eyelids grass green and put on a pair of long false eyelashes. 'Baby, you ma great big beautiful doll!' Black Mamba grinned. 'You knock 'em all dead, honey.'

'I hope so,' Lilywhite said. 'Though I don' want any of them to join us as ghosties for the rest of eternity. I want make them all rush back to swinging London with their tails at half-mast.'

A great number of people came to the Happening. Mrs Courage and her staff had sent invitations to all the bigwigs of Sussex. Famous intellectuals of all denominations, poets, artists, actors and novelists, as well as what was left of the landed gentry, started to arrive at Ardmore Manor about seven o'clock. Lilywhite, frisky in her fleeced flummeries, mingled freely with the guests, introducing herself as the exiled Princess of Badelmandib. The Countess, completely invisible, kept close beside her. Baron Charles de Riveaux, also invisible, sat in Jeff Gayheart's sitting-room, drinking ghost free whisky. Black Mamba, immersed in his skull, grinned on top of a table in a small room, waiting until Giles, the scruffy art student who was arranging the Happening, was ready for him. Giles, wearing a mangy musquash coat that might have belonged to his grandmother, was already high on marijuana.

At seven-thirty the lights were dimmed. The guests sat on

flimsy gold lacquered chairs in front of a platform raised against the french windows of what once had been the great drawing-room. A large fat seventy-year-old novelist sat in the front row, his programme held in podgy hands between thick thighs. He had been awarded the Nobel Prize for Literature, even though he had bad breath, thick ankles and a compulsive habit of patting young men's bums. Lilywhite sat on one side of him; an evil-looking youth with a wispy beard, wearing the uniform of a sergeant in the regiment nicknamed the Duke's Canaries of the year 1870, sat on the other. As soon as he sat down the Nobel Prize Winner turned to this youth, clapped his hands loudly and said: 'Isn't this tremendously exciting!'

'What exciting about it?' Lilywhite said to the Countess. 'Jus' wait till we start, missy. I give him something so exciting he make a mess in his pants.'

The pseudo-sergeant said nothing. He stared with dull eyes at the platform. He didn't know he was staring through the Countess, who was sitting on the edge of it keeping an eye on both the audience and the performers gathered in the impromptu wings.

A juke box began to play a pop record. A painfully plain and conceited youth with a greasy shoulder-length bob minced across the platform holding up a large white board on which was scrawled 'A Happening'. He opened the french windows, glanced back at the audience, tossed his head, gave a little snigger and went out with a wriggle of his thin hips.

The old novelist applauded and said: 'My word, isn't this fun!'

The young man in the uniform stroked his beard and stared ahead. The novelist turned to Lilywhite and said: 'Where do you come from, my dear?'

'Swinging Chelsea, love.' She giggled and fluttered her false eyelashes. 'Full of beatnik beardies and ole queens.'

Giles, who had taken off his granny's fur coat to reveal a pair of Grenadier Guards trousers and a grubby white shirt that foamed with Shelley-like lace frills, came onto the platform clutching a microphone. 'This, ladies and gentlemen, is a happening,' he said in a cockney voice. 'It will bring you all on to the contemporary scene and show you its psychedelic motivations. If you aren't trendy you won't understand it, and if you don't understand it it's your loss. But if you're in the groove it should be a great psychomatic experience. This rave has been imagined and devised by Chris Cooper-Riordan, and it will begin with Chris reading some of his own poems.'

Three youths bounded onto the platform; two were blowing trumpets, the third banging a toy drum. They were followed by a willowy beanpole with lank platinum hair who wore a Second World War army greatcoat dyed bright green. He grabbed the microphone from Giles, held it close to his mouth and gabbled:

Riding on a Lambretta
Round and
Round
Piccadilly ...
We will not lick policemen's arses.
We will smoke pot if we want to.
The policemen can sit on their potties
And lick lollipops.

'Isn't this marvellous?' the Nobel Prize Winner whispered. 'These young people are so original. They have so much more imagination than we had when we were young.'

'You speak for yourself, mate,' Lilywhite muttered.

While Chris Cooper-Riordan, with eyes shut, was gabbling more poems into the microphone, half a dozen girls ran onto the stage. They had white frilly caps perched on top of their long hair, black shoes with spike heels and tiny white lace aprons tied with black velvet ribbon. Otherwise they were naked.

'Topless waitresses!' the Nobel Prize Winner breathed. 'My word, how original! How really marvellous!'

He clapped wildly. A number of others joined in his applause.

Some waitresses carried bags of soot, some carried bags of flour. They dipped in their hands and started to throw it at each other and at Chris. He took no notice; he went on gabbling into the microphone. The trumpeters and the drummer stood outside the french windows and blew and beat tunelessly.

'Isn't it trendy!' screamed someone behind Lilywhite.

'Isn't it fab!' cried another.

'Bravo!' the Nobel Prize Winner shouted. 'Bravo!'

Two youths pushed a dustbin onto one side of the platform; another two pushed another dustbin onto the other side. Two waitresses clambered on the tops of the dustbins, smeared themselves with soot and began to scream. They went on screaming relentlessly, rocking themselves in complete abandonment, their faces alight with ecstasy.

'Isn't this tremendous fun!' cried the old novelist.

The big black woman with the orange hair nodded regally and said: 'Sure is. 'S what I calls smashin'.'

'Oh, we're living it up!' the novelist shouted. 'It's fab. Absolutely fab!'

'I'm on the banana!' screamed Lilywhite, who had heard a weirdie use the expression.

The topless waitresses rushed about the stage, screaming and throwing soot and flour. The trumpeters were blowing wildly; the drummer was banging madly. Chris Cooper-Riordan was still clutching the microphone, still gabbling a stream of meaningless words into it. The four youths, who had disappeared into the wings, came back carrying balloons tied to the ends of sticks and belaboured the waitresses. The waitresses ran off, pursued by the youths. The plain youth with the greasy hair minced on again, carrying a large card that proclaimed 'There is No Godot But Beckett.'

The lid was thrust off one of the dustbins and Giles stood up in it and cried: 'Allah il Allah! We are the truth and the light. Any gods before us were bums. All gods are bums except the young. Their motivations are purer than the lilies that bowed down before Solomon in all his non-glory ... '

'How brilliant! How clever!' the Nobel Prize Winner cried. 'Isn't this exciting! Isn't it madly exciting!'

'Ole fool,' Lilywhite muttered. 'You cuttin' your own throat, man. And not only that – you cuttin' the throats of other oldies at the same time.'

'I'm a product of my environment,' Giles whined. 'There are five elementary ingredients – air, water, fire, earth and psychedelic upheavals. The young are motivated by pure aesthetic joy, with a belief in each other. They will have no

truck with the out-dated, moth-eaten fuddy-duddies of the
past. They look forward. They look upward. They move
onward with the machines that have freed men from the
tyranny of the oppressor. Only the young know the joys of free
and beautiful and worthwhile experience. Only the young are
fit and capable of leading the tired old world into new
boundless joys and unheard of happenings ... '

The old novelist felt a hand on his thigh. He turned to
Lilywhite. Her seat was empty. He turned with delight to the
young pseudo-sergeant. He was sitting with hands clasped
beneath his weak thinly bearded chin, gazing entranced at the
stage and Giles's top half swaying in the dustbin. The hand
moved up between the old novelist's legs and squeezed. He
squealed.

'That the stuff you want to give the troops,' a voice
whispered. 'Lilywhite havin' a ball. What you havin', mate?'

The hand squeezed energetically, and the old novelist
shrieked with anguish.

Several youths ran through the french windows, carrying
swords. They were naked except for riding boots and
guardsmen's plumed helmets. Giles went on speaking, then he
looked at the other dustbin and yelled: 'Like our twin spirits!'

The naked guardsmen leapt off the platform, and ran
among the audience, slapping each other's bottoms with the
flats of their swords. 'Like our twin spirits!' Giles yelled. 'Like
our twin spirits! Like our twin ... ' He began to gasp for
breath, his eyes popping.

The lid of the other dustbin rose in the air and fell with a
clatter. But the youth who should have appeared like a jack-
in-the-box didn't. He could not take his cue.

All the lights went out. The Countess, her skeleton covered
with phosphorescent paint, floated through the french
windows. The Baron, dressed in his tattered centuries-old silk
coat and breeches, rose out of the same dustbin as Giles,
leering wickedly. Two black skulls joined to the same skeleton
leapt out of the second dustbin, swayed across the platform
and went down among the audience. Their mouths were wide
open and their teeth gleamed as they screamed bloodthirsty
African slogans.

The old Nobel Prize Winner had fainted, but nobody took

any notice. Too many other people had fainted at the same time. The others were running towards the exit, scrambling over each other to get out. 'Get your big arse out of my way, you fat whore!' a famous Shakespearean actor yelled at an opera singer from Glyndebourne.

Giles, freed from the Baron's hand on his windpipe, fell out of his dustbin and staggered across the platform. When he saw what was in the second dustbin he screamed and fainted.

The body of the youth who had been taking the part of the second Beckett-like character was lying curled up in his dustbin. He had been strangled.

'Silly boy,' Lilywhite said to the Countess. 'He got a fright when me and Mamba join him. Lilywhite try to make him hush, but he struggle too much. Lilywhite couldn't help it. She got enthusiastic.'

*

By three o'clock in the morning the Inspector in charge of the investigation felt that he was turning as daft as the weirdies he'd been interviewing for hours. At least six people swore they'd seen the dead youth, Benny Alper, get into the dustbin, that they'd put on its lid and then had trundled it onto the platform. Another fifty swore that nobody had lifted the lid; all the time it was in full view of the audience until it had gone up in the air like a rocket and the two-headed black ghost had come out. The Inspector would have been inclined to think that Benny had died of asphyxiation except that the marks of manual strangulation were too strongly imprinted on his throat.

At last he said wearily: 'It's an outside job. No doubt about that.'

'I agree with you, Inspector,' the old Nobel Prize Winner said pompously. 'I was assaulted myself by a strange young man. Someone who definitely is not a member of this party. He must have come through the french windows when the lights were dimmed.'

'Yes, sir,' the Inspector said even more wearily. He said to one of his constables: 'Where's that identiti-kit of the bloke who did that job at Strawbourne Heath last week? The one that knocked the old girl on the head and got away with the seven hundred quid she'd sewn in her mattress.'

The policeman held up an identiti-kit drawing of a youth with a sullen face, vacant eyes and shoulder-length light hair. He held it in such a way that nobody could see it properly. The Inspector said: 'Have any of you seen anybody that looks like that?'

All the long-haired youths looked vacantly at it, looked at each other and shook their heads.

'Don' look like nobody,' Lilywhite said. 'Looks like them all.'

'What this dentikit palaver anyway?' Black Mamba said.

'It's one of them do-it-yourself pictures, you ignorant nigger. Only you doesn't do it yourself. The police does it for you. They takes a bit of you – your nose maybe – and then they takes a bit of me – my eyes maybe – then they takes a bit of missy – her mouth – and they strings them all together and say: "Has anybody here seen Kelly? K. E. double L. Y See, this the bad man what did the murder." '

'Funny,' said Mamba.

'Not so funny for the poor cow that looks like everybody else. Lilywhite don't like when the police does things. She like to make her own dentikit like the book missy tell me about – How To Make Your Own Canoe.'

'I paddle your canoe for you, baby!' Mamba grinned.

'If you try that caper, man, Lilywhite paddle your black bum. You wish you was back with your old Arab sheikh.'

'But I know this man,' the Nobel Prize Winner cried, snatching the identiti-kit picture from the constable. 'He sat next to me. He was the one who assaulted me.'

The youth with the wispy beard and the Victorian uniform began to look alarmed.

'Yes, this is the one,' the old novelist said. 'He had very bright orange-coloured hair. A murderous-looking thug. He told me he came from Chelsea. A most extraordinary young man. He wore a white mini-skirt.'

'Mine,' screamed the Sex Symbol from Room Sixteen. 'I wondered who'd stolen it.'

'That'll be our man,' the Inspector said with relief. 'Write this down, constable. "At nineteen hours forty-five minutes when the lights were extinguished, the suspected person was seen to assault this gentleman and then proceed onto the platform towards the dustbin, where he promptly carried out the crime of manual strangulation on the person of Benjamin Abraham Alper of Studio 5, Wildrose Gardens, etc." You've got the address and all the other particulars. Send this identiti-kit to all the stations in the district. Now, let's get cracking. I need some shut-eye.'

*

'There's something evil about this place,' Mrs Courage said the following evening. 'I've always felt it ever since I came here. All sorts of funny things have happened.'

'Evil? What she mean, missy?' Lilywhite said. 'She evil. She and them arty-crafty whiz kids the onliest evil things here. We good old time ghosties.'

'Nothin' evil about us, man,' Black Mamba said.

'I should think not,' the Countess said. 'We mind our own business. We interfere with nobody – unless they interfere with us first.'

'Let's drive the *canaille* into the sea,' said the Baron, taking a pinch of snuff.

'Good ole Charlie boy!' Lilywhite said. 'How we goin' do it, mate?'

'I'm sure there are uneasy spirits here,' Mrs Courage said. 'I can sense them. I can feel the poor crazy creatures creeping about, miserable because they're excluded from our happy carefree activities. They want to join in our revels. They ache to be part of our huge family circle. They want to be trendy and kooky like the rest of us, but they can't, poor dears. They're inhibited and old-fashioned. They want to get in the groove and be swinging with us all, but their past lives won't let them. We must do something to liberate them.'

'Why not hold a seance, madam?' said Molly, an Irish member of Old Mother Courage's sycophantic staff. 'I know a medium in Brighton, madam, who'd be only too glad to come here and help those poor unhappy creatures to find peace.'

'An excellent idea,' Mrs Courage said, nodding her pink-haired head sagely. 'Perhaps you could ask your friend ... '

A few days later Madame Wanda, a small, shrivelled woman in a lavender twin set and a lavender tulle hat arrived.

Her beady brown eyes were half hidden under hooded lizard-like lids, and her false teeth seemed ready to fall out every time she grinned, which was often. She carried a large black plastic handbag that contained, Lilywhite soon found, a half bottle of gin, a packet of mints, a roll of white muslin, a spare set of false teeth, nail scissors, two packets of Woodbine, a cigarette-lighter, a grubby comb, an even grubbier compact and a purse with seven pounds, nine shillings and tenpence and a return bus ticket to Brighton in it.

'I'm ever so pleased to meet you, love,' she greeted Mrs Courage. 'And I do 'ope I'll be able to solve your little problem. I feel sure I shall. I always 'ave great success with unhappy spirits. I think you'll find after we've 'ad our sitting and I've called our friends out of astral space that we'll come to an understanding with them. Poor things, maybe they just need a little sympathy and encouragement to 'elp them to move on to an 'igher sphere and then they won't trouble you no more.'

The seance was held in Mrs Courage's private sitting-room, and about a dozen of the under-privileged weirdies, those who'd been close buddies of Benny Alper, attended it, along with Molly and a few members of the staff who were anxious to keep in with madam. Before it began, Madame Wanda said coyly to Mrs Courage: 'Excuse me, love, but I must go to the toilet. I always get ever so nervous before we 'ave a sitting.'

She didn't know that Lilywhite and the Countess accompanied her to the lavatory. As soon as she'd got inside and bolted the door, she rummaged in her plastic bag for the half bottle of gin. But Lilywhite had already taken it out, and she and the Countess had drunk most of it. They hadn't been able to share it with the Baron and Mamba, for the Baron had refused to attend the seance, preferring to amuse himself in the Sauna Baths instead, and they hadn't seen Mamba since that morning when they'd buried his skull in the hole by the river where Lilywhite's own skeleton lay so that the art students couldn't take it back to London.

'Bloody 'ell, I been robbed,' Madame Wanda cried. 'Thievin' lot ... '

At that moment the bottle materialised on the washbasin. Madame Wanda's eyes widened and she looked around her like a frightened sparrow. But her thirst was so great that she did not trouble to investigate; she took off the stopper, put the bottle to her mouth, and had a great gulp. After peering around, she took another swig, put the stopper back on the bottle, put it in her bag and unbolted the door, muttering: 'It's like everything else, gin ain't what it used to be. Or is this place a bloody sight rummier than what I thought?'

'This a funny one, missy. She give Lilywhite the creeps,' the black ghost said.

'She gives me the creeps too. Something strange came into this house with her. I can't see what it is, but I can sense it. All this talk of hers about unhappy friends from "some world far from ours". What does she mean? What other world is there?'

'Maybe she mean people from outer space, missy?'

'Och, don't haver,' the Countess said. 'You've been watching too much science fiction on the telly. You'll be telling me next you believe in men from Mars. Have you ever seen what they call a flying saucer? You know as well as I do there's only this world. I wonder if she means that there're ghosts here that even we ghosts can't see?'

'Shoulden be surprised,' Lilywhite said. 'Somethin' funny certainly happen when this ole bag come in the front door. It make Lilywhite's bones rattle.'

Mrs Courage and the weirdies were already sitting round the table. Madame Wanda drew the curtains and sat down, saying: 'Please all put your 'ands flat on the table and let your pinkies touch the pinkies of the ones next you. Now, if you will all please try to think about nothing … '

'Shoulden be difficult,' Lilywhite giggled, and she viciously tugged the hair of one of Jeff Gayheart's boy friends.

He yelped and kicked out.

'Watch it, mate,' Jeff snarled, looking under the table at the trousers of his Crimean War uniform. 'You're muckin' up me gear.'

'Quiet, please,' Madame Wanda said. She closed her eyes, tilted her face ceilingwards and said in a voice that was much stronger than her usual tone: 'If there are any unhappy friends here who want to communicate with us, will they please tap on the table?'

There was silence except for a giggle from the Sex Symbol.

'Don't be afraid,' Madame Wanda said. 'We are all friends here and we only want to 'elp you. Are you here, Sheikh Abdullah Oman? If you are, please tap on the table.'

There was a loud tap.

'Sheikh Abdullah Oman is my spirit guide,' Madame Wanda said in her normal tone. 'I shall now go into a trance and 'e will enter my body and take over.'

The Sex Symbol giggled again.

Madame Wanda closed her eyes. Suddenly she gave a jerk and her body stiffened. Her mouth opened and she began to gasp as if struggling for air. Then a man's deep voice said: 'I am with you. I have come a long way this evening to help you. I have come from the fields of larger life, from that finer realm where my spirit has lived happily for over seventy years. If you wish to get in touch with any dear ones, will you please speak freely? ... What? What was that? There is somebody here, a spirit – I can scarcely see it, so it must be someone who has only recently departed, for it has not yet reached the higher realm but is hovering in that limbo into which we all go before we achieve entry into the greater fields. Who are you, my friend? And who do you want to speak to? Will you please tap out your message? One tap for yes, two taps for no. Does your name begin with A?'

There were six or seven frenzied taps on the table.

'This ghost can't count, missy,' Lilywhite said.

'Don't boast, you brazen black besom,' the Countess said. 'I don't like this Abdullah Oman creature at all. I can't see any sign of him, but maybe he can see and hear us.'

'You know as well as me it all a fake, missy. It all come from that funny little woman. See, she was kickin' under the table. It all palavers.'

But Madame Wanda's feet were lying slackly on the floor when Sheikh Abdullah said: 'Does your name begin with C?' and there was one loud tap.

'It is a man, I can see him now,' Abdullah said. 'Is there anybody here with a dear departed whose name began with C?'

Mrs Courage gazed through her cigarette smoke. 'Perhaps ... my husband. He was Llewellyn Courage. He passed over five years ago.'

'Is your name Llewellyn?' said the Sheikh.

There was silence.

'It must be another C,' said the Sheikh. 'Who are you, my friend?'

There was such a frenzied tapping that the table shook. Lilywhite grinned at the Countess, leaned over Jeff Gayheart's shoulder and started to tap too.

'Stop, stop! Not so fast,' cried Abdullah. 'What? Yes, his name is Courage. His other name is ... I can't make it out. It begins with a T. Is it Tom?'

'Take,' gasped Mrs Courage, and her cigarette fell from her mouth. 'Oh, God, no! It can't be Take.'

'It is Take Courage,' Sheikh Abdullah said solemnly.

'My brother-in-law,' Mrs Courage whispered. 'It was the name we always called him. He liked Courage's beer, so we nicknamed him that after the advertisements. Oh, Take, Take!' she said. 'Is it really you? Show me you're here. Show me!'

'He has gone,' the Sheikh said. 'He's gone back into limbo.'

Mrs Courage screamed.

Lilywhite had lifted off her pink wig and was holding it high above the centre of the table.

'Oh, Take!' Mrs Courage moaned, putting her hands on her scalp. 'Why've you done this to me? Not even Llewellyn knew. Only you. It was our secret ... '

As Mrs Courage slumped in her chair in a faint, Lilywhite replaced the wig, and Madame Wanda jerked up and said in her normal voice: 'There's nobody 'ere who wants to get in touch with the dear departed, Mister Abby love. We are 'aving this sitting tonight to find what un'appy friends are disturbing the peace and quiet of this gracious mansion. We want to 'elp those un'appy people to move on to another sphere.'

'My mistake,' said Sheikh Abdullah Oman's voice.

'Granted,' Madame Wanda said.

Molly and another of her staff tried to revive Mrs Courage by slapping her hands, but she didn't open her eyes until Lilywhite gave her face a hard slap. 'That bloody Take!' she cried, sitting up and straightening her wig. 'Oh, I feel so unwell. I must have some brandy.'

'I'll get it for you, madam,' Molly said, and she scuttled quickly out of the room.

The Sheikh's deep voice said: 'There is one unhappy spirit here tonight. I can see you there in the shadows. I can see you. I don't know who you are. I have never seen you in the finer realm, but I know you want to communicate with us. Will you come forward? If you don't wish to speak through the body of our medium, will you please answer my questions by tapping. Are you a spirit that has been long departed from this physical plane?'

The Countess suddenly cried with alarm: 'Oh, my God! I see a ghost! An odd-like creature in a wimple has just materialised.'

'Your eyes better 'n mine, missy … Ooooh!' Lilywhite shrieked. 'That ole woman, she comin' to get me. She comin' straight for pore Lilywhite.'

A tiny shrivelled ghost with a skin as brown as her shapeless garment hovered above the table, bright mouse-like eyes glittering beneath her white headdress. She leered malevolently at Lilywhite and the Countess, who clung together and backed away into a corner. The old woman cackled. But none of those seated around the table seemed to see or hear her. The young man next the Sex Symbol was feeling her under the table. Jeff Gayheart was trying to rub a spot out of the arm of his uniform. Mrs Courage was slumped in her chair, mouth slightly open.

Lilywhite shook herself. 'Maybe she not a real ghost, missy. Maybe she one of them dentikit ones the police make to frighten us.'

'She's real enough,' the Countess said, shivering. 'A pox on her! She's trying to put the evil eye on us.'

'Real or not real,' Lilywhite said. 'She a tattie ole number.'

'I do wish you'd stop watching the telly, Lilywhite. You do pick up the quaintest expressions. It's really got to the stage where I can't take you into decent society with any confidence.'

A thin high voice came through Madame Wanda's lips: 'I am Gudrun, the Wise Old Woman of Ardmore. It is many hundreds of years since a wicked knight and his men dragged me away from my hovel of mud and wattle and tied me to a stake on the village green and burnt me as a witch. This wicked knight wanted the land on which my hovel stood. He built this mansion on it. For over seven hundred years my ghost has been imprisoned beneath this house, which has grown and grown since then, every stone, every brick forcing poor old Gudrun even deeper underground. I have tried and I have tried to escape, to make myself known. I have tried and tried, seeking revenge on that wicked man and his descendants. But not until tonight has my ghost been freed from bondage. Tonight, thanks be to God and that good foreign spirit, Sheikh Abdullah Oman, I have been able to materialise. I am free! Free! Ah, you poor earth people, you may not be able to see poor old Gudrun. She is too old, too thin to be seen by mortal eyes. But she can be seen now by her fellow ghosts. Ay prithee, for there are other ghosts here – wicked ghosts ... '

'Spirits,' said Sheikh Abdullah's deep voice. 'There are no ghosts in God's Celestial Garden. We are all spirits ... '

'We are ghosts, I tell you,' Gudrun screamed. 'I am a good ghost, but there are others here whose souls are black with wickedness. There is a big fat black woman with a poisonous mind and tongue. There is a fair-haired man, a swaggering brutal soldier, a dirty foreigner who takes snuff. And there is a woman, a beautiful proud wicked Jezebel, who is a descendant of that knight who burnt old Gudrun until not even her bones were left. Lack a day, lack a day! For over two hundred and fifty years I have tried to haunt them, but they have ignored me. I have screamed at them, I have touched them, I have tried to strike the fear of God into their black hearts. But they have never heeded me. They have looked through poor old Gudrun as though she were the dust beneath their feet. They have been too proud, too full of their own importance as ghosts to notice the existence of a poor burnt old woman. But now I can manifest. Gudrun, the Wise Old Woman of Ardmore has come to life again. She's free! And now I will have my revenge.'

Madame Wanda cackled so venemously that those around the table, who had been listening with popping eyes, clutched each other's hands and shivered. Jeff Gayheart quickly swallowed three purple hearts.

Lilywhite and the Countess clung together in the corner.

'Don' let that ole witch get near me, missy,' Lilywhite pleaded.

'I can't do anything about it, you silly cow,' the Countess cried, backing against the wall until both she and Lilywhite passed through it into the next room where Molly was drinking a large brandy before refilling the glass and taking it to Mother Courage.

Old Gudrun was too carried away by her harangue to follow them. This was the first audience she'd had for centuries; she was determined to make the most of it. She knew, anyway, that she could plague Lilywhite and the Countess for evermore.

'My fellow ghosts have never seen me,' she screeched. 'But now they can, and I will make them pay. Ay, how I will make them pay! I will haunt that big black woman until she wishes she were back in her native land. And I'll haunt that wicked Margaret Torryburn, her that calls herself a Countess, until she howls for mercy. Oh, revenge is sweet! I will make them pay for all their own sins, as well as the sins of their ancestors. I will pay them again and again – hundreds and thousands of times – for every flame that crept up towards poor old Gudrun's face ... '

'Now, see what you've done!' the Countess cried. 'You're to blame for this, you pestilent doxy. You should be burnt at the stake too. If you hadn't tried your daft capers to get rid of Old Mother Courage and her brood they'd never have held this seance and all this would never have happened.'

'Lilywhite issen to blame. You make the balls, missy, and she fire them.'

'It's your fault entirely. I wouldn't have bothered to try to get rid of these weirdies. I have nothing against them. I quite like them, in fact. They add to the gaiety of nations. They amuse me immensely. But you, you big fat black jade! You can't bear them. You loathe the sight of them. So they must go. To please the great Lady Lilywhite! And see what you've done now! Your plan's misfired. We'll be saddled with this vitriolic old hag for the rest of eternity.'

'We have to get rid of her somehow, missy. We must make a plan ... '

'You and your plans!' the Countess screamed. 'That's what you said about old Ma Courage and the whiz kids. And look at the mess you've made of it!'

'You want to get rid of them as much as me. Don' you try to wriggle out of this, missy. You and that dirty Frenchy as much to blame as pore Lilywhite. You think you so clever, missy, because you a Countess and can read and write good and dance 'n curtsy at ole fat Anne's palace. But you jus' a stupid bitch of a ghost now – a lot stupider than Lilywhite.'

'Oh, you snake-tongued limmer!' The Countess seized Lilywhite by the hair and shook her.

'Who you callin' snake-tongued, you Scottish hoor?' Lilywhite cried, catching the other by the throat. 'Lilywhite a babby in arms compared with you and lee Baron. You a viper, Margaret Torryburn. I go file a complaint with Mr Cameron of the National Union of British Ghosts and sue you for libel. I get big damages, so jus' you watch your step and your forked tongue.'

Madame Wanda was now giving eldritch screeches while the ghost of old Gudrun danced in the air above her, clawing at the skull of Black Mamba grinning a foot away from her face.

Lilywhite released the Countess. Margaret gave her throat a rub, and then they moved slowly through the wall.

'That ole crone didden know about Mamba,' Lilywhite said. 'Funny,' she said, reflectively picking her nose. 'You woulda thought she'd knowed.'

'He mustn't have been on her wave-length,' the Countess said.

'He on it now.' Lilywhite grinned. 'Maybe he scare her so good she go back underground.'

'He can scare her to kingdom come as far as I'm concerned,' the Countess said. 'Come to that, I think he's scaring more folk than her.'

By this time Mamba and old Gudrun had become manifest to those around the table as well as to the other ghosts. Jeff Gayheart screamed and passed out. All the others, except Mrs Courage, rushed to the door, fighting each other to get away.

'Do you recognise me, granny?' Mamba leered at Gudrun. 'It's your lil' grandson, sweetie pie – the one you strangle at

birth with a cord when my mammy that was yo' daughter
have me when my black daddy come to England after the last
crusade.'

'Get thee hence, you black devil!' Gudrun shouted. 'You
are sent by Satan, the Unholy One, to terrorise a poor old
woman. I had no grandson.'

'Oh yes, you had, granny! You think nobody know. You
hide my mammy in yo' lil' hut and you give my daddy poison
meat so he get the bellyache and die. Maybe you manage to
hide it from all stupid peasants in village, because they
frighten of the Wise Ole Woman, but you can't hide it from
me. I saw deep into yo' black heart, sweetie pie, when you put
the cord roun' my neck and pull.'

'Liar! Liar!' Gudrun screeched.

'You bury me deep under yo' hut,' Mamba said. 'But five
hundred years after that I gets borned again in Africa. I's
what they calls a re-in-car-nat-ion. And I gets killed again
when I's a grown man. But soon as I die second time I
remembers ma firs' life of few hours in this cole, cole country.
You can't fool Mamba, granny. I here now to haunt you for
ever and ever amen. I got two heads here. A lil' babby body
with a head buried away deep under this big house, and a big
skull without a body buried in a secret place where them arty-
crafty students won' find it. I be able to haunt you good now.
You won' know which way to turn. Two heads is better than
one!'

Gudrun shrieked again and again, then her body flew
downwards and disappeared through the floor.

One of Mamba's empty eye-sockets winked at Lilywhite.

Madame Wanda, who had been sitting stiffly with eyes
shut, suddenly sat up and yawned. 'Oooo, my 'ead!' she
muttered, and she reached into her plastic bag and took a swig
of the watered gin. She belched, put a hand on her flat bosom
and said, 'Pardon.' She looked around and said 'Manners!'
but the word broke off abruptly when she saw the overturned
chairs and the slumped figures of Jeff Gayheart and Mrs
Courage.

She stood up, pulled down her lavender skirt and walked
round the table to Mrs Courage.

'Well, it seems to 've been ever such a nice sitting, love,' she said. 'Very successful. I knew that Mister Abby would be able to bring things off all right. I do 'ope you're pleased with our little efforts.'

Mrs Courage did not reply. She was staring with blank eyes at the brandy glass on the table. Madame Wanda coughed and said: 'Well, I suppose, love, I should be thinking about getting back to dear old Brighton. My last bus leaves in 'alf an hour, so maybe if we could get the question of the fee settled now ... '

Mrs Courage went on staring. Madame Wanda coughed again and touched her on the shoulder. 'I was saying, love ... '

She screamed.

Mrs Courage's body fell forward on the table. She had been dead for nearly ten minutes.

'Now you've done it, you black besom,' the Countess said bitterly. 'Now we've not only got that noisy hag of a Wise Woman for company, but we've got Old Mother Courage – and we've probably got her bloody brother-in-law as well.'

3

He Took Me Among The Rhododendrons

'He took me among the rhododendrons,' the Countess said. 'And then he laid his hands on me.'

'What happen, missy?' Lilywhite said.

'What could happen, you daft bitch?' the other ghost said. 'Like us, the poor childe's been dead for years.'

'What a disappointmen',' Lilywhite said.

They were sitting on the roof of Ardmore Manor.

'One of the white slaveys once took me among the rhododendrons too,' Lilywhite said. 'Long long ago. A footman. Jonathan something. A big man with blondy hair an' brown eyes. He a village boy.'

'Spicer,' the Countess said. 'I think that was it.'

'Culpepper,' Lilywhite said. 'I 'member now. Your memory not what it use to be, missy.'

'Maybe not,' Margaret Torryburn said. 'But I remember Jonathan. He was quite a dish.'

'He a dish right enough. Such a dish! Ummm ... ' Lilywhite smacked her lips and sighed. 'But pore Jonathan. He not a dish any longer. Dust to dust and ashes to ashes like that ole preacher man say.'

'Stop drooling, you sentimental cow,' the Countess said sharply. 'What happened among the rhodies?'

'We walk along and we walk along and then Jonathan stop and take a pinch of snuff. Then he put his arm round Lilywhite and say he like a cuddle. And then he claw Lilywhite's leg.'

'And what did you do, you black slut?'

'I claw his face, missy. Lilywhite not like to be rushed.'

'More fool you,' the Countess said. 'I wish I'd been with him. I'd soon have had his breeks down.'

'He woulden have let you, missy. You forget what you threaten to do to him jus' a few days before that. He ragin' wild about it that night among the 'dendrons. He say to Lilywhite when she defend her honour, "You like yo' mistress, you black whore. You a bitch that should be hung from the gibbet!" '

'Well, I declare to God!' the Countess cried. 'I always thought he liked me. I had quite a fancy for him, and I once considered taking him into my bed – only for a one-night stand, of course.'

'He knew that, missy.' Lilywhite laughed. 'And he more than willing to get between your sheets. But that temper of yours, missy. That what done it.'

'Did what?'

'Like I say,' Lilywhite said. 'Your memory not what it use to be. You failing.'

'I'm as good as ever I was, you insolent bitch. By God, I wish it was the good old days. I'd show you whether I was failing or not. I'd crack my whip across your fat backside.'

'That what you try to do with Jonathan,' Lilywhite tittered. 'That the mistake you make, clever missy. You say to him when he upsets some wine over the tablecloth, "Take down yo' breeks, you clumsy fellow." An' you pick up you riding crop. But Jonathan grip yo' wrist and say, "No woman ever whip Jonathan Culpepper." I remembers it, missy. I standin' behind yo' chair at the time and I thinkin' what a pity I not get the chance of seein' that big white bum bent over.'

'Well, why didn't you take the chance of seeing it when it was offered to you on a plate among the rhododendrons?' the Countess said acidly.

'It wasen' the same thing, missy. When he claw Lilywhite's leg she not in the mood. And after she claw his face Jonathan was never in the mood again either.'

'A pity,' the Countess said. 'Still, you can console yourself now with Black Mamba. He's more in your line.'

'He no good,' the buxom black ghost said dolorously. 'And you know that well, you Scottish jade. You just takin' the micky out of pore Lilywhite. How can Mamba be any good when his body's buried somewhere in deepest Africa? So deep even his pore head don' know where it is.'

'No, Mamba hasn't got what it takes,' the Countess said.

'And he hadn't when he die either,' Lilywhite giggled. 'If your memory wasen so bad, missy, you'd 'member what the Arab sheikh did to pore Mamba before he chop his head off.'

'A pox on him,' the Countess said. 'For Mamba must have been quite something if he kept all the sheikh's wives happy.' Then she giggled too.

'And what evil mischief are you two harpies thinking up now?' a voice said behind them.

It was the ghost of Old Mother Courage who'd died of fright three months ago.

'We wasn't thinkin' up no mischief, Williamina love,' Lilywhite said.

'Mrs Courage to you. if you don't mind.' The icy draught of her voice whistled through Lilywhite's shade, but she shrugged it off and said:

'We was just sayin' how lovely it was to have you with us and all be palsie-walsies together, Minnie dear.'

'Lovely! You murderess!' Mrs Courage spat. 'You're the one that caused me to pass over so quickly. You and that wicked old Wise Woman, Gudrun. If it hadn't been for you I'd still be in the land of the living.'

'You were never in the land of the living,' the Countess said. 'You've always been dead from the neck up.'

'As for you, you Scottish whore,' Mrs Courage whirled like a wasp. 'What were you doing with my man in the rhododendrons last night?'

'I wasn't with your man,' the Countess said.

'You were with Take.'

'Took,' said the Countess.

'Take, if you don't mind. Take Courage.'

'Are you presuming to teach me grammar, my good woman?' Margaret Torryburn said. 'His name is Took.'

'I think I should know his name better than you. After all, I *am* his sister-in-law.'

'Was,' the Countess said. 'And although I understand you were his mistress and although he may have been Take Courage when he was alive, he's Took Courage now, for he's in the past tense.'

'But not past enough to keep you from making a pass at him, eh?' Mrs Courage laughed nastily.

'He made the overtures, but he was incapable of carrying on,' the Countess said. 'And he's neither your brother-in-law nor your lover any longer. He's number BXG9, 999, 803 on the books of the National Union of British Ghosts.'

'Well, he won't be a number on the books much longer, and neither will any of us. I've just heard – '

Mrs Courage was cut short by a cackle from a cloud above them. 'Whoooo, thou fine high-and-mighty dames! Whoooo! Get thee into the dungeons where thee belong. Into the lower depths with thee and say thy beads and clank thy chains and prepare to meet thy lord and master, the Evil One! Whooo!'

Gudrun, the tiny shrivelled Wise Woman of Ardmore, hurtled down from the cloud on her broomstick, the toothless gap in her brown wrinkled mask leering at them. 'Prithee, my not so pretty ones, what's afoot?'

'Nothing that concerns you, you pestilent beldam,' the Countess said.

Gudrun placed her broomstick carefully against a chimney stack. 'And why not, Margaret Torryburn?' she shrieked. 'What concerns thee concerns me, you prideful strumpet, so do not hasten to draw thy skirts aside. For better or for worse, old Gudrun is one of thee now and she must be party to thy conclaves. What's afoot, I say?'

'Ain't nothin' afoot, Gudry love,' said Lilywhite. 'We was just enjoying the moonlight and thinking how smashing it was to be old-time ghosties and be able to get away from it all up here in the quiet and peace.'

'Ah, my black friend,' Gudrun cackled. 'I harbour a soft spot for thee since it was because of thee and that dame who calls herself a medium that poor old Gudrun's spirit was at last released from bondage. But if thou art telling me an untruth ... '

'I know that Lilywhite is a liar,' the Countess said. 'But even she would not waste her time and breath on an old harridan like you. Will you kindly go away, my good woman, and leave us to our meditations?'

'Don't thee try to treat me like a serf, Margaret Torryburn,' Gudrun hissed. 'It was your ancestor that burnt old Gudrun as a witch. And I will see that thee burns in hell fire for ever and ever because of it. On the day the last trump sounds Gudrun will be there in the forefront of the host before Our Lord to accuse thee of all thy evil deeds.'

'Och, away and not haver, woman. The knight who once owned Ardmore and tied you to a stake and burnt you – and rightly too – was no ancestor of mine, though you seem to have got that rooted in your empty skull. It's true that I married one of his descendants, but my own ancestors were Scottish lairds and dukes who would not have soiled their hands touching a stinking old trollop like you. And if it's any consolation to that mass of maggots you call a heart an ancestress of mine was burnt as a witch too. And she was a high-born Highland lady who wove spells and held communion with the Evil One, not a half-daft cratur' like yourself that dealt in charms and simples.'

'Simples!' Gudrun screeched. 'I would have thee know, Margaret Torryburn, that my simples gave aid to many a poor downtrodden peasant.'

She picked up her broomstick, whirled it above her wimple, and rushed at the Countess, crying: 'I can scarce wait for the Last Trump. Methinks I'll kill thee now.'

The Countess wafted slowly to six feet above the roof and hovered there, laughing mockingly. 'Save your breath, you old fool, you know perfectly well you can't harm me.'

'When you've all finished arguing,' Mrs Courage said, 'I have a little piece of news that will take away what wits you've got left.'

'Hark to the cat that's stolen the cream,' the Countess said.

'Bad news,' Mrs Courage said.

She gave a hollow laugh and said: 'I've just come from the new Lady Superintendent's sitting-room. *My* sitting-room. With that woman, Mrs Loveday – Mrs Priscilla Loveday if you please – sitting in my chair drinking the brandy I bought and paid for before I passed over. Jeff Gayheart and three of his boys were with her. They were holding a committee meeting.'

'A committee meeting!' the Countess cried. 'And what do these dolts know about committees? That callant Gayheart has nothing in his noddle but psychedelic dreams brought on by drugs.'

'Jeff's a very clever young man,' Mrs Courage said stiffly. 'He's a great pop singer, the idol of millions, and as the oldest inhabitant of Ardmore he has every right to attend the meeting.'

'The oldest inhabitant!' Gudrun screamed. 'I would have thee know, brazen jezebel with a pink wig that thou art, that *I* am the oldest inhabitant. The Wise Woman of Ardmore has been here for over seven hundred years even though she has only been visible for the past three moons.'

'A pity you hadn't stayed invisible for another seven hundred,' Mrs Courage said. 'Anyway, as I was saying, they were holding a committee meeting about all the hauntings that have happened since that seance, and it was decided – at least that woman Loveday decided – that we must all be exorcised.'

'Lilywhite, do you hear that?' the Countess cried. 'Lilywhite! Where is the black cow?'

Lilywhite was sitting behind the gable of the East Tower cradling Black Mamba's skull in her arms and crooning: 'You made me love you, I didden wanna do it, I guess you always knew it ... '

'You wan' something, missy?' she called.

'Stop that stupid canoodling and come here and listen to this. You should know better at your age anyway – especially with a man who's no damned good to you.'

'That ole Take Courage he not much good to you either,'

Lilywhite grumbled. 'Well, what all the excitement?'

'That woman,' the Countess said. 'That thin-blooded minion, that bureaucratic meddler, Loveday, is going to have us exorcised.'

'Exercised? What you mean, missy? Like horses?'

'No, you fool. Exorcised.'

'I heard you the first time, missy,' Lilywhite giggled. 'Coo, what fun! Can't you see ole Minnie Courage here gallopin' round and round in circles!'

'Ex-OR-cised,' the Countess said. 'Exorcised by a clergyman with bell, book and candle. An old ceremony to get rid of ghosts and make them disappear for ever.'

'She can't do that to *us*. Not on your bloody nellie,' Lilywhite said. 'Why, we was here long before her. She got no authority over us. Lilywhite got her union card. See, here it is. I always keeps it stuck in my boosie. When Mr Cameron of the NUBG give it to me he say, "Lilywhite, you stick closer to that than a flea stick to your bottom, and you'll always be all right. No human be able to touch you."'

'I doubt that union cards won't be much good to us in an exorcism ceremony,' Margaret Torryburn said.

'What they do at this ceremony?' Lilywhite asked.

'I've never seen one. Thank heavens I've never needed to circulate in such low class superstitious circles.'

'I attended one once,' Mrs Courage said. 'I've never been so high and mighty as your *ladyship*. I've always been interested in psychic affairs.'

'A lot of good it's done you,' the Countess said acidly. 'If you hadn't meddled in a seance with that funny little medium you might still be alive and kicking.'

Mrs Courage sniffed. 'This exorcism ceremony was carried out by a priest of the highest integrity, Canon Jessop. It was quite an elaborate affair, and was held in an old castle that had been troubled by a ghost for centuries. First of all the priest said a prayer in the room the ghost was always seen in, then he sprinkled holy water around it, and then he lit a candle and called upon the ghost to leave the castle and never come back. I remember it all so vividly. There were about a dozen of us at the service. I went with my great friend, Mrs Boxley-Adams – at least she was my great friend at that time –

and I remember she said to me … '

'I don't want your life story, my dear woman,' the Countess said. 'All I want to know is: Was the exorcism successful?'

'Of course it was. Canon Jessop was a most able and most persuasive man. The unhappy ghost gave one shriek and was never seen or heard again.'

'So you think the same thing will happen here?' Margaret said pensively. 'That some silly little parson will do a bit of mumbo-jumbo and he and Mrs Loveday and Jeff Gayheart – for that moronic show-off will naturally have to be in the centre of the stage – will walk about with candles, and *pouf!* We will all be forced to take to our heels and vanish.'

'That is what I expect,' Mrs Courage said. 'Oh, dear God, whatever's going to become of me? I don't like being a ghost but at least I'm *here* in a manner of speaking. I don't want to be exorcised into nothingness. God curse the day when I set my eyes on you three evil bitches.'

'Dost thou mean that after poor old Gudrun struggled to become a visible ghost for seven hundred years and has been a free spirit for only three moons that now she will be made invisible again by an interfering cleric?'

'Your guess is as good as mine,' the Countess said. 'You've heard what this woman has just said. If you believe her you're free to think the worst.'

'Oh, lack a day! Lack a day!' Gudrun shrieked. 'That a poor old soul like me should come to this after all my tribulations! To disappear into nothingness … A murrain on all of thee! What is poor old Gudrun to do?'

'There's only one solution,' the Countess said. 'Come, Lilywhite.'

She and Lilywhite floated across the remains of the great park and came to rest beside the river, near the hole where Lilywhite's bones had been mouldering for centuries.

'We must emigrate,' the Countess said.

'What you mean? Lilywhite don' like them long words.'

'I forgot you were still in the four letter stage,' the Countess said. 'We must leave Ardmore. We must leave the country. We must become part of this Brain Drain they're always talking about.'

Lilywhite said: 'You flatter yourself, missy. You got no

brains. You got even less than pore Lilywhite.'

'None of your old-fashioned sauce, you nigger besom.'

'Don' you call me a nigger, Margaret Torryburn. I as British as you are.'

'I'm Scottish, thank God. But don't let's argue. We must work this thing out. Secretly. We must keep it to ourselves, so don't let your tongue drop a hint to Old Mother Courage or Gudrun. We don't want to take them with us. It'll be a damned good thing for everybody if this exorcist manages to free Ardmore of them.'

'What about Take Courage?' Lilywhite said slyly. 'We takin' him with us?'

'Not on your nellie, as you yourself would so inelegantly put it. It's high time you got away from the influence of this pernicious television. I hope and pray there'll be no such devilish machines where we're going.'

'Where we goin' then, missy?'

'My family used to have estates in Jamaica,' the Countess said musingly.

'I know. Lilywhite been there once with you.'

'I wonder? Yes, I think we should go there. You'll feel at home there among your black brothers.'

'But Lilywhite got no brothers, black or white. Lilywhite don' want to leave Ardmore.'

'Neither do I, you stupid cow. But needs must when the Devil drives. I have no wish to emigrate, but it's either that or be exorcised. We can always come back to Ardmore after that interfering bitch Loveday and her minions have gone, and if this exorcism's a success we won't find Courage and Gudrun waiting for us.'

'Nor Take,' Lilywhite said.

'Nor Take,' the Countess said sadly. 'He must have been a fine figure of a man at one time before the drink got him. I saw that when he took me among the rhodies.'

'As fine a figure as Misyew lee Baron?'

'No, hardly. Charles was really ravishing.'

'I never like him, missy. Lilywhite have hate lee Baron ever since that ole Battle of Blenheim time. She be glad to see the last of him.'

'But he's coming with us.'

'Over Lilywhite's dead body.'

'You haven't got a body any longer, you stupid whore. Must I always keep drumming that into your thick skull? Naturally the Baron will come with us. We died together, and we can't join the Brain Drain without him.'

'Well, if he come, then Lilywhite bring Black Mamba too. Maybe he not much cop for this Brain Drain but he always good for a laugh.'

'I expect he'll feel at home in Jamaica,' the Countess said. 'And we won't need to pay a fare for him. You can easily smuggle his head there in your handbag.'

'Lilywhite got no handbag.'

'Well, you're going to get one, you fool.'

'But why we pay fares anyway? We ghosties don' need to pay our way like the common herd.'

'Unfortunately we'll have to manifest in order to get to Jamaica,' the Countess said. 'You know the rules as well as I do: that no ghost can cross water. In case you don't remember, we've got to cross the ocean to get to Jamaica, so we'll have to go there in human form.'

'How we goin' manage that? You know 's well 's me, missy, that we not due to have our week's holiday in human form for two months yet.'

'We'll get by somehow or other,' the Countess said. 'Let's go and consult with the Baron.'

The Baron Charles de Riveaux was in the Sauna Baths. Leaning nonchalantly against a steam heater, he was watching two of Jeff Gayheart's naked boy friends beating each other with birch twigs.

'Ah, Charles my poppet, at your favourite occupation,' the Countess gushed. 'The eternal *voyeur!*'

'At your service, *madame*, as always,' the Baron said, bowing over her hand and kissing it. 'This is a very poor night for *le sport*. It is usually much gayer at this time, but there has been nobody here all evening except these silly boys. Even though their hair is longer than the hair of most of the girls it isn't quite the same. I have never been a lover of *garçons*,' he added sourly, taking a pinch of snuff and watching the youths manoeuvre into an elaborate sexual contortion. 'And now that they imitate the girls so much there is something repellent, something most *outré* about them. *Faugh!*'

'Coo, look at that, missy!' Lilywhite giggled. 'I give them larriday, eh?'

She twisted a wet towel into a rope, materialised, and skelped each pink bottom. The youths screamed with pain, then they screamed even louder when they saw the large black woman leering at them, and they helter-skeltered out of the Baths.

'They'll have something to tell the Committee meeting,' the Countess said. 'It wouldn't surprise me if that busybody Loveday got the parson here tomorrow. We must join the Brain Drain at once, Charles.'

'But the Brain Drain is only for scientists, *ma belle*,' the Baron said. 'How can you possibly hope to qualify?'

'The Brain Drain is open to everybody who wants to get away from this sinking island and that President Welfare or whatever his name is who breeds labradors – a dog I never could abide – and eats scampi for breakfast.'

'I don't see why we need to leave England,' he grumbled. 'Even Sussex for that matter. Why don't we move to Carstairs Castle and stay with old Lady Carstairs until this exorcist has done his little mammy-palaver?'

'Because the castle is a complete ruin and we'd never be able to thole the draughts,' the Countess said. 'Besides, old Lady Carstairs is dreary company these days. She spends all her time working on that same bit of tapestry she was at when Lilywhite gave us those toadstools that made us all kick the bucket.'

The Baron glared at Lilywhite and said: 'I'll never forgive you for that, you *bête noire*. Cutting me off in my prime. The only thing that makes Jamaica possible is that you will not be coming with us.'

'Of course, she's coming with us,' the Countess said. 'Don't act dafter than you really are, Charles. We all died together, so we must all emigrate together.'

'I shall not go one step then. I'll kill that big fat sow first.'

Lilywhite grinned malevolently and swung the wet towel. 'You and who else, Frenchy? You know the rules as well as me. If you touch me, Mr Cameron goin' to have somethin' nasty to say to you, and then you get what-for in a big, big way.'

'Stop it, you two,' the Countess said sharply. 'We have enough trouble on our hands without your eternal squabbling.'

'In that case, I shall go to Carstairs,' the Baron said. 'I'd rather put up with the old lady's embroidery than go to a strange island with this poisonous wench.'

'Have it your own way,' the Countess said. 'But I'm warning you, Charles. I'm afraid the parson's exorcism will stretch as far as the castle, for you must remember that Lady Carstairs died in the Ardmore dining-room along with us, and she only haunts the castle because of the bounty of the Council of Ghosts.'

'You mean the NUBG, missy,' Lilywhite said. 'It's like I told you. Your memory's failing.'

'Little wonder in this technological age,' the Countess snapped. 'I shall be glad to get away from it. I trust there are no technologists in Jamaica, nor daft fools rushing around madly in those awful motor cars. Come, to horse! To horse! We must ride this instant to London and see our friend, Mr Cameron.'

Reluctantly the Baron followed her to the building that was on the site of the old stables where the ghosts of several Torryburn horses still munched phantom hay. Lilywhite went to the shed and took the motor scooter she always pinched when she wanted a joy ride. She had never been able to bear horses, and even tonight, she preferred to travel by modern transport. 'Good job I'se a ghostie,' she chuckled up at the moon. 'If I kills somebody on this contraption no polisman is goin' be able to make Lilywhite take that new breathalyser test.'

4

The Ghost Drain

Along with other fugitives from the Welfare State, the Countess, the Baron and Lilywhite boarded a plane at

London airport a few hours before the exorcist was due to arrive at Ardmore. By special dispensation of the National Union of British Ghosts, they were travelling in human form. Mr Cameron had told them they could remain like this for exactly a week after they arrived in Jamaica. 'But only a week,' he said. 'After that ye become wraiths again – though ye'll be out o' my jurisdiction. Ye come then under the control of the Jamaican Voodoo Board or the League of Duppies, and as ye're immigrants on the island ye'll have to knuckle under and put up wi' their ploys. Ye canna come back here without their permission.'

'And who would want to come back here?' the Countess said haughtily.

'Weel, I dinna ken, my leddy,' said Mr Cameron, a courteous old Covenanter who had been tortured and executed in Edinburgh after the Battle of Bothwell Brig in 1679. 'Every cock craws best on his ain midden, and I doubt ye may get hamesick. Whiles I get hamesick mysel'. Though I suffered a cruel death on the orders o' Bloody Claverhouse and have no pleasant recollections o' my end in the Grassmarket, I widna like to gang far from Scotland.'

'I'll miss Ardmore,' the Countess agreed. 'But it's got unlivable in lately. So it's better to uptail and seek fresh woods and pastures new as yon poet callant said.'

'Ay, but I wonder if Mr Milton would have said that so blithely if he hadna been so doucely settled at Chalfont St Giles?' Mr Cameron said. 'I hope ye'll no' regret becoming part o' the ghost drain, my leddy. For ye're not the only spirits that are emigratin'. A good wheen o' long established Scottish and Welsh ghosts are already awa' because they canna put up ony longer with life in the affluent state. Lady Kate Kilcheviot, a bonnie lassie that got murdered a whilie after you, and her maid, Mercy Milligan, left yesterday for the United States. They're awa' to Chicago no less. Just because they canna bear to bide in the ruins o' Kilcheviot Castle and put up with the Glasgow keelies that are building a new town on top o' it.'

Mr Cameron had obtained passports for them. The Countess was travelling as Mrs Margaret Torryburn, and the Baron, much against his will, as Mr Torryburn. 'I cannot see why I cannot retain my title,' he said. 'Nor why I should

assume *madame's* name when I have a perfectly good old
French name of my own. I would have you know that I am not
a gigolo, *monsieur.*'

'Stop havering, Charles, and be content that you've got a
passport,' the Countess said. 'Personally, I'd be glad to travel
as Felix the Cat so long as I got away from here.'

Mr Cameron gave them a large bundle of Bank of England
pound and five pound notes. 'They're part of the money
hidden after the Great Train Robbery a few years syne,' he
said. 'One o' our men was on that job. That's why the bobbies
've never been able to catch him. They have his picter
plastered up all over the place, but nobody'll be able to claim
the reward, for nobody's ever seen him properly. The
photograph was one he had taken for a lark, and of course it's
not his right face. He passed over hundreds o' years ago. Ye'll
maybe know him? Colonel Blood that stole the crown jewels
from the Tower o' London. He likes to materialise every now
and then and have a wee crack at difficult safes and such like
when he's on holiday. It keeps his hand in. He got a lot o' fun
out o' organising the train robbery.'

Lilywhite's passport was in the name of Miss Lily Blanco.
She was wearing a purple coat and a cherry-coloured dress
she had stolen at midnight from the Outsize Women's
department of an Oxford Street store. A white tammy, in
which she'd stuck a pheasant's feather found in the park at
Ardmore, was perched on top of her head. The Countess had
on a pale grey silk costume, and over her shoulders was
draped a mink coat she'd not been able to resist taking while
Lilywhite was trying on hats. 'I can't see what good it will do
you in Jamaica, *ma chère,*' the Baron said. 'I understand it's
very hot there.'

'Och, it'll maybe come in handy at nights,' she said. 'You
may be glad of a share of it yourself if it gets cold. That's a
very thin suit, my bonnie mannie.'

More than the Countess thought the Baron was a bonnie
mannie. While they were waiting in the airport lounge all the
women, as well as some men, kept looking at him, and several
women did their best to get into conversation with him. Even
Lilywhite had to admit unwillingly that his blonde
handsomeness, unimpaired by over two hundred and fifty

years of ghosthood, was intensified by a short modern business man's haircut, a dark grey suit, a white shirt and a discreet maroon tie, though she sniffed loudly when she heard a woman say: 'What a devastating bit of beefcake!'

When it was announced that their plane would be late in taking off, the Countess looked anxiously at the diamond bracelet watch she had nicked from Asprey's. 'I hope that parson doesn't arrive early and that his incantations don't reach as far as this,' she said. But her attention was diverted by watching the arrival of a planeload of West Indians. 'Here's a lot of your black brethren, Miss Blanco,' she said. 'They're a prosperous-like bunch, aren't they? I wonder if they've been home on holiday, or if they're just immigrants arriving to see what goodies they can pick from President Welfare's table.'

'Lilywhite coulden care less, missy. All she wants is get on this plane and get it over. I think I take some more of them planesickness tablets.'

'You've already taken nearly a dozen, you daft cow. Why don't you wait till we get in the air and see if you really need them?'

'Seeing all zose black peoples makes me wonder if there will be any left in Jamaica,' the Baron said.

'It's a sort of shuttle service, I expect,' the Countess said. 'Like one of these swing-doors. When one comes in, another goes out. I daresay we'll see some familiar faces in Jamaica. I just hope that Old Mother Courage and Gudrun haven't had the same bright idea as ourselves and we find them waiting for us.'

When eventually they got on their plane Lilywhite was the only black passenger. She sat across the aisle from Mr and Mrs Torryburn, and nobody showed any inclination to take the vacant seat beside her. Most of the passengers were earnest-looking young men with horn-rimmed glasses and brief-cases. Two sat in front of Lilywhite, and as soon as she'd recovered from her fright at the plane's take off and had got settled comfortably after the air hostess had to disentangle her from her safety-belt, she listened to their conversation. At first she could not understand their jargon but gradually she gathered that they were scientists. The one in the

Glenurquhart check suit was going to an executive post in bauxite, and the one wearing a beige suede jacket and Bedford cords to an executive post in alumina.

'Jamaica is the largest producer of bauxite in the world,' Glenurquhart suit said. 'I've got a great future in front of me. I'm starting at five and a half thou.'

'You're laughing,' beige jacket said. 'I'm only starting at four and a half, but I expect to get it raised to seven and a half in less than two years.'

'Jolly good, old boy,' Glenurquhart suit said. 'I wonder if that luscious bird can rustle up a brown ale? I could do with a noggin.' He signalled the air hostess and ordered a drink. She was preparing to go for it when he said as an afterthought: 'Oh, would you care for a wet, old boy? Make that two browns, miss.'

Lilywhite turned her attention to the other passengers, wondering if any were ghosts. But they looked too solid for any such frivolity, so after a quick look downwards at what she could see of the sea beneath the clouds she took three more airsickness tablets and closed her eyes.

They were halfway across the Atlantic before she opened them. The Baron and the Countess were sipping gin and tonic. The two young men had drunk several brown ales, had worn each other out with their jargon, and they were now reading paperbacks. Lilywhite slipped out of her human body, though she knew she was taking a big risk in case Mr Cameron's radar-like eyes were on her, for a few minutes to kneel in front of them to see the titles. Glenurquhart suit was reading a Mickey Spillane, his nose almost glued to the pages. Beige jacket was reading a Hank Jensen. Lilywhite took the opportunity to put her hand on Glenurquhart's genitals and caress them. Afterwards she was amused to see him look suspiciously every now and then at beige jacket, who had a rise but seemed to keep his hands firmly on his book. She thought of playing about with several other passengers but decided it wouldn't be amusing enough. She took another three airsickness tablets, belched loudly and closed her eyes. At Miami she opened them long enough to see what was going on. She didn't open them again until the end of their 5,200 mile journey.

But they opened widely enough when the plane landed at Palisadoes airport at Kingston. While she was waiting in the queue for the customs, a tiny black man leered at her from behind the barrier and cried:

'Well, nigger, has yo made yo millions and come back here to queen it over us pore trash?'

'Hush your mouth, black man, or I get the Race Relations Board on your track,' she said.

'Belt up, honey,' a coffee-coloured customs man said, grabbing her handbag. 'Don' you start throwing your weight around here.'

He opened the handbag. Then he let out a yell and dropped it when he saw Black Mamba's skull grinning up at him.

" 'S all right, man,' a big black buck said, thrusting past him and taking Lilywhite's arm. 'This my friend. This big obeah woman. Best not upset her, man, or she put the hex on you.'

The customs man quickly passed Lilywhite and the Countess, hesitated at the Baron, but let him pass too when the big buck growled: 'They all friends a mine, I tells you. If Samson Truelove say they okay, then they okay, nigger.'

Mr Truelove, in white silk suit and a panama hat with a wide scarlet band, took Lilywhite by the arm and said: 'You come along a me, Miss Blanco. I take you and yo friends to yo hotel.'

As he led them to a sugary pink Cadillac Lilywhite whispered: 'Oh, missy, I's scared. All them black faces!'

'It's a judgement on you,' the Countess said. 'Just think of all the poor folk you've scared with your own ugly black physog for centuries.'

Lilywhite jerked her thumb warningly at Samson Truelove. He laughed and said: 'Don' pay no attention to me, folks. I's a ghostie like yoselves. I's the reception committee. The chairman of the local branch of the League of Duppies, and I's been deputised to make yo first week in Jamaica memorable. But memorable!'

He settled himself at the wheel, squeezed Lilywhite's knee, rolled his eyes at the Countess and the Baron in the back seat, started the Cadillac and shot off at sixty miles an hour. 'You folks all right behind there?' he shouted, twisting round to grin at the Countess.

She was terrified. All the way across the Atlantic she'd been thinking about the principal condition of their release from ghostdom in Sussex. 'Ye will assume human form before ye gang to London Airport,' Mr Cameron had said. 'And ye'll retain this form for exactly one week after ye reach Jamaica. Ye will not be allowed – nor will ye be able – to disappear into ghostliness for more than a few seconds, and this will be only three times in that week. For emergencies, like. And if, by some mischance in that week, ye meet with an accident fatal to your corporeal body, ye will have to make a fresh start as a ghost and ye'll ha'e to haunt the spot where ye last drew breath in the guise o' a human being. That's the law and ye're bound to it.'

Margaret Torryburn had no desire to spend the rest of eternity hovering above this crowded Kingston street, so she was relieved when the Cadillac skidded to a stop in front of a hotel. Mr Samson Truelove leapt out, again took Lilywhite firmly by the elbow, and ushered them into the hotel with a flourish of his panama. He handed them over to the receptionist and went to speak to the manager.

The receptionist was a small, elderly, coffee-coloured woman with sharp, snappy, little black eyes and a thin mouth. A huge Alsatian dog sat upright on a high stool beside her. It started to growl when the Countess was signing the register. She scrawled 'Margaret Campbell of Torryburn' in such huge letters that her signature took up nearly a quarter of the page. 'Yo might try to leave room for other people,' the little woman sniffed, pushing the book at the Baron. He was so busy looking at the dog, which was growling more loudly, that he signed his real name. Lilywhite, agitated by the dog, which had thrust itself now onto the desk almost on top of her, its fangs bared, laboriously wrote: 'L. Blanko. Made'.

'Has yo no pride, nigger?' the receptionist sneered, looking at Lilywhite's signature. 'What for yo calls yoself a maid and lets yoself be trampled on by them white trash?'

She peered at the Baron's signature and said: 'Dis man not even put the same name he has on his passport. He a fraud. Get the polis pronto.'

'Hold your tongue, *méchante*!' the Baron cried.

'Watch it, Josephine Mary, you old windbag,' Samson Truelove said. 'Them people my friends.'

He grinned at Lilywhite and said: 'She uppity because she daughter in London who a big bug. She manageress in big restaurant and she make the whiteys stand in line before she give them der food. She crack the big whip over them.'

'De law is de law,' the receptionist screeched. 'Dem is bad peoples, Sammy Truelove. Yo just got to look at dem. I knows evil when I sees it. Polis! Polis!'

The Alsatian's snarls accompanied her cries, and it leapt at the Baron.

Truelove grabbed it by the collar, swung it up and held it a few feet from the floor.

'See! Winston Churchill here – he knows dey's bad peoples. Polis! Polis!'

'Belt up, you ole bitch,' Samson Truelove said quietly. 'Button yo mouth or I buttons it for yo. My friend here, Miss Lilywhite Blanco, she a big obeah woman from Constantinople. She only got to lift a l'il finger ... '

The receptionist's lips stretched in a thin line. 'Winston!' she snapped. 'Winston! Yo a naughty boy, Winnie, to bark at dose nice peoples like that. Yo should be ashamed o' yoself. Yo go back and sit on yo stool.'

'That's settle that ole fart,' Samson Truelove muttered to Lilywhite. 'Now you folks, go to yo rooms and have a bit of shut-eye. I comes back later to show yo the joys a Jamaica.'

'I don' think I goin' to like this place, missy,' Lilywhite said when they were safely in their rooms.

'Och, we'll get used to it,' the Countess said. 'Once we get this Samson Truelove to take us to my old family plantation we'll be all right.'

Lilywhite shook her head. 'I don' believe it. Lilywhite sees bogey-mans everywhere already. The black spirits don' like us.'

She lay on top of her bed and brooded. She had been brooding for about an hour when there was a soft tap on the door, then it opened quietly and Samson Truelove came in with his panama set rakishly on the back of his head.

He grinned: 'Miss Blanco, you done been a naughty girl.'

'Who? Me?' Lilywhite sat up, giggled and rolled her eyes

provocatively.

'Yes, you,' he said, coming forward and sitting on the edge of the bed.

'You got no manners, nigger,' Lilywhite said, arranging her skirt over her knees. 'You got a sauce comin' like this into a lady's boudoir with yo hat on.'

'You no lady,' he said, pitching the hat into the corner of the room and taking off his bright red tie. 'I saw what you done on the plane.'

Lilywhite stiffened.

Samson said: 'You done change into a ghostie and interfere with an innocent young man.'

'I never done no such thing. Lilywhite as pure as the undriven snow.'

'Balls,' Mr Samson Truelove said.

'Lilywhite don' like that word. She a virgin of the purest ray serene.'

'Don' hand me that line, Miss Blanco. Sammy knows better. And don' prevaricate. I saw you. I was sittin' behind you.'

'But there was no darkies on the plane,' she said.

'I was incognito. I was playactin' as a whitey. I was that ole man with the grey beard.'

'Him!' Lilywhite sniffed.

'I saw yo stirrin' up dat young fellow's evil passions,' Samson said. 'You know yo got no right to appear as a ghostie over water. You was breakin' the law, Miss Blanco.'

'It was only for a minute,' she said.

'You know it was against the rules,' he said. 'Anyways, you was puttin' evil thoughts in that young science fellow's mind.'

'It wassen his mind I was puttin' it in.'

'No matter,' he said. 'You was breakin' the rules. You got to be punished. And Samson Truelove's the boy to punish you.'

He grinned lasciviously. Lilywhite grinned back and said: 'What you suggest, nigger?'

'You a real ripe chick, baby,' he said, reaching out for her. 'You and me goin' to have some nooky so long as we in the human state and can enjoy it. But good!'

'Tha's all right with me, honey,' she said. 'Lilywhite haven't had a fuck for two hundred and sixty-three years.'

*

And so Lilywhite became Mr Samson Truelove's mistress, and for the next few months they assumed human form every now and then and gave way to their animal passions. But soon Lilywhite began to tire of Mr Truelove's insatiable ardour. 'He don' give me no rest, missy,' she complained. 'I don' know what it is, but I don' seem to get the enjoyment out of it I used to get in the good ole days.'

'It's a very over-rated pastime,' the Countess said.

'He such a weight,' Lilywhite said. 'And all that gruntin' and groanin'. It take all the romance outen it. I just lies there thinkin' I be better employed scarin' the pants offen some of them damn-fool niggers.'

'Instead of them scaring the pants off you!' The Countess sighed. 'You've deteriorated badly since we came to this pestilent island. You aren't the same wench.'

'Don' seem to have any go left in me,' Lilywhite agreed. 'Feel all washed up. Don' like all this sunshine. Don' like all them black faces. Don' like them ole voodoo tricks. And I don' like Sammy Truelove. I only puts up with him because I's scared to make an enemy of him. He a bad man to cross.'

'Ah well, I suppose you should count yourself lucky you've got a man,' the Countess said. 'The Baron's been a slack tool for years as far as I'm concerned. And every time I manifest into a beautiful young woman and manage to get a young mortal he always sheers off before the crucial moment. I don't know what it is.'

'Prob'ly he smell the mustiness of the grave, missy. Why don' you set yo cap at big Samson? I bet he'd go for a bit of white meat. He might like a change – like me.'

'I never did fancy blacks. You know perfectly well that even when we came over here to look at the plantation when we were alive and it was the fashion for ladies of high degree like myself to take the biggest buck slave as a lover I just couldn't face it.'

'I remembers.' Lilywhite sighed. 'I remembers you left them to me. Samson may think he the answer to a maiden's prayer, but he never reach the heights some of dem ancestors of his done. Ah, dem were the days ... '

The Countess sighed, too. The return to the old Torryburn plantation had been a grievous disappointment. She'd expected to find some changes after nearly two hundred and seventy years, but when she'd seen the shanty town the place had been turned into, the hovels with tin roofs, the little gardens where hens scratched and half-naked piccaninnies played, she'd wept and had never gone near the place again.

She loathed Jamaica as much as Lilywhite did. The Baron was indifferent; so long as he could watch pretty coloured girls bathing and spy on them and their big bucks in bed he did not complain. The only one who was happy was Black Mamba, who had become friends with a zombie and spent most of his time with this creature at voodoo ceremonies.

At first, when they arrived in Jamaica, Lilywhite had gone to some of these ceremonies with Samson Truelove. Sammy, who sometimes acted as a *bocor* or cult-priest, was anxious to initiate Lilywhite into the religious customs of the island so that she could do a good trade in haunting. 'We a superstitious people in Jamaica, Miss Lilywhite,' he'd said. 'We wan' keep the good ole times goin'. We don' like this new hippy trash. We wan' dig everythin' that belong to dat ole time religion. Peoples believe in spooks and when they goes to a voodoo meetin' they wan' *see* spooks.'

Lilywhite was quite willing to give the voodoo worshippers their money's worth, but after frightening the wits out of a few old black mammies and little girls she grew tired of the game. There wasn't much fun in frightening simple black peasants who fell down flat and screamed hysterically at the slightest touch of an ice-cold hand. She kept longing for the good old days on Brighton beach when she'd often had to run through most of her repertoire before it was noticed and appreciated by the sullen-faced, longhaired youths, their sullen-faced short-skirted girl friends and the moronic, beer-bellied, middle-aged factory mates who usually went on rolling their cigarettes phlegmatically before they said to their wives: 'Tell me, missus, do you feel anythin' funny goin' on here?'

Lilywhite disapproved of Mamba taking up with a low-class zombie. But she disapproved even more of the way Samson Truelove kept encouraging him to greater and greater efforts in ghostly high-jinks. 'Them pore peoples,' she said. 'It ain't fair to make them go into them trances and froth at the mouth.'

'Hark at her!' the Countess said, laughing sarcastically. 'Dinna tell me you're turning over a new leaf in your auld age, my bonnie lassie. It's not so very long ago since nothing could hold you back from gallivanting in the wee small hours screaming like a banshee and giving folk heart attacks.'

'Lilywhite don' mind doin' that in England where they got no nerves. But she don' like to frighten them pore black peoples.'

'Yes, I must say it's not much cop,' the Countess said. 'Life doesn't seem to have the same flavour here.'

'Let's go home to England then.'

'Don't be daft, woman. You know fine we can't go back to Sussex. We'll never see Ardmore again, so you'd better reconcile yourself to the fact. Anyway, I couldn't bear to set foot in the Welfare State again. But maybe we might consider going somewhere else. France maybe … '

'Over my dead body. One Frenchie in Lilywhite's life is too much. She coulden bear to cope with forty million more.'

'There are plenty of other countries in Europe,' the Countess said. 'We have all the time in the world to think about it. In any case, we have to get permission from the League of Duppies before we can leave Jamaica. You'd better sound your friend Mr Truelove about it.'

'Oh no, no! Mum's the word to Sammy. He never forgive Lilywhite if he think she want to get away from him. He the great lover. He coulden bear to be jilted. He stop us from goin' like an old Victorian daddy.'

'Well, wench, you'd better go and see Mr Shakespeare K. Milton, the President of the League of Duppies.'

'Why don' you go and see him yoself, missy? You better at the ole mammy-palaver than pore Lilywhite who didden even get a cestificate from that evenin' school in Brighton.'

'You'll manage him better than me, girl, so don't argue. I have my reasons for not wanting to interview Mr Shakespeare K. Milton. The principal one is that he was a slave on the family plantation in the time of my father-in-law and he was tortured to death to entertain some of the old Earl's lady friends. I understand that he doesn't bear any kind feelings towards the Torryburn family.'

'Okay, missy, Lilywhite go and beard him in his den. Better not mention what we plan to do to you-know-who before we gets it done in case he spills the beans to big Sammy.'

'I shall say nothing to Monsieur le Baron,' the Countess said grandly, 'until I am able to put his aeroplane or his sailing ticket into his hand and say, "Fall in and follow me." I'm sure he will approve of our plans, anyway; he would like nothing better than to go back to Europe.'

Lilywhite wasn't sure where she'd find Mr Milton, but after some discreet questioning she found herself sitting in the office of the President of the League of Duppies and made her request.

Shakespeare Milton, a handsome big buck about twenty-nine years of age, smiled and said: 'So you don' like our pleasant li'l island, Miss Blanco? Since I was murdered about three hundred years ago I've travelled all over the world and seen many beautiful places, but I always come back here with joy. Why don' you stay here a little longer and get used to the place?'

'I wants to get back to Europe, Mis' Milton. Lilywhite was borned in dear ole Constantinople and she want to get nearer home sweet home. I guess you understan' that.'

'Of course, I appreciate your sentiments. The trouble is that there are several very stringent regulations to be adhered to before the League can authorise you and your two friends to leave here.'

'Three friends,' Lilywhite said.

'Two,' said Mr Milton. 'I'm afraid the League can only authorise exit visas for the departure of yourself, the Baron de Riveaux and the Countess of Torryburn – though personally I would like to keep that high and mighty harlot here to suffer as I had to suffer at the hands of her wicked father-in-law. But we can't authorise the departure of the head of the man called Black Mamba. In the first place, he is an illegal immigrant, having been smuggled into the country by your own fair self. In the second place, he is not in possession of his body, and one of the rules of exit is that the emigrant must be in full physical condition and fit in wind and limb.'

'Oh, pore ole Mamba!' she cried. 'Still, I daresay he be

happy enough to stay here. He like all the mumbo-jumbo and the voodoo and he become great pals with that zombie what tell him hair-raisin' tales about Baron Samedi and Damballa, the snake god, and werewolves and other funny things.'

'There is nothing funny about Damballa or Samedi or any of these people, Miss Blanco,' Mr Milton said coldly. 'I do not mock your religion, so please do not mock the religion of the people of Jamaica.'

'Lawdy me, Lilywhite ain't got no religion, man,' she said, giggling. 'She a free thinker.'

'Too free sometimes, I imagine,' Mr Milton said.

Lilywhite was about to retaliate, but she thought better of it and said meekly: 'What them rules and regulations you say we got to do before we can leave here?'

Shakespeare K. Milton grinned: a distortion of his finely-boned handsome face that suddenly turned it into an evil mask.

'The first regulation, Miss Blanco,' he said slowly, 'is that you and your friends consent to become spies for the League of Duppies?'

'Spies?' Lilywhite gasped, and then she giggled: 'Coo! You mean you wan' us to be like James Bond in them films?'

'In a way,' Mr Milton said, toying with his fountain pen. 'Though only in a way. It will not, of course, be exactly in the manner of the dashing Mr Bond.'

'I think he smashing,' Lilywhite said. 'He a dish.'

'Yes, I agree that Mr Sean Connery, who plays the role in the films, is quite spectacular. But I'm afraid your roles as spies will not work out in quite the same way.'

'What you mean?'

'Precisely this.' Mr Milton began to doodle with the pen on the writing pad in front of him, not looking at Lilywhite. 'For some time past the League of Duppies has been sending agents behind the Iron Curtain so that we can be kept informed about various matters that will help us black people when eventually the inevitable war comes between black and white. We ghosts, naturally, have no colour, so this makes it easier for us to get information. While carrying out their investigations, however, our spies often have to do things that otherwise they might not wish to do as peace-loving citizens.

Our spies must have strong stomachs. They must be prepared to disregard human life and kill – to kill always when it is necessary, and to kill sometimes when it is unnecessary.'

'Is that all?' Lilywhite sighed with relief and sat back. 'You can count me in, man. I has said it before, and I'll say it again,' she said with a deep chuckle. 'What's a few more deaths between friends?'

5

What's A Few More Deaths Between Friends?

'I'm afraid you won't be a spy according to Bond, Miss Blanco,' Mr Milton said, smiling ruefully. 'It will not be a business of carrying an automatic in your handbag or putting cyanide in the Soviet ambassador's champagne or scaling rope-ladders into the Kremlin. Nothing so thrilling and romantic and colourful. Not at first, anyway. You may be able to do these things to your heart's content later – if by that time you wish to continue to be a spy – but for the first six months you will be in bondage. You will have other obstacles to surmount.'

'Look, honey, James Bond always surmount obstacles,' she said. 'If he surmount them, so can we.'

'I'm not so sure about that. There are a number of conditions about this assignment. I must warn you that your life as a spy may not be exactly a pleasant one.'

'What them conditions, bud?' Lilywhite said, acting tough.

Mr Milton smiled sadly and said: 'The first one is that you must spend the first six months of your – shall we call it secret servitude? – in the form of an animal. That is so that you can leave this country and enter a continental one in disguise, also that you can cross the ocean in a corporeal body.''

'I don' mind, baby,' Lilywhite said. 'I often think I like to be nice li'l white Persian pussy. How about that for an alibi?'

He played with his fountain pen and said: 'I fear not, Miss Blanco. You and your friends have no say in the choice of animal body you must assume. The first rule is that you leave this island in the forms of animals that won't be subject to quarantine at the other end. Animals for whose transport licences have already been obtained by their owners. It so happens that three show jumpers are due to leave Palisadoes airport the day after tomorrow for a destination in East Germany. If you and your friends agree to the rules, you can be transformed into their bodies and begin your journey.'

'Show jumpers? What you mean, lover?'

'Horses,' he said laconically.

'I don' mind bein' a horsey,' she said.

'Maybe not. But what about your friends?'

'I don' suppose they mind either.'

'None of you will in theory perhaps, Miss Blanco. But in practice … Well, such a position has its drawbacks.'

'What you mean?'

'Human nature being what it is, you are not to know what kind of hands you may fall into. I don't think I need tell you that man's inhumanity to animals is even greater than man's inhumanity to man.'

Shakespeare Milton gave such a great shudder that his body almost heaved out of the chair. He said: 'Have you ever been a horse, Miss Blanco?'

'No, Lilywhite never been very keen on horses, so she never even think of manifestin' as one even for a bit of fun.'

'There will be no fun in it,' Mr Milton said. 'I can assure you of that. Many years ago when the League found it difficult to procure secret agents I assumed the body of a racehorse so that I could do some spying in Italy. International racecourses and show jumping meetings are the best places to find foreign agents who mingle with the wealthy jet set, and as people speak freely in front of horses it's amazing the secrets one learns. Like all our agents, I had to submit to the rigid six months rule, and I must say that I've always regretted it. I was raced in Italy, France, Germany, England and other places. I was ridden by dozens of jockeys of all nationalities, and each of them had nothing to learn in the art of coercion. Often when a slave in my human condition I'd thought I had dredged to the depths of men's cruelty – the old Earl of Torryburn had a most fertile imagination in thinking up tortures – but – ' he shuddered – 'I had not known then what it is to be a horse. I carry the scars on my back and sides to this day.'

He closed his eyes for a few seconds, then he said: 'You must think very carefully, Miss Blanco, before you decide. You must realise, in the first place, that once you become a horse you will have to remain as a horse for the statutory six months. There is nothing you can do about it. You can buck and rear, of course. You can kick your groom or your rider, and you can bite them. You can take all the means that a horse takes to get his own back on his master. But you cannot use any ghostly or supernatural methods and tricks to help yourself. You will be able to speak in ghostly language to your fellow ghosts, but that is all. Otherwise, you will be a chattel, an animal, in the hands and at the mercy of all the human beings you come in contact with during your period of bondage. I want you to think this over very carefully before you agree to become a secret agent.'

'Don' make me nervous, man,' Lilywhite said, rising with a swagger. 'I guess I be able to hold my own. It'll be a lark maybe.'

'Maybe,' Mr Shakespeare Milton said, rising and shaking hands. 'But before you take the oath and sign the necessary papers, I suggest you consult your friends and tell them exactly what lies in front of them.'

The Countess didn't like the sound of it, but she was so anxious to get away from Jamaica that she decided to agree. 'I don't think we need tell the Baron all the conditions, however,' she said. 'We'll just tell him he has to assume the form of a horse. We'll keep our own counsel about the disadvantages.'

'That okay by Lilywhite, missy. We to give Shakey our decisions by midnight so he can arrange for us to go into the bodies of the horseys – two mares and a stallion – what's to be put on the plane the day after tomorrow.'

When the Baron heard he was to be a stallion he was delighted. 'Ah, *mes belles*,' he cried, 'I shall be *enchanté* to give the East German mares a good time. Oho, a brave new life is beginning for De Riveaux!'

Lilywhite looked sourly at him and said nothing.

'You are sure you don't want to change your mind, Miss

Blanco?' Mr Milton said in his office at midnight. 'You are sure you will be able to bear it?'

'Lilywhite guess she can manage. After all. what's six months in a lifetime of centuries? I guess I get used to bein' a horsey for that short while.'

He looked sympathetically at her. 'It's unfortunate that you don't care to spend the rest of your ghostly existence on our lovely island, Miss Blanco. Still, you must dree your own weird, as those horribly smug Scottish people keep saying.'

He drew some papers towards him and said briskly: 'I will repeat the rules. You will not be able to assume any form other than that of a horse for the next six months. Anything that may happen physically to you in that period will remain with you when you become a wraith again. You will have to go wherever your master takes you, and should you be in, say, China when your horse-time is up you will have to find your own way back to Western civilisation without any help from the League. During your six months servitude the League will keep a very close eye on you, so don't try any hanky-panky. You will collect as much information as you can about activities detrimental and antagonistic to our black race, and you will transmit this information to another of our agents who will reveal himself to you in due course. I think that is all.'

Mr Shakespeare Milton stood up and put out his hand. 'Good luck, Miss Blanco. I fear you will need all the luck that's going. And never forget that I warned you.'

*

As soon as she'd got used to having four legs instead of two Lilywhite enjoyed her first day of being a horse at a stud farm near Kingston. She was now a beautiful sprightly white mare. A name-plate above her stall announced that she was 'Sargasso Star'.

'Classy name, ain't it?' she said to the Countess, now a chestnut mare in the stall on the right-hand side. 'Better than yours, missy. Tawny Jemima! What a come-down for you. It sound like a tabby cat.'

'Be quiet, you scurrilous slut,' the Baron said from the stall on the other side. 'Or I shall bite your fat rump as soon as we're taken out for exercise.'

He neighed lustily and kicked the side of his stall. He was now a seventeen-hands four-years-old black stallion with a white blaze on his face. He was called 'Barnaby's Demon', and he could hardly contain himself with excitement; the body he had inherited, even though for only a temporary period, was bursting with strength and sexual vigour.

'Demon! That is a good name for me, is it not?' he nickered. 'I can hardly wait till I get to the stud farm in Germany. It is like being born again!'

All that afternoon Alvin, a good-looking young mulatto, groomed and petted Lilywhite until her coat shone. 'Make yo beautiful for yo new home,' he crooned. 'Yo a lovely gal an' I hates to lose yo. I sure gonna miss you, honey.'

Lilywhite arched her neck under his caresses, and she nibbled daintily at the sugar he held on his smooth pink palm. She nuzzled his chest and shoulders, and he put his arm around her neck and laid his face against her mane. Lilywhite hadn't experienced such acute sensual pleasure since she was a girl. This youth reminded her of her first lover: a page in the household of Barbara, Duchess of Castlemaine. That youth had been several years younger than this one, but he'd had the same slim, wide-shouldered figure, the same beautiful features, the same soft caressing hands. Lilywhite whinnied with enjoyment. What was Shakey Milton making all the fuss about? If life as a horse was going to be like this she'd have nothing to complain about. Although she wished she were a woman again and could enjoy his caresses properly and respond to them in a fitting manner. If only, instead of being a beautiful mare, she were a beautiful girl of sixteen again. If only she'd met Alvin instead of Sammy Truelove when they came to Jamaica ... If it came to that, why hadn't she met Alvin when she was young instead of that page who'd been sold to a French princess and taken to Paris before he and Lilywhite had been able to consummate their love? It was too late now. Everything always came too late. She would always be a big fat woman of forty-three, and no young man like this would ever look at her except in derision, even if she were a human being again.

In the evening, three grooms, who had just arrived from Europe, came with Alvin to inspect their new horses. The head groom, a small ginger-headed Scot with a much-lined red face and bulging green gooseberry eyes, nodded with appreciation when he saw the Baron. 'My my, but this yin's a braw big lad,' he said, patting the Baron on the haunch. 'Ay, man, ye're a bonnie cratur'. Me and you's goin' to be great pals.' He rubbed the Baron's neck and head, hissing unintelligibly and sniggering. 'I can see you're a right big randy rascal. Me and you'll get on fine as long as you behave yourself, cock.'

He gave the Baron a proprietory pat, saying to the other male groom, a young German with long fair hair and a sickly pretty face with violet shadows under the eyes: 'I'll take complete charge o' this yin, Dolf. You can take that yin.' He pointed to Lilywhite. 'And Gerda can look after that frisky-like chestnut.'

The girl groom, who had a short mannish haircut and a hard weather-beaten face, nodded and strode into the Countess's stall. '*Ja*, I look after her goot, Villie,' she said in a deep voice.

Alvin went into Lilywhite's stall and stroked her neck. 'This ma favourite horse,' he said. 'I desolate to lose her.'

'Is that a fact, then?' Willie said, entering the stall and patting Lilywhite. 'Ay, she's a lovely mare. I'm sure ye'll miss her. But don't worry, son. Dolf'll look after her well, won't ye, Dolf?'

The German youth, leaning listlessly against the wall, was examining his nails. He did not answer.

' 'S a pity you're not comin' to Germany wi' her,' Willie said, eyeing Alvin up and down. 'Have you ever thought of goin' abroad, eh? I could get ye a job in Germany. It's a grand place, cocky. I'm from Leith myself – in Scotland, ye ken – but I've lived in Germany ever since I finished ma national service. When my best pal, Alec, married a German lassie and settled in Dresden I decided to bide with them – to keep a fatherly eye on him, like. Me and him was very close. I never liked her, but I was that fond o' him I managed to put up wi' her. Me and him was – well, ye ken what I mean, eh? Maybe you like a bit of fun and games with a pal? Ye'd get plenty in Germany. I wouldn't think there was much scope here, eh?'

He squeezed past Alvin, taking the opportunity to pat the

young mulatto's handsome well-developed bottom. 'Ay, any time you want to make a change, cock, just you let me know and I'll arrange it.'

*

Next morning Lilywhite and her fellow horses were taken in horse-boxes to Palisadoes airport. Alvin went with Lilywhite, petting and soothing her on the journey. 'Be a good gal, ma beauty,' he whispered as he handed her over to Dolf, who was to lead her onto the plane. 'Maybe I see yo again sometime.'

In her stall on the plane, Lilywhite, nervous after being half-led, half-pushed up the ramp, suddenly realised with terror that on this journey she would have no air-sickness tablets. That was the best of being a human. You could ask for what you wanted. She was growing sick with anticipation of the flight ahead when she heard voices in the Baron's stall.

'Give us a hand to hobble this big bugger,' Willie said. 'Look, we'll do the back legs first. A bit tighter, I think. He's got a big reach and I dinnie want to be kicked from here to kingdom come.'

'Vhy is it you want to hobble him?' Dolf said.

'Well, it's to keep him frae kicking, like I said. I want to give him a good rub down and get to know him a wee thing better, like. Now we'll do the front legs. Watch him now! So you'd try to bite me, would you, ye big black bastard? Take that!'

Lilywhite heard a loud slap, then the Baron snorted with fury as he bucked and reared to try to get rid of the hobbles. After a lot of noise and muffled shouting, Willie said: 'Now that's him well tied up. Shove off now, cock, and see to your own mare.'

'I don't vant to. Please, Villie. You know I do not like lady horses. I vant to have a share of yours. Please! Do not be mean.'

'Shove off,' Willie said. 'Leave me in peace to rub him doon.'

'There is much horse to rub. I vill help you.'

'Shove off like I said.'

'Oh, come on, Villie dear, let me stay. Remember all the goot times you and I have had. He is big enough for us both.'

'All right, cocky,' Willie said. 'You take that side. I'll take this.'

Lilywhite heard the Baron snorting and heaving. She could feel the powerful vibrations through the wall. She heard Willie cry: 'Steady there, Demon! Steady there, my bonnie big stud!'

Lilywhite heard more snorting and plunging. Then Willie cried: 'Whoa now, whoa there, Demon! What're you makin' all the fuss about? Behave yoursel', you rascal, or I'll tickle your dock wi' the whip.'

'You enjoyin' yoself, Charlie boy?' Lilywhite called. 'What happenin' in there? You havin' a ball?'

Lilywhite did not understand the Baron's reply in French *argot* but his squeals of rage showed he was not enjoying himself. She neighed maliciously.

*

The Baron was still quivering with outrage at the indignities perpetrated on his person by the grooms when they arrived at Colonel Thadeus Syzmanski's stud farm midway between Dresden and the Polish border. 'I will kick that Willie to death at the first opportunity,' he snarled to the Countess while they were being led out of the horse-boxes.

'Control yourself, Charles. Please!' she said. 'Otherwise you may find yourself controlled … unpleasantly.'

The Colonel, a tall thin man with a monocle, was waiting to inspect them with his wife and daughter. 'This mare is mine,' he said, putting his hand on Lilywhite. 'She is a beautiful creature. She and I will have great success together in the ring.'

The Colonel's daughter, Irina, was a slight young woman of nineteen or twenty, with a flowerlike face, large grey eyes and long ash-blonde hair. She had the kind of delicate beauty that artists go into raptures over. She paid no attention to the Countess and Lilywhite. She walked around the Baron, taking in every muscle rippling under his sleek black hide. Aware of her admiration, the Baron preened himself, arching his neck, tossing his head and lifting his tail while he pawed the ground. Irina gripped his halter and stroked his muzzle. Then she placed her hand on his neck and gently drew it down his withers. As she moved along his side, stroking his barrel, he whinnied with delight. He quivered with ecstasy, holding himself as rigidly as possible in case he made the slightest movement that might upset this fragile creature.

'I like this big fellow, father,' she said. 'This one's mine.' And she slapped the Baron's hindquarters. 'I'll train him good. By the time I've finished with him he'll be a champion jumper.'

'I can rely on you, my dear, to put him through his paces,' the Colonel said.

'*Voilà, mes belles!*' the Baron said, prancing on the way to the stables. 'That lovely young lady appreciates me. Oh, what gentle hands she has!' He was drooling with delight. 'I will be proud indeed to have her on my back and gallop and gallop at her slightest command. I'm proud to be chosen to serve such a fair young mistress.'

'Blind peoples can see how you feel, Charlie boy,' Lilywhite said. 'You forget you ain't got no clothes now to hide yo passion.'

As soon as he'd led the Baron into his stall, Willie started to groom him. When the Baron kicked and reared, Willie shouted to Dolf to bring the hobbles.

'You black cow!' the Baron screamed, struggling futilely. 'It's your fault. This would never have happened if you hadn't made us leave Ardmore.'

'Not my fault, Charlie. And Lilywhite not a black cow. She a nice white horsey.'

A piebald mare in the stall next to Lilywhite's, who'd been watching the proceedings with enjoyment, suddenly squealed: 'It's you, is it? You vile bitch! So our paths cross once again!'

It was the old queen from Hove, the one Lilywhite had frightened to death on Brighton beach a long time ago.

'We – ell … ' Lilywhite said. 'How you like Africa, mate?'

'Not any more than he likes being groomed by Willie,' the piebald queen-mare said. 'Though I wish I was in his place.'

Lilywhite craned her neck, trying to see what was happening in the Baron's stall, and repeated: 'How you like Africa, you ole frizzle?'

'I didn't. Too many black devils like you there. So I gave them the slip and stowed away on a plane going to the USA. New York is wonderful. Such a lively place, my dear! So many gay young people! But do you know something? I don't mind telling you this – though I hate your guts for taking me away from Hove, and I'll never forgive you – young men now aren't like what they used to be. All that long hair! It makes life so difficult. Sometimes I followed a pretty faggot and he turned out to be a girl, and then other times I paid no attention to what turned out to be a real cosy boy. All this long hair takes away the kick. Still, I did enjoy America, and I wouldn't have missed it.'

'What make you leave then?'

'Alas, I got caught in a raid on a male striptease club. My dear, you never saw such ongoings! I thought we were pretty advanced in Brighton, but – oh, words fail me! I was so *disgusted* by what I saw that I was coming out when the police came in, and I was nicked by the ghost of a Puritan policeman – a member of the Watch Committee or whatever they were called then – who had come along with the human fuzz for kicks. And so he grabs me and claps on the cuffs before I could cough. What a brute! One of the great human brutes of all time. He had gone over in the *Mayflower* and was one of those that arrested the Salem witches. Well, to cut a long story short, he hauled me in front of the Ghost Control Commission. And, seeing I was an illegal immigrant, they were all for sending me back to Africa. But I do have my moments, and I do know how to handle men. So the upshot was that the Commission made a bargain with me. They would send me to Germany if I consented to be a spy for WASPs.'

'What that?'

'Really, you are an ignorant bitch.' The old queen-mare tut-tutted, but without taking her eyes away from the Baron's stall where there was a pandemonium of outraged squealing, heaving, slaps and sibilation. 'It means White Anglo Saxon Protestant. That's the bunch I'm working for.'

'You shoulden tell me you's a spy,' Lilywhite said.

'Why not? You're a spy too, aren't you?'

'Yes, but I don' work for the same side. I work for Black Power.'

'What difference does it make?'

'It mean you break your oath, you false ole flibbertigibbet. Oh, jus' you wait till them Ghost Control boys get their hands on you!'

'I couldn't care less, dear. At least they would take me away from this bloody hole.'

'You might land in Siberia,' Lilywhite said. 'I hears the Commies got some lovely concentration camps.'

'Sufficient unto the day is the evil thereof,' the queen-mare said. 'Well, to continue my tale – and I don't mean a horse's – when they put up their proposition I got ever so excited. They told me they'd send me to a Household Cavalry depot. I often used to have flutters with boys in the Blues when they came to Brighton on leave, and I was so excited at the thought of having a big strapping trooper astride me again it never dawned on me to ask what kind of horse I'd be.'

'What happen to change it?'

'That Puritan watchman knew I wanted to be with the Blues. He said he wasn't going to encourage immorality and altered my papers at the last minute and sent me here. And then he played the filthiest trick by making me a mare. I couldn't believe it when I found I hadn't my masculine appendages. Some of those German grooms are very sexy – I once had a very gay time with one in Hamburg – and I thought if I couldn't have a guardsman I'd have a groom.'

'What you complainin' about?' Lilywhite said. 'You got those two who're givin' Charlie such a good goin' over. What more you want?'

'Them! They're only interested in studs. They never lay a hand on me. I'm groomed by that bloody lesbian. And I'm always ridden by that fat smelly woman, Madame Olga Syzmanska. A curse on you, you black bitch, for doing that to me on Brighton beach. Sometimes I wonder if my six months 'll ever end ... '

*

Next morning the Baron whinnied with delight when Irina walked into his stall. He stretched his neck and nuzzled her shoulder. 'Stop that, horse,' she said, slapping him on the muzzle.

'Hurry up, Gerda,' she called.

The girl groom, who had been curry-combing the Countess, sidled into the stallion's stall, carrying a saddle, a bridle and a riding switch. 'Throw those down just now,' Irina ordered.

'We've got time for something else before I put this brute through his paces.'

The Baron backed, horrified, when Irina seized Gerda round the waist and kissed her passionately. His nostrils distended with disbelief; his ears became as flat as his fieriness at the sight of Irina fondling Gerda's breasts.

'Now, *Liebchen*, let's get this brute ready,' Irina said.

She slung the saddle on the Baron's back. 'Stand still, horse,' she shouted, pulling the girth so tightly that the Baron felt he'd never be able to breathe again. The weight of the saddle and the constriction made him rear. 'Enough of that,' Irina said, picking up the switch and slashing his hindquarters.

He squealed with pain. Gerda gripped one of his ears, twisted it with her strong hand, and pushed the fingers of her other hand into his nostrils to make him open his mouth wider. Irina quickly shoved a double-bit into it, pulled the bridle over his head and fastened it. The Baron was so anguished at feeling the weight of cold steel on his tongue that he was scarcely aware of Irina tightly fastening the chain of a curb under his chin. He shook his head, trying to get rid of the affliction in his mouth, as Gerda led him out of the stable.

'Behave yourself, animal,' Irina said, striking him with the switch again. She leapt into the saddle, lifted the reins, drew them tight and, almost before the Baron realised she was on his back, she kicked her spurs into him.

He squealed and dashed forward. Irina headed him towards a paddock where there were a number of jumps. A few yards from the first jump she cried 'Up, horse!' and struck his flank with the whip. The Baron was so astonished he leapt in the air and got over the three-feet obstacle without touching it. He was trying to get enough breath to snort with temper when Irina wheeled him round with a wrench on the bit and cried 'Up, horse!' And at another slash of the whip the Baron leapt over the jump again. Another wrench round, another 'Up, horse!', another slash and he leapt the third time. Then she dug in the spurs and headed him for the next jump, a higher one.

When he was taken back to the stable the Baron's flanks and backside were covered with weals. He was quivering with shock, pain and fury. And his fury reached bursting point, insult being piled on injury, when Willie made a great fuss of him. 'So ye got a thrashin' eh?' Willie clucked. 'Well now, you randy big rogue, it serves ye right for not bein' a wee bit more amenable like. Aw, what a mess she's made o' yer lovely bum ... Never mind, I'll do all that I can to soothe it.' The groom sniggered. 'I notice our bonnie Miss Irina didn't succeed in makin' you brandish your weapon this mornin'.'

The Countess and Lilywhite had also been getting their first training as show jumpers and, although neither had been maltreated, they were tired and outraged at the indignities they'd had to suffer – jumping and wheeling, cantering and trotting at every touch of heel or pressure of knee and reins – and all the time they'd been terrified and apprehensive, watching what the Baron was undergoing and wondering how soon it would be before they suffered in the same way.

'There's no need to worry,' the old queen-mare said when they were back in the stable. 'Although that Irina's a lesbian she never rides mares. She's not interested in them. She likes to vent her spleen on the masculine sex, to have them in her power. I expect there's some psychological explanation.'

The Countess repeated this to the Baron, saying: 'You must be reasonable, Charles.'

'Reasonable! Reasonable!' He was hysterical. 'Suffering like this at the hands of those vile people, and you ask me to be reasonable!'

'I know you're having a dreadful time,' she said. 'But I warned you to behave yourself. You elected to be a horse. You had to take a chance. We all had to take a chance. It was all in the luck of the draw that the fair mistress you were enraptured about last night has turned out to be such a sadistic whore. After all, you didn't treat your own horses with consideration when you were alive. You had a very free and heavy hand with the whip. And it was not only horses ... I remember once you thrashed a groom because he remonstrated about the way you were ill-treating your own stallion.'

'What a pity you couldn't be ridden by one of those nice boys in the Blues,' the old queen-mare said. 'They would never treat you like this. They are all so *fond* of their horses, giving them sugar and carrots and beer ... and even bars of chocolate. And tickling their ears ... '

'You keep out of this, you piebald monstrosity,' the Baron shouted, trying unsuccessfully to rear. 'You should see where this *cochon* is tickling me.'

'Better that than having your fair mistress tickling you with her whip,' the Countess said tartly.

'Tickle! The woman's an Amazon. If this goes on for six months I'll be black and blue for eternity.'

'Perhaps her correction won't be so strict tomorrow,' she said.

It was even stricter. For the next few weeks, day after day, there was a never-ending battle of wills between the young woman and the stallion. At first, taking the Countess's advice, the Baron pretended to submit docilely to Irina's mastery. But to no avail. He soon learnt that his mistress was as ready to lash a docile horse as a recalcitrant one. So he changed his tactics. He fought her with bitter brute cunning. Always, after she'd given him a brisk work-out over the jumps, Irina would head him towards the farm gates and gallop him fully extended into the open country. After a week of this, with the Baron seemingly under control, Irina relaxed a little so that she could enjoy the gallop. The Baron took his opportunity. In mid-gallop he stopped suddenly, reared and unseated his rider, wrenched the reins from her, kicked up his heels and galloped away to freedom. But he had not reckoned on the conspiracy of humans against the animal world. He was cornered by some farm-hands and brought back. Irina tied him to a post in the stable yard and thrashed him with a carriage whip.

The struggle went on. Sometimes the Baron was successful in throwing Irina and escaping to temporary freedom. It always ended with him being tied to the whipping post.

Even Lilywhite watched her old-time enemy's punishment with horror. She was thankful that Colonel Syzmanski had none of his daughter's sadism. He rode Lilywhite firmly, but his training was fairly gentle, and by the time Irina said it was a thankless job training the Baron for show jumping Lilywhite was declared ready to take part in an event.

Before this came about, however, she received a pleasant surprise. The young mulatto groom, Alvin, arrived at the

Syzmanski stud farm.

'I surprise you, baby?' he said as she nuzzled him with joy. 'That Willie he *inveigle* me to come here. Such winning letters he write. He a man who like young studs, and he beg me to come. He think he get some sweetness from me, he think again, baby!'

Lilywhite bloomed under Alvin's care: a wonderful change from the perfunctory ministrations of Dolf, who was now put in charge of a young bay gelding that had just been bought and was being trained by Irina. Finding this bay quicker and a better leaper than the Baron, Irina transferred some of her vigour to him. And since he did not show such a vicious temper as the black stallion, she had the Baron gelded. 'It will maybe tame the brute,' she said.

When the vet arrived with his gelding instruments, Lilywhite shuddered and said to the queen-mare: 'Poor ole Charlie. Lilywhite thought she want revenge for what he done to me, but not now. It shoulden happen to yo biggest enemy. Life never be the same for him again. They shoulden do it to no animal. Charlie be better to be shot stone cold dead in the market.'

*

A few weeks after he was gelded the Baron took the opportunity when Irina came into his stall to gloat to give her such a kick that he broke her leg in two places. 'That horse is useless,' she said as Willie and Dolf carried her on a stretcher to the ambulance. 'It's a dead loss. I'll sell it.'

While Irina was laid up with her broken leg, the Countess and Lilywhite went to their first show jumping event at Rotterdam. Lilywhite, ridden by Colonel Syzmanski, was entered for the same novice competition as the Countess, ridden by Madame Olga Syzmanska. In the ring Lilywhite responded to every pressure of the Colonel's hands and knees. She leapt and leapt and gained enough points to qualify her for the next round. The Countess, petulant and sweating under Madame Olga's bulk, also qualified for the next round. Halfway through the second round Lilywhite realised that the Colonel was trying to restrain her and she thought: 'Oho, he don' want me to win. He want his ole woman to win. But

Lilywhite don' want Olga and missy to beat her. No sir, that ole Countess Torryburn she ain't goin' be able to crow over Lilywhite.'

So, despite the Colonel's pressure, she leapt and leapt over the jumps, clearing them all against the clock, and won. As the rosette was pinned on her bridle she crowed to the panting Countess: 'I's a nice white horsey! Better than you, you ole done chestnut mare!'

In her box behind the show ring, Alvin rubbed down Lilywhite, put on her blanket, petted her and left her chewing two lumps of sugar. Standing with her head over the half-door, she was savouring the last grains as well as her triumph over the Countess when two very horsey-looking men came up. Even Lilywhite, a newcomer to the sporting world, guessed there was something phoney about them. Their breeches and leggings looked as though they'd never been near a horse's hide. The tall one wore a deerstalker with checks that clashed with the checks of his over-checked jacket; the short one had on a large cap that practically hid the top of his face.

The short man looked at the name on Lilywhite's door and said: 'This is the one. Sargasso Star.'

He shoved away Lilywhite's head and opened the door. 'Back there, horse,' he ordered. 'Gid back there!'

'Whoa, whoa!' the tall man shouted. 'Is he all right?'

'Oh yes, he's a quiet one. That's why Comrade BA37 chose it for the job.'

'I don't like the look of it. See those teeth!'

'She'll be all right, comrade. But let's hobble her to be on the safe side.'

They shut both halves of the door behind them, switched on the light, and the short one took some straps out of his bulging pockets. At the sight of them, Lilywhite backed into a corner, ears flat with alarm. After hobbling her – and Lilywhite kicked and plunged with fury before the job was done – the short man took a small object out of the lining of his cap. Lilywhite trembled, thinking it was either a syringe or a chloroform pad. While the tall man held her firmly by the halter, the short man bent down, lifted her left forefoot and squeezed the object under her shoe. 'Steady there, nice horse steady there!' he cried as he pushed it securely between the horn of her hoof and the steel plate.

Suddenly Lilywhite realised what was happening. These men were spies. They were using her as a decoy to smuggle something behind the Iron Curtain. She snorted with suppressed laughter. They were such amateurs, shouting so much it was a wonder the police were not here already.

'Listen to her neighing!' the tall man said. 'She *likes* us.'

'Goodbye, horse,' the short man said. 'Be sure and deliver the goods safely to Comrade BA37.'

Lilywhite laughed as she watched the comrades scurry away.

'What was all that noise in aid of?' the Countess shouted from the neighbouring box. 'It sounded as if you were entertaining a dozen men.'

Lilywhite giggled: 'No, only two Russian spies.'

'Spies?'

'Yes, missy. Has you forgotten our assignment? The job what we endurin' all this for?'

'But spies here?' the Countess cried. 'In a horse box!'

' 'S not as funny as it sound, missy. Even the animals spyin' on each other nowadays.'

'What 're you going to do?'

'Just wait and see what happen,' Lilywhite said. 'Shakey Milton tell me our contact come see us one of them days. So we wait and see.'

They were still talking about it when Alvin and Gerda came to fodder them. 'Wonder what this contact man be like?' Lilywhite shouted through the wall.

Alvin said: 'He be a black man, sister.'

Lilywhite stopped in mid-neigh.

'What you say, man?'

Alvin laughed. 'He a black man, sister. He your lover boy.'

'Well, shiver ma ole bones!' she said.

'Yes, I's a ghostie like you,' Alvin said in the *lingua franca* of the nether world.'You not guess that, baby? You not penetrate ma disguise? Shakey Milton not takin' no chances. He send his Number One agent to keep an eye on you all.'

'Well, shiver ma ole bones!' she repeated.

'Let's see this secret thing,' Alvin said, lifting her hoof and prising out the packet.

It was a microfilm. Alvin held it up to the light and squinted. 'I no scientist man,' he said. 'But I guess this Western Nuclear secrets. This more useful to Black Power than Russia.'

He put it in his pocket and grinned: 'Now we jus' wait and see who come to inspect your hoof, ma pretty gal.'

But nobody came while they were in Rotterdam, and they returned to the Syzmanski stud farm without anything happening. On the journey to Dresden Alvin told Lilywhite and the Countess his life story.

He had been a slave on a plantation in Georgia before the American Civil War. 'But I done get tired of the overseer man,' he said. 'So I runs away. They chase me through the woods with them big snarling dogs, but I gets away north to freedom. Then, would you believe it, only a week after that ole Civil War start I get shot dead.'

'My goodness!' Lilywhite nickered. 'you a hero of Gettysburg, man, like that Abraham Lincoln?'

'No, I never gets near no battlefield,' Alvin said. 'I gets me a job as a porter in a hotel for travellin' gents in a town in Illinois. And I thinkin' I come to the land of Canaan, overflowin' with milk and honey, with no overseer, no ole massa shoutin' Boy do this, Boy do that. Then one of them travellin' gents gets pistol-happy drunk because he goin' to fight for the Union and he starts shootin' and I gets a bullet right through ma head.'

*

Irina was walking about slowly with a stick, her leg in a heavy plaster. Unable to ride, she turned over the exercising and training of the Baron to Willie. But the change of rider did not make the Baron's life any less miserable. For, if anything, Willie was an even sterner taskmaster than Irina. Ever since the stallion was castrated the groom had transferred his affections to Alvin. The mulatto was kept busy skipping out of the way whenever Willie sidled into a corner beside him. Laughing gaily, he always kept Willie at arm's length. And because he was frustrated, Willie tried to get satisfaction in thrashing the Baron.

On the night they returned to the stud farm Lilywhite reared with shock and apprehension when Irina came unexpectedly into her stall. She felt a great sickness in her belly. It was the first time Irina had ever come near her. Was the old queen-mare maybe wrong when he said Irina wasn't interested in mares? Maybe she was going to choose her to ride because she'd won that prize at Rotterdam?

'Stand still, you swine,' Irina said, slapping Lilywhite's side.

She bent down, lifted Lilywhite's left forefoot and probed beneath the shoe. Lilywhite was so surprised that she started to shudder violently.

'Stand still, damn you,' Irina shouted. Then, as she went on searching and found nothing, she began to swear in Polish.

'You find somethin' wrong with Star's shoe, Miss Irina?' Alvin said, appearing suddenly beside them.

'No,' Irina said. 'I just thought it looked a little slack when she came out of the box this afternoon.'

'It not slack, missy,' he said. 'But it done get a bittie somethin' – some kind of funny paper – caught in it when we was in Rotterdam.'

'A piece of paper? What did you do with it, boy?'

'I throwed it away, Missy Irina.' Alvin grinned. 'But natch! It only a bittie ole dirty paper.'

'You bloody fool! You interfering nigger!'

Irina gave Lilywhite a vicious jab in the belly with her stick and limped out of the stable. At the door she turned and said: 'Once this bloody leg of mine is better I'll be riding this creature. It seems she's quite a good jumper. Better than that black brute, anyway. I'm selling him.'

Next morning Willie passed on the news to Baron. He came into his stall and took over the grooming from Alvin. 'I'll give him a wee rub down for the last time,' he said. 'There's a man frae the Argentine comin' to look at him the day. Ay, my braw laddie – if we can call ye a laddie any longer!' He giggled. 'Ye're goin' on a long journey, we hope. The Colonel was for shootin' ye, but Miss Irina said we might as well get some money for you, you cantankerous brute. Oh, I don't suppose we'll get much for ye. Ye're a bloody washout as a show jumper, and you're nae good as a hack. So what this man from the Argentine can want with ye I don't know. I hear tell he's got a real bad reputation for the way he treats his horses. He soon wears them out. So I imagine he'll not be long in sendin' ye to the knacker's. Ye'll likely end up as a tin o' corned beef.'

Senor Luis de Gonzales, a fat man with a greasy face, gold teeth and hands flashing with diamonds, had the Baron paraded up and down several times before he said: 'I'll take him. He'll make a good carriage horse. I will have his tail docked first, of course. My coachman does not like horses with long tails.'

Senor Luis then asked for the piebald queen-mare to be paraded. 'I will buy this one too,' he said. 'My little daughter is getting too big for ponies. This old hack will suit her quite well for a few months until she gets something livelier. It will be nice for this black one to have his friend with him. I do not like to think they should be separated.'

Within an hour the Baron and the old queen-mare were boxed and on their way to the airport.

Lilywhite said: 'Pore ole Charlie. He been better killed in that ole battle of Blenheim, poor sod.'

*

The Countess pined so much her coat lost its lustre and she drooped. 'You better buck up, missy,' Lilywhite said. 'You go in a decline like this, and that bitch Irina sell you too.'

'I miss him so much,' the Countess sobbed. 'We've been together for such a long time.'

'We all been. But Lilywhite not gonna let it get her down. She gonna think up ways and means of gettin' our own back on that ole Irina.'

After some more training the ghostly show jumpers were taken to Ireland to show their paces at the Dublin Horse Show. And there Comrade BA37 was in evidence again.

This time it was the Countess's loose-box the two Russians visited. This time it was the Countess's left hindfoot that received a microfilm between the horn and the shoe.

The Russians were scarcely out of sight before Alvin, in ghostly form, arrived in the Countess's box. The microfilm showed maps of Hottentot arms dumps all over Ireland and plans for using English tourists as slave labour once the

Hottentots came into power.

'I don't know what use this to us in Black Power,' Alvin said. 'But Miss BA37 sure not gettin' it.'

He had scarcely spoken when Gerda ran into the box. She picked up the Countess's left hindfoot and searched beneath the shoe. Alvin and the Countess giggled at the expression on Gerda's face; and when she lifted each of the Countess's other feet and examined them they became hysterical. Suddenly Gerda rushed out. She went into the box of another chestnut mare a few doors away. After a few minutes she dashed out and went into the box of a brown mare that might also have passed for chestnut. Then she went into the box of a chestnut gelding. 'She sure don' trust them Russians,' Alvin said. 'She guess them agents don' know one horse from another.'

Lilywhite won two prizes at Dublin; the Countess won one. Irina's delight about this turned to rage when Gerda told her there was no microfilm. Irina shouted: 'I told you to keep near Tawny Jemima's box and to collect the paper as soon as the men left.'

'But there was nothing there,' Gerda protested. 'I looked at all her feet, then I looked at the feet of other mares in case those men had made a mistake.'

'Soviet agents never make mistakes,' Irina said. 'I've been double-crossed.'

Gerda went on: 'Nobody else was in the box and nobody was near it.'

'The truth is, you double-dealing whore,' Irina said, 'that you were having trade with another groom in another box and weren't watching for the agents. Somebody will suffer for this. Bring me a whip!'

'Oh, my God!' the Countess cried. 'My hour has come!'

When Gerda brought a thin riding switch the Countess laid back her ears and prepared to kick. But Irina said to Gerda: 'Drop your breeches, bitch. I'll teach you to be so careless.'

*

'I expects Irina in bad now with her Russian masters,' Alvin said. 'Guess we kin kiss goodbye to Comrade BA37.'

Not long after, however, when competing in Nice, where Lilywhite won the Puissance by clearing a wall of seven feet and got her picture in all the international papers, the two horsey-looking Russians appeared again. Irina took over Alvin's duties as a groom during the event, and Lilywhite shivered with apprehension when Irina led her to her box after she'd won the prize. Instead of rubbing her down, Irina left on Lilywhite's bridle and saddle and went into a corner and lit a cigarette. Alvin, there in his ghostly form, whispered to Lilywhite: 'Don' you worry, honey. I got ma eye on her.'

The two horsey-looking men came into the box and, without looking at Irina or speaking to her, hid a microfilm in Lilywhite's saddle, between the flap and the seat. The short one patted Lilywhite and said: 'He is a very goot horse, yes?'

The Russians left. Irina ground out her cigarette on the floor, but before she could put her hand on the microfilm she saw it appearing from under the flap and disappearing into the air. Alvin had put it in his ghostly pocket.

'Great God in Heaven!' Irina screamed. 'I saw it with my own eyes, yet I've been double-crossed again. I shall write to the Kremlin and complain.'

*

Back at the stud farm, Lilywhite counted the days until their period of servitude would be ended, but the Countess sank into the deepest depression.

'For the sake of sweet Jesus you snap out of it, missy,' Lilywhite implored. 'We got only seven more weeks to go. You behave like this and that Irina bitch done sell you too. She flamin' mad because the doctor man tole her she be lame for life and never ride again. That sure was somethin' ole Charlie did with a great big bang. Do cheer up, missy! Irina fit enough to try to take it out on you.'

'It's such a long way to South America,' the Countess sobbed. 'I think of him all the time, and his poor docked tail. My darling Charles, he'll never be able to find his own way back to me.'

'Aw, sure he will,' Lilywhite said. 'We ghosties got a lot of low cunnin'. And Charlie, he got great gumption. He come back to you all right.'

'If he doesn't, what 'll I do?' the Countess snivelled. 'We've been together for all those hundreds of years.'

'You still got me, missy.'

'You!' The Countess sprang into life and her eyes blazed. 'You wicked black besom! You're to blame for all this.'

'Now then, missy, no re-crim-in-at-ions,' Lilywhite said. 'I got you away from Jamaica and all that voodoo, didden I?'

'Yes, and see the result!'

'I gets you away from here too,' Lilywhite said. 'But you watch that Irina cow. I don' want her to sell you, and then we lose each other. Me and you's been such great pals all them hundreds of years I woulden want to lose you. I be desolate without you.'

'Desolate my arse!'

'Now then, Margaret Torryburn, don' you go and re-vert to your coarse Scottish ancestry,' Lilywhite said. 'That no way to talk to an ole friend who only thinkin' of your good. You and me have our ups and downs all them years, but I never forgets we closely linked in this vale of bloody tears. I stick to you closer than a flea.'

'I gets you away from here,' she said later on. 'And I helps you get Misyew lee Baron back safe – though not sound like he might of been, pore ole geldin'. I feel very friendly to him too. Though I don' know yet how I goin' to manage our blessed re-un-ion.'

'Maybe Alvin will help,' the Countess said. 'He's sweet on you.'

'Sweet?' Lilywhite giggled. 'You know what, missy? That Alvin say he want to marry Lilywhite after we done our term as horseys. What you know about that? Alvin seem to forget, though he such a big bug in the Black Power world, that there ain't no givin' and receivin' in marriage in the land of us ghosties.'

She nibbled delicately at some hay. 'I don' think I accept his offer. He a nice boy. Oh, he ever such a nice boy, and I love him dearly. But Lilywhite don' want to be accused at her age of cradle-snatchin'.'

'Besides,' she mused, 'he a secret agent of Black Power, and if we marry he want Lilywhite to go on bein' a spy. I don' want to be Secret Agent Number CT69. I guess I had enough of spies. Ain't you, missy?'

'I never want to hear that word again.'

'Neither does Lilywhite. But before we leave this land of the evil livin' and goes back to the good ole ghostie times again, we must have re-venge on that Irina. Don' you want to give Comrade BA37 somethin' to make her re-mem-ber us by?'

'Of course, you fool,' the Countess said. 'But what?'

'We think up somethin', missy,' Lilywhite said. 'We think up somethin' real good. When the time come for you and me to become ghosties again we kick that wicked Irina in the guts and kill her. We arrange it with Alvin so it happen in the last few minutes before we get our bodies transform'. So if they shoots the pore horseys whose bodies we jus' been in they don't shoot me and you. Then maybe we go to Con-stan-ti-nople? Jus' a little trip so's Lilywhite can see the Land of her Fathers. And maybe we could stir up somethin' among them Turkeys heathen? Somethin' good before we goes off to South America to find Iee Baron. We might even do somethin' for that pore ole queen from Hove. I regrets what I done to her. Poor ole thing, she sure does love them boys in the Blues. We arrange somethin' for her. But before we goes, missy – and you give this the front place in yo mind – we kick that Irina to death. What it matter about another death between friends? We do a great ser-vice to hum-an-ity. And if she lucky enough to become a ghostie, we *per-se-cute* her for the rest of eternity. Won' that be lovely? Oh, what good times me and you will have, and poor ole Charlie will get his revenge.'

VI

The Lady of Sweetheart Abbey

The first great wave swelled in with such a swoosh that it engulfed her whole body and she strained against the ropes that tied her to the stake. She closed her eyes and opened her mouth to scream. The salt water flowed into her mouth, choking her. She was still choking and spluttering when the wave ebbed. She opened her eyes, shook the water from her head and, looking down, saw that the tide had not yet risen to her ankles.

'Mammy! Mammy!' she screamed. And then she whispered: 'Oh, God, dinnie let me dee like this.'

The other Margaret, tied to a stake seven feet away, was saying the Lord's Prayer in a loud voice. She stopped in the midst of it and cried: 'Wheesht, Maggie! Dinnie ask God to do something he cannie interfere with at this late stage. He cannie save us noo. Have courage, lassie, and let's hope we droon quickly ... Forgive us our trespasses as we forgive them that trespass against us. For thine is the Kingdom the Power and the Glory. In Jesus's name, amen.'

As the second great wave rose like a mountain over her, Margaret heard mourning wails from the people gathered on the shore behind her. She could not turn her head, but she knew the village folk were berating the dragoons who had brought the prisoners from Wigtown. Her ribs were still aching from the jack-boot of the big brawny brute with piggy eyes to whose stirrup-iron her hands had been tied while they walked the miles to the shore. She had stumbled along, trying to keep pace with the horse. The trooper had laughed as she began to lag, and he had kicked the horse, then kicked her, saying: 'Get up, ye Covenantin' limmer! Run if ye dinnie want to be dragged to yer death.' And so she had been forced to run until they reached the wide stretch of Solway, where she had been untied from the stirrup to be tied again in a few minutes to the stake on the sands. The piggy-eyed dragoon had chucked her under the chin after he had tied her, and he had leered and said: 'What aboot a fareweel kiss, hinny?'

When the third great wave came and engulfed her, Margaret shrieked. Then, as it subsided, she looked down and saw that the water had reached only the bottom of the calves of her legs. She whispered: 'Forgive me, oh Lord, for being so feared, but I cannie help it – I want my mammy!'

While the fourth or maybe fifth or sixth waves were flung over her, out of them, suddenly, there appeared an old woman dressed in weird other-worldly garments. A tall peaked hat with veils that were swathed under her chin towered above a sweet, lined face with compassionate cornflower blue eyes. She touched Margaret on the forehead and said: 'I have come to comfort you, my daughter. Have no more fear. 'Twill soon be over, and in a few moments I shall take you to a far more pleasant land. I am the Lady of Galloway, Devorgilla of Sweetheart Abbey. Courage, my child. You will soon be in another country.'

She floated over to the other Margaret, touched her and murmured the same words. Another great wave engulfed them all a second later.

*

Maggie Campion screamed. She awoke and gazed into the darkness, terrified, and then she realised she was safely in bed beside her husband, stout comfortable Cass. She clutched his shoulder.

'What's wrong?' he mumbled. 'Heard you yelling. Had a bad dream?'

'Yeah, but I'm okay now,' she said. 'Go back to sleep.'

Cass did so, but Maggie lay sleepless for a long time. She had not had this nightmare since her marriage twenty-five years ago, though as a child she had had it frequently. It scarcely ever varied in detail. The approach of the great engulfing waves; the sweet face of the old lady in the high peaked hat; the voice of the other Margaret; and her cries of

'Mammy! Mammy!' – these were always the same. And so was the awakening, drenched in sweat as clinging as the salt water of the Solway.

Maggie did not know how many times she had the nightmare over the years between the ages of five and nineteen, but the first time was engraved on her memory. It was while her father's mother, who had a small farm in Nebraska, was visiting them in their home in Oklahoma. It was the first time Maggie remembered seeing Granny Maitland. The old woman had visited them when Maggie was a baby, and then again when she was two years old. But Maggie only became aware of her as a person on this third visit, which was to be the last.

Maggie knew already that her father's ancestors were Scottish. It had been well drummed into her by her mother, who also had some Scottish blood. Rosemary Maitland had been a schoolteacher in a little prairie town where several of her pupils were of Scottish descent.

'They were always the wildest kids,' she said often, 'but there was something about them that kind of got me. Something that made me a l'il bit sweet on them. I guess they appealed to the Celt in me. I used to read them the old ballads and Robert Burns and Sir Walter Scott. "Breathes there the man with soul so dead, who never to himself hath said, this is my own, my native land" and all that. And they used to get me so excited, so carried away by it all, that I'd forget how God-damned awful they could be sometimes when they got mulish and stuck in their toes when I was trying to teach them something they didn't want to know about. I guess it was remembering this kind of *exuberance* that made me marry your Daddy when I heard his folk came from Scotland 'way back. I didn't know then that every Scotsman doesn't come off the same bonnie rowan tree.'

Her mother always stopped there. She could tell Maggie no actual facts about her father's ancestry; her own was based on a Scots great-grandfather who had emigrated from Inverness to Chicago in the 1870s. It was not until Granny Maitland's visit that Maggie learned that the Maitlands had come to what was then the American colonies near the end of the 17th century.

'I dunno whether they came with a free will or whether they was transported,' Granny said. 'Transportation was a terrible bad thing to happen to any young man or woman in them days, but it was better than bein' killed. In Scotland them days was called "The Killing Times". I dunno whether the first Maitland to settle here was kin to one of the Wigtown Martyrs or whether he married a girl who was kin to one of them women, but there's always been talk in the family about them. What's for sure is our early folks came from Covenantin' stock, and ever since then the Maitlands – bein' what they call clannish – have always married folks who have Scottish blood too. My own grannary was an Urquhart from some place called the Black Isle.'

And then Granny Maitland told Maggie the story of the Wigtown Martyrs: Margaret Wilson, a girl of eighteen, and Margaret MacLachlan, a widow aged sixty-three. The way she told it was a rambling old wife's tale, full of asides and speculations, sighs and lamentations about her own health and the sorrows of old age, with many dramatic screechings and warnings to her little granddaughter about what to expect from life and what to do to avoid similar tribulations when she, in her turn, came to Granny's great age. Although she did not understand a lot of it, Maggie sat, entranced and terrified, at the telling in her grandmother's flat Nebraskan voice of the saga of the two Galloway women Covenanters who had been dragged, in the year 1685, by the red-coated dragoons to their deaths at the stakes sunk in Solway sands thousands of miles from Oklahoma.

Granny Maitland's discourse was so rambling, her lamentations and asides so many, that little Maggie never learned whether her blood came from the family of Margaret Wilson or the family of Margaret MacLachlan. And so, when she had the nightmare for the first time, a day before her grandmother's visit ended, she did not know which Margaret she was. And throughout all the years she still did not know from which martyr she stemmed. Sometimes she thought she was one Margaret, sometimes the other. Always she was herself, Maggie Maitland, but the figure tied to the other stake was sometimes an old woman wearing a mutch, sometimes a girl whose long hair was drenched with sea water.

Because of the recurrent nightmare the Solway tide and the stakes haunted Maggie's imagination, and as she grew older she looked forward to asking her grandmother more about the martyrs on her next visit. But before she could see her again the old woman died in faraway Nebraska. Maggie's father, a dour, phlegmatic man uninterested in history and tradition, was either unable or unwilling to enlighten her; he told her to forget all this history nonsense and concentrate instead on her school work, especially on writing and arithmetic so that she'd grow up to get a good post as a stenographer.

To spite her husband's boorishness, Rosemary Maitland recited every Scottish ballad she could remember and she got Maggie to learn them off by heart, too. And she encouraged the child to read all the Scottish books she could lay hands on. In this way, when she was only seven or eight, Maggie read *Old Mortality*, Walter Scott's novel about the Killing Times and Grahame of Claverhouse, who was called Bloody Clavers by the Covenanters and Bonnie Dundee by the royalists. She read, too, the poems of Robert Louis Stevenson, and at nights before going to sleep she would recite her favourite to herself:

> Blows the wind today, and the sun and the rain are flying,
> Blows the wind on the moors today and now,
> Where above the graves of the martyrs the whaups are crying
> My heart remembers how!

*

Now, listening to Cass's low, reassuring snores, Maggie Campion, who was close on her forty-fifth birthday, knew she'd had the nightmare again because of association of ideas and proximity to the place where the martyrs had suffered. She snuggled against Cass's broad back, remembering she was safely in bed in a small inn on the outskirts of Wigtown. The inn had only two guest rooms. She and Cass were the only guests that night. Mrs McClure, the snippet of a landlady with rimless eye-glasses and blue-rinsed shingle, had informed Maggie that she let rooms only to visitors if she liked the look of them.

'I have no use for the ordinary tourist,' she said, briskly wiping imaginary dust or fluff off the bosom of her dusky-pink silk blouse. 'If I don't take to folk, Mrs Campion, I just cast a cold eye and say we're expecting very important people and we're bookit up. That soon settles their hash, I can assure you.'

Maggie wondered what Mrs McClure would have said to Bloody Clavers if he had come knocking on her door. Would he have withered beneath her cold eye? Or would Bloody Clavers have recognised Mrs McClure as somebody with Covenanting sympathies and finger-pointed her for a martyr's grave on the moors? Suddenly Stevenson's poem, long forgotten, came into her mind. And crowding upon it came a line from another poem she hadn't thought of since childhood either: 'Love swells like the Solway but ebbs like its tide.' She could not remember who wrote it, though she must have known his name once. Was it Scott? She did not think it was Stevenson, but maybe it was.

It was extraordinary, she had not thought of either of these poems since she was – what? Eleven or twelve probably. It was about then that she had discovered the dream world of the movies, and because she started to go to the cinema at least three times a week her reading, except for school text-books, suffered. Her mother nagged encouragingly that she ought to read the novels of J.M. Barrie and D.K. Broster if she could find them in the public library, and while she did her household chores Rosemary Maitland kept on reciting the Scottish ballads aloud. But the Second World War and names like Okinawa and Guadalcanal and Rommel and Tobruk were more exciting than Bonnie Prince Charlie and Sentimental Tommy. And then, when Maggie graduated to high school and became aware of the joys of boys, of necking in their cars, of dancing cheek to cheek, and cheering them on in football matches, neither the war nor her text-books received much of her attention, and every now and then her father took time off from his war work to lecture her about lost opportunities and the struggle ahead being a dark one and full of pitfalls.

In all this time she had the nightmare about Solway sands only about three times a year; she was so occupied with boys that she did not have time to dream about anything else. And when the great pash of her life, Cass Campion, star football player and four years her senior, came home from the army of occupation in Germany and proposed, she never had the nightmare again.

She and Cass were married in 1949. They had lived ever since above his family's grocery store in Valley Springs, where they had reared their five children. His father had died when Cass was abroad, so he took over the store from his mother who was only too happy to go and live with her sister Nellie in Southern Illinois.

Now, a year late, Maggie and Cass were celebrating their silver wedding by a three months tour of Europe. Cass had wanted to come last year, immediately after their anniversary party for family and friends; but Maggie, making one excuse after another, had got the trip postponed until, at last, she could not cajole Cass into putting it off any longer. Cass wanted to see the glories of Italy before he was too old to enjoy them. He had visited Rome for a week when he was on furlough from the army in Bavaria, but it was not enough; he hankered to go to the village in Sicily from which his grandfather, Salvatore Campiopamoni had emigrated to the States in 1907. Although his name had been Americanised, Cass was still very aware of being an Italian. Like Rosemary Maitland, he was ancestor-conscious. He wanted to visit Sicily to find unknown relatives who would be able to tell him about Salvatore Campiopamoni's antecedents.

On the other hand, Maggie had no feelings now, whatever she may have had as a child, for ancestor worship. She did not want to leave Valley Springs and her family, except maybe once a year for a short visit to Aunt Nellie, who was rich and had no other close kin. Maggie was enveloped in her family. Genevieve and Julie were engaged, and Maggie wanted to be on hand to steer them safely to their wedding days, which she had planned completely already and was determined to carry out without outside help or interference. Two of their three sons were married, but so far there was only one grandchild: Georgie-Cass, a bright little boy called after both grandfathers. He was three years old. He visited Maggie and Cass every day and dominated their lives. Maggie did not want to leave him even for three months; she felt the time they spent in Europe would include an important period in Georgie-Cass's development, and she wanted to stay at home and participate.

In the long run, Cass took matters into his own hands. Without telling her, he arranged plane flights and everything else for a three months tour of Scotland, England, France, Italy, Greece and Spain. Then he told her they were leaving next day and she had exactly five hours to pack.

Maggie was still seething with outrage at his duplicity when they landed at Prestwick airport, and while they drove to Glasgow in the car Cass had hired she hardly drew breath once. At last, when he could get in a quiet word, Cass said: 'Your Ma always wanted to come to Scotland, Maggie. It was one of her greatest ambitions but she never achieved it. So please, honey, even if you don't want it for your own sake, can't you try and sit back and enjoy it for hers? She'd be mighty happy in her grave if she knew where you are now.'

'You must remember, dear, that I'm my father's daughter, too,' Maggie said. 'He was never as keen on the Scottish links as Ma was.'

She said no more. She settled down to enjoy the beauties of the Highlands and, like a good American matron who'd tell her family all about it when she got back home, she took turn-about with Cass in photographing each other on the banks of the Caledonian Canal, in Inverness, on the moor of Culloden and against the sparkling granite of Aberdeen's fine buildings. They spent a happy week in Edinburgh, and in Holyrood Palace Maggie remembered a film about Mary, Queen of Scots that she had seen when she was a child. Katherine Hepburn had played the Queen. Maggie suddenly became nostalgic remembering dear Fredric March, one of her favourite stars, wearing a kilt in the part of Bothwell.

This nostalgia grew as they drove south-west towards Galloway. They were heading for Port Logan on the western coast of Wigtownshire because a Texan encountered in Edinburgh had told Cass about the fish pond built in the rocks there: a pond to which fish came in from the sea and became so tame they could be fed by hand. 'It sure is worth seeing,' the gentleman from Texas said enthusiastically. 'I wouldn't have believed it if I hadn't seen it. Great cod come to the edge of the pool and open their mouths wide and wait for you to pop a sandwich into them. I fed one, a great whoppin' brute with scales bigger 'n my thumb nail and cold ugly eyes. I tell you, buddy, it was an experience – but an experience I never wanna repeat. I let the guide feed it the rest of the sandwiches.'

Before they reached Newton Stewart it began to rain. It rained so heavily that Cass said there was no point in driving through it, and they looked for a hotel. All the hotels were full, however. The manager of the last they tried suggested that perhaps a friend of his, Mrs McClure, who had an inn a couple of miles on this side of Wigtown, might be able to put them up. He made a phone call; Mrs McClure said she would have a room waiting for them.

As they drove to Mrs McClure's Maggie's memories of childhood took such a strong hold on her that she started to think of herself as Maggie Maitland again. She had not been conscious of this last night, but now, after that fearsome girlhood nightmare, she realised how weird it was. A feeling of dread and great desolation came sweeping through her. Maggie Campion whimpered and clutched Cass, burying her face against his shoulder in an attempt to fend off the uncanny foreboding that was pressing upon her.

*

Mrs McClure joined her for a cup of coffee after breakfast. Cass had gone out early for a walk. Today Mrs McClure wore a powder-blue twin set, and her hair looked as though it had just been marcelled. If it were not for her shaven neck Maggie would have suspected that the landlady wore a wig.

'Excuse me for mentioning it, Mrs Campion,' she said, probing with shrewd little eyes. 'I hope you don't mind me asking, but did I hear you give a bit of a skirl through the night? About half-past two this morning?'

Maggie stiffened. 'I guess you did. I – er – cried out. I was ... '

'You would be having a nightmare?' Mrs McClure said. 'I knew it! Bob aye had a nightmare when he slept in that room. Bob was my husband. He's been dead and gone six years, and oh how I miss him! However, that's by the way. Your nightmare now. What was it if I'd be so bold as ask?'

'I dreamt I was being drowned.'

Mrs McClure's eyes sparkled. 'I knew it! I jaloused it! You

would be tied to a stake on the sands and the Solway tide would be gallopin' towards ye?'

Maggie nodded.

'Oh, God alone kens how often my Bob had that dream,' Mrs McClure said. 'Time and time again he'd waken up skirlin' as if the De'il and all his bogies were chasin' helter-skelter after him. Oh, I ken that dream off by heart, he's tellt me about it that often. He was aye dressed as a woman, and tied to another stake a bittie awa' frae him was another woman. And then when the waves were comin' up to their waists an auld wifie wearin' a tall peakit hat like a witch would arise out of the waves and comfort them. And it was then Bob would waken skirlin'.'

Maggie nodded again. She seemed to have lost her voice. She knew she wanted to tell Mrs McClure what obviously she knew already, but she could not find the words.

'The funny thing is,' the landlady said, pouring out more coffee, her pinkie still held out elegantly in the way she had drunk the first cup,' Bob aye averred it was not only the clothes, he even felt like a woman. And I can assure you, Mrs Campion, there was never a more *manly* man than my Robert.'

She sipped her coffee genteelly. 'It was a most uncanny experience he aye said, and one he could never fathom. Of course, Bob was descended from one of the Wigtown Martyrs. I don't suppose you've ever heard tell of them, but they were two women ... '

'But I have,' Maggie cried. 'I'm descended too ... '

'Oh, you poor soul!' Mrs McClure put her hand on her flat chest. 'What an affliction for ye! An affliction and an abomination – that's what it was for my Robert, and I have nae doubt it is for you too. Dear oh dear, I had no idea when you came to my door yesterday that you and my Robert were kin. But I can see it now – ye have the mark of the Margarets upon ye!'

Maggie's stomach turned over and began to churn. She tried to take another drink of coffee, but the cup clattered against her teeth. 'It was the Killing Times,' she whispered. 'I've read so much ... '

'Oh ay, yon were terrible times,' Mrs McClure said. 'And thankful I am that I didn't live in them. Three hundred years ago when your life wasn't worth a docken, for ye never knew when the door would be flung open and the moss troopers would stride in and drag ye out by the scruff o' the neck and – before ye could say Jack Robinson – ye'd be dead. Either with cauld steel in yer belly or by hangin' at a rope's end on a gibbet.'

Mrs McClure resettled her glasses on her nose. 'It was dreadful about these two puir women, the Margarets. They didnie deserve such a fate. No wonder their spirits still haunt us. But as the Bible says, the evil that men do lives after them.'

She took another sip of coffee, pondering. 'Now, was it the Bible? I don't think I'm right. D'you ken, Mrs Campion?'

Maggie shook her head. She had been listening subconsciously to the way Mrs McClure's genteel accent was giving way to the doric that evidently was her natural speech. She clutched at a forgotten school-memory. 'It couldn't be Shakespeare?'

'I have no use for him.' Mrs McClure's eyes glinted frostily, and Maggie wished she had kept her mouth shut. 'We were forced to do his plays at school, but I was never able to take to them. *As You Like It!* Feech! What a lot o' silly blethers! Would ye believe it, Mrs Campion, I was *forced* to play yon simperin' wee besom Titania in an end-of-term school play, and I got belted with the tawse when I said I didnie want to play her. Oh no, I have no use for Mister Shakespeare. The English are welcome to him. Now Rabbie Burns is a different kettle o' fish. *There* was a man who knew and understood everything about human nature and its ills. Ay, Rabbie's the lad for me. Well, as the Bible says – and it must be the Bible – the evil that men do lives after them. This whole town reeks o' the cruelties perpetrated by Bloody Clavers and his troopers. But of course, ye'll not ken that much about them, Mrs Campion, you bein' an American like, and havin' a different kind of history.'

'But I have the same kind of history,' Maggie whispered. 'Some of it, anyway.'

Mrs McClure picked up the coffee tray. 'Ay, so ye have,' she said. 'I suppose we're a' Jock Tamson's bairns in the long run.' She cleared her throat and said briskly: 'You ken that the graves of the martyrs are in the auld kirkyard here? You must go and see them. Ask the sexton – Jimmy McLeish, he's a second cousin o' mine – to show them to you. Be sure and tell him I sent ye.'

'We certainly will, ma'am,' Cass said, coming in at that moment. 'And we're mighty obliged to you for telling us.'

Maggie said nothing. She had never told Cass about the nightmare; there had been no cause, for she had never thought of it once throughout their married life until it had returned this morning in the small hours. She did not know whether her mother had ever told Cass. She and he often used to have long talks, so God knows what intimate things Rosemary might have revealed. If she had, Cass had never mentioned anything to Maggie.

*

While Cass was looking for the sexton, Maggie wandered around the old churchyard, peering at the faint, nearly indecipherable inscriptions on the sunken moss-encrusted headstones.

'You are looking for the Margarets, daughter,' a voice said.

A long pale hand was laid on her arm. It was the old lady who had arisen out of the waves in her nightmare. Maggie opened her mouth to scream, but no sound came. The old lady wore a tall peaked headdress of scarlet, with a long scarlet veil flying from its peak; parts of the veil were fastened at her throat by a great diamond brooch. Her beige silk dress, flecked with gold, swept the ground. She was tall and dignified. Her finely wrinkled face was calm, except for mischievous quirks at the corners of her mouth.

'I am Devorgilla of Galloway,' she said. 'I am a long time dead, but I know who you are and what you want to see.'

She took Maggie's hand. Hers was cold and as brittle as the skeleton of a bird. 'Do not be feared,' she said, and she gave a low laugh. 'I will not harm you. I shall show you the grave of one to whom you are related even though you may not be directly descended from her. Come!'

She led Maggie to the graves of Margaret MacLachlan and Margaret Wilson. As Maggie looked at them, hands clasped over her handbag, not knowing what emotions she was expected to show, aware only of terror and desolation,

Devorgilla lifted one hand in a regal gesture over the graves and said: 'Man's inhumanity to man has made countless thousands mourn ... Do you know the poems of Robert Burns, my daughter?'

Before Maggie could reply, they heard the voices of Cass and the sexton. Devorgilla smiled. 'Do not think it strange that I know the works of Burns, though I lived long centuries before. My body may have turned to dust, but my mind remains as clear as ever it was.' She gave another low laugh. 'I will see you at Sweetheart, daughter,' she said and vanished.

An overwhelming sense of doom and a fervent desire to get away at once from Scotland came over Maggie. She was trembling when Cass and the sexton, Mr McLeish, joined her. Neither appeared to notice her state, and neither said anything about having seen Devorgilla. Mr McLeish, a loquacious drone, talked on long after he had intoned his official spiel about the graves of the martyrs.

Maggie was so full of foreboding that she scarcely heard a word until, suddenly like a pebble plopping in a pool, she heard Mr McLeish say: 'There used to be a monastery in this town. It was built by a lady called Devorgilla in the 13th century. Devorgilla was descended from the auld Scottish kings, and she was the mother o' John Balliol, the king just before Robert the Bruce. Ye can read all this in the history books, of course. I learnt it all at the school, but I've forgotten a lot o' it. It takes me all my time to remember the stories about this auld kirkyard without havin' to bother about a monastery that's disappeared long syne. I have nae doot that Devorgilla was a guid Christian woman. She built a wheen churches. Ye can see the remains o' a big one called Sweetheart Abbey that she built near Dumfries. I've never been there mysel', but I hear tell she's buried there. Maybe if we're interested, ye should pay it a wee visit.'

After they extracted themselves from the clutches of Mr McLeish and he extracted a good-sized tip from Cass, they got into the car. They had driven for about half an hour in silence when Maggie, whose hand had been clenched against her knotted stomach all the time, said: 'I thought we were going to Port Logan?'

'Aren't we?' Cass said.

'No, honey, we're going in the opposite direction.' She pointed to the open map on her lap. 'We're heading for Dumfries. I just realised it.'

'Well, I'll be damned,' Cass said, drawing into the side of the road and stopping the car. 'I knew there was something wrong, but I haven't been able to do anything about it. I feel as if somebody else is driving. I seem to be wrapped in veils and there's a hand on top of mine, manipulating the steering wheel.'

'We'd better turn back,' Maggie said, 'if we're going to get to Port Logan today.'

'Aw hell! Why should we turn back now? We've come this far, we might as well go on and see Dumfries and be done with it. It'll save us doing it tomorrow. We can go to Port Logan tomorrow instead.'

'Have it your own way,' Maggie said. 'You're the driver.'

'I don't think I am,' he said. 'I feel kinda funny.'

Maggie thought she heard a low laugh as they drove on. Neither spoke until they came to Dumfries, and then Cass said: 'We'll go and see Burns's grave first.'

'Okay,' she said.

They saw, in St Michael's churchyard, the grave where Burns was buried in 1796. They saw the grand Mausoleum to which his body was removed in 1815. They went through Burns's house and looked at the things he had been familiar with. They visited the Globe Inn, which had been his drinking 'howff'. Guide book in left hand, forefinger inside marking the place, his other hand supporting the camera slung around his neck, Cass moved from one historic spot to another. Maggie walked beside him, taking in nothing. Her mind was at home, in Valley Springs.

It was not until they came into the High Street and were looking at the statue of Burns that Maggie was jolted back into consciousness of the time and the place. While Cass, the dedicated tourist determined to get his money's worth, was photographing Burns from different angles, Maggie drifted away a short distance to look at a tablet that had caught her attention on a wall. She shivered when she read that it commemorated the place where Devorgilla had built a

Franciscan monastery and that on its altar steps Robert the Bruce had killed the Red Comyn in 1305.

Was there no escape from Devorgilla? Maggie wished they were safely away from Scotland and the bloodstained past. She looked forward to moving into England where, thank God, the Campions had no associations. If there were any ghosts in Italy, it was Cass they would affect, not her.

Hurrying to rejoin him, she thought she saw a scarlet veil floating among the people around the monument.

Back in the car, they had crossed the bridge over the River Nith and had driven nearly two miles before Maggie was able to say: 'Where are we going?'

'Back to Mrs McClure's place, of course.' Cass sounded surprised. 'Where else? We'll go on to Port Logan tomorrow.'

'I won't go back there,' she said. 'I refuse to go back. I couldn't sleep another night there. Stop the car.'

'Now, sweetheart,' Cass protested. 'What's come over you?'

'I don't want to go back to Mrs McClure's. I don't want to go to Port Logan. Turn the car and let's cross the border into England just as fast as we can.'

'But sweetheart ... ' Cass began wheedlingly to sing in his tuneless tenor: 'Sweetheart de-dum ... Sweetheart de-dum-de-dum ... ' All he could remember of a song they used to sing in their teens.

'Don't think you'll get round me,' Maggie said. 'Turn the car.'

'I can't,' he said. 'Somebody else seems to be driving.'

'Go on to Sweetheart,' a low voice said.

Cass's hands tightened on the wheel, but he could not control the vehicle. Maggie's heart sickened at the sight of a signpost *Sweetheart Abbey 4 Miles*. Cass was breathing so heavily she could hear the tubes of his chest whistling. She knew he was as conscious as she of the presence of an unseen third person. Yet when they reached the beautiful 13th century Cistercian ruin, she could not help admiring it despite her fearsome feeling of dread. They sat for a moment, looking at the ruin, then Devorgilla opened the car door for Maggie. 'Welcome to Sweetheart, my children,' she said.

'That's mighty nice of you, ma'am,' Cass said, coming

round the front of the car and holding out his hand. 'Our name's Campion and we come from a small town in Oklahoma, USA.'

'I know all about you, Mr Campion,' Devorgilla said. 'Come, I shall show you around my home. I built it in memory of my husband, John Balliol, who was a great and good man and was the founder of Balliol College at Oxford. You have not visited Oxford yet, Mr Campion, but when you do I want you to be sure and look at Balliol College.'

Maggie dared not look at Cass's face. Instead, she looked at the silver casket Devorgilla was holding in her thin white hands. Seeing her gaze, Devorgilla said: 'This casket contains the heart of my husband. It is buried with me in my coffin.'

'I beg your pardon, ma'am?' Cass said. 'I didn't quite catch what you said.'

'You heard me plainly, Mr Campion.' Devorgilla gave her low laugh. 'Only you do not wish to believe what you heard. Come, I will show you my tomb.'

'Maggie!' Cass gasped, and he gripped her arm. 'Maggie, let's get outa here. Quick!'

'Do not panic, Mr Campion,' Devorgilla said. 'I will do you no harm. I must show Margaret the tomb, for she is descended from the Balliol family. The sight of it will give her a memory that will hearten her in the years to come.'

She led them into the ruins. As they stood at the spot where she is buried, Devorgilla said to Maggie, ' 'Tis a pity, daughter, that we have to meet beside graves, but it is in the Balliol tradition. My son, John, who was king for such a short time, lost his kingdom in a graveyard at Strathcathro, far away from here in Kincardineshire. He was stripped of his crown and regal ornaments and was dressed in a penitent's garb. Then he was forced to kneel and beg for mercy before yon monster, Edward Plantaganet, who called himself the Hammer of the Scots. My poor John, he died in exile.'

The late afternoon sun glinted on the silver casket when they walked beneath the arches of the nave. Devorgilla laid the casket on top of a broken pillar and said softly: 'Rest there a while, sweetheart, until I return for you.'

She held out her hands to Maggie and Cass, saying: 'Come, I will escort you to your carriage. You have seen all of

Sweetheart that you need to see. I hope it will give you strength and comfort, daughter, on the road that lies before you. Remember that death is not the end but the beginning.'

Maggie could see that cold sweat was pouring down Cass's forehead at having his hand held by Devorgilla. His mouth was half open and he was swallowing like a fish with a hook in its gullet. She did not dare look at the bewilderment in his bulging eyes.

They were approaching the car when they heard the barking of dogs and the cries of a shepherd. A flock of sheep ran past, pursued by two collies.

'*Grâce à Dieu!*' Devorgilla exclaimed pettishly. ' 'Tis Donnert Donald. He and his sheep have plagued my existence for centuries. When both of us were alive, his flocks were a great source of income for the Abbey, of course. We had well nigh seven thousand, and we sold their wool to the Flemish trade. If he speaks to you, do not believe a word he says. Forbye being daft, he is but a poor ghost like myself.'

The hands of the lady of Sweetheart Abbey dissolved in theirs. Maggie looked round and saw she had gone. Cass wiped the sweat off his forehead.

'Good afternoon to ye, sir!' the shepherd called to him, ignoring Maggie in the customary Scottish male manner. 'Ye'll be takin' your ease for a wee whilie? Will ye have been lookin' at the Abbey?'

'We certainly have, sir,' Cass said. 'We certainly have. We have seen something today we never expected to see in all our lives.'

'Ye'll be a Yankee?' the shepherd said. 'We get a lot o' them hereabouts. Nice like folk, maist o' them, and very generous.'

'Who was the old girl in the fancy dress?' Cass asked. 'She showed us round the Abbey. Then she was here one minute, and gone the next.'

'I've seen naebody in fancy dress, sir,' the shepherd said. 'As sure as I put up ma hand to the livin' God, I've seen naebody but yer guid selves this afternoon.'

'Well, there was an old lady that looked like a witch in a tall red hat with us a minute ago,' Cass said, looking around as if he hoped to pluck her out of the empty air.

'A red hat, did ye say, sir?' The shepherd laughed. 'Ach,

that would be the auld daft body that's aye moochin' about here, among the ruins. A witch did ye call her? I would call her somethin' else. An auld limmer in a long brown coat and a red tammy? Is that whae ye mean?'

'I guess so,' Cass said.

'Ach, I met her away up the brae. She bides in a wee cottar hoose ahint yon clump o' fir trees. I've kent her all my life, and I'm near seventy. She has never worn anythin' else but yon brown coat. She sometimes changes the tammy for a red sou'wester on wet days. She maun be a great age – gettin' on for ninety or a hunner, I should think. She has aye looked the same to me. Oh, she's an auld limmer, as sure as ma name's Donald Purvis. Aye stirrin' up trouble and frightenin' folk.'

'She sure frightened me,' Cass conceded.

'Ach, she's a harmless enough auld body,' Donald Purvis said. 'Her long tongue's worse nor her bite. She doesnie ken what truth is. She aye carries a wee tin boxie and tells everybody her husband's heart's inside it. Sic blethers! As far as I ken, she's never had a husband and there's never been anythin' in yon tin but an ounce o' tobaccy, and that must ha'e been smoked long years syne.'

Maggie, whose legs had turned to water, got into the car. Donald Purvis took no notice of her; his long red nose was quivering with mingled malice and the Celtic desire-to-please a few inches from Cass's almost snub North American one. Maggie's heart was thudding so heavily she was aware of every beat. She wished Cass would stop speaking to this awful man, who was far too big and solid to be a ghost, and drive them away from this terrifying place. But instead of getting into the car, Cass was moving away to look at some view Donnert Donald was showing him.

She did not know whether she turned on the car radio in a rage, or whether an unseen hand turned it on. Gradually she became aware of ugly elocution-veneered English voices in some programme of current events, and then she leapt to full consciousness when out of them she heard someone announcing:

'Here is an SOS message for Mr and Mrs C.L. Campion of Valley Springs, Oklahoma, USA, who are touring Scotland in a car of which the number is unknown. Would Mr and Mrs

C.L. Campion please telephone the American Embassy in London, telephone number 01-499-9000 about their grandson, Georgie-Cass Campion, aged three, who is dangerously ill. This is the end of ... '

'Cass!' Maggie screamed. She stumbled out of the car. 'Cass! Take me away from here! Take me away!'

He looked at her and waved, then he turned and resumed his conversation with Donnert Donald.

Maggie clung to the car door for support and screamed 'Cass!' again, but her voice seemed to her to be barely above a whisper.

'Your lady-wife seems a wee bit upset, sir,' the shepherd said.

'Yeah, she's had a kinda disturbed afternoon,' Cass said. 'So have I if it comes to that. That old lady in the red hat – is she quite ... ?'

'Ach of course, she's no' all there,' Donnert Donald said. 'Did she tell ye she was a ghost?'

'She certainly did. She frightened the life outa my wife.'

'She's nae mair a ghost than I am. There's no' a balmier auld wife in the whole o' Dumfries. I'm surprised at your wife bein' taken in by her blethers.' Donald wheezed with laughter. 'But ye ken what women are, sir. They're like sheep, a bit chancy. Ye only need to look at them frae the wrong direction and they go into a panic and have hysterics. They need a dog aye at their heels to keep them in check.'

Cass was laughing in man-to-man way at this when, turning round, he saw Maggie lying on the ground beside the car. Running towards her, he just caught a glimpse of a scarlet veil disappearing behind one of the Abbey's arches.

VII

Cleopatra Had Nothing On

I reckon there hadn't been such a sensation in hell since Lady Godiva got her hair shingled. It was stupendous, colossal, gigantic. Just think of all the things Hiram's gonna say about your new picture and you'll have some idea of what it was like, baby. I've seen lots of Reception Committees in my time, but I guess I never seen a Reception Committee like the one that met me when I got off the boat that took me over the Styx.

There was Lucretia Borgia and Doctor Crippen and Mary, Queen of Scots and Bill Shakespeare and – oh, everybody who was anybody in Hell. I always knew I was a pretty important guy, but, gee, I got plenty of proof now. All them folks was big guns, folks who'd plastered themselves all over the historical map. I guess my old mother would of felt mighty proud of me if she'd been there to see. And I dunno what the folks in my home town would of said. They always was jealous of me, anyway.

How do I know they was historical personages?

Say, baby, ain't I directed more historical epics than anybody else in Hollywood? Ain't I a con- con- oh, you know, and if you don't, ask Hiram.

When I came down the gang-plank a guy came forward and said:

'Welcome to our fair country, Mr Von Valdron. Allow me to introduce myself. I'm Benvenuto Cellini, sir, at your service.'

'Howdy, Ben,' I said. 'Mighty glad to know you. I ain't read your book, but I know it by reputation. It's in the drawing-room of every lady in Hollywood and some who ain't ladies.'

'That's swell,' he said. 'Let's hope they read it.'

'Well, they all read some of it,' I said.

They was all pressing around, wanting to shake my hand, but Ben shoved them all back. 'Just a minute, folks,' he said. 'We gotta take Mr Von Valdron's picture first.'

So I posed obligingly and Ben posed beside me. And while we was bein' took he said: 'How about the low-down on your death, Von? I wanta write up an interview with you for the Hellish Hot News.'

'How much?' I said.

He laughed sarcastic. 'You gotta remember you're in Hell now, big boy,' he said. 'Not in Hollywood.'

'Looks pretty much the same to me,' I said.

The picture was took, so Ben got out his notebook.

'How long do you aim to stay here?' he said.

'Stay here?' I said. 'Ain't this Hell? Ain't I here for eternity?'

'You can please yourself,' he said.

Before he could say any more and explain hisself a whole buncha dames came jostlin' around us. Real classy dames. 'Oh, Mr Von Valdron,' they cried. 'Will you give us your autograph?'

Well, I guess I should be used to dames askin' for my autograph, but this bunch sure made me dizzy, baby. I was tickled pink. Honest I was. Here was me, Gus Von Valdron of Great Smoke, Ohio, late of Hollywood, Cal. and all them famous dames was mashin' around me like I was the Great God Pan. Gee, I sure wish the hicks at home could of seen me.

'Do you aim to make any pictures in Hell, Mr Von Valdron?' Cleopatra said.

'Will you give me a leading rôle?' Nell Gwynne said. 'I sure got what the boys want.'

'I always wanted to be a tap-dancer,' Queen Elizabeth said.

'I gotta swell scenario,' Charlie Dickens said.

'Me too,' Lord Byron said.

Well, you know how it is. Before I knew where I was they'd got me taped to make a film in Hell. I always thought I'd get a rest when I died, but them folks didn't aim to give me one. It was kinda selfish of them, I guess, seein' most of them had been dead for centuries and had had a rest.

Ben Cellini, Bill Shakespeare, Tommy Hardy, Willie Thackeray, Charlie Dickens and Sammy Pepys got together on the scenario. They stayed so long in conference that I began to think we'd never get started, so I told Georgie Eliot and Janie Austen and Lottie Brontë to see what they could rustle up together in case the boys couldn't think of nothing. But there wasn't no need for the dames to worry, the boys showed up on time.

'We gotta swell scenario, Mr Von Valdron,' Ben said.

'Stupendous, Mr Von Valdron,' Bill said.

'Colossal, Mr Von Valdron,' Tommy said.

'We're gonna adapt Genesis,' Charlie said.

They all stood back waitin' to see what I'd say. So I said: 'OK boys, go ahead.' But to myself I said, Now, what the hell's Genesis, anyway. I'd a kinda hunch it had somethin' to do with Einstein or one of them guys you hear about when you get culture, but I wished Hiram had been there so's he could of told me.

'We gotta adapt an awful lot, of course,' Bill said. 'It ain't classy enough as it is, so we aim to write in a whole lotta more scenes. Nobody would stand for it the way it is just now. It's too slow.'

'You gotta have action in films nowadays,' Tommy said.

'And we must have comedy-relief,' Charlie said.

'And a bedroom scene,' Sammy said.

'And a mother-love scene,' Bill said. 'I always wanted to write a mother-love scene. Somethin' like what was in *Over The Hill*.'

'How many's in the cast?' I said.

'Five,' Willie said.

'Five!' I said. 'Five!' I near lost my voice. 'This is an epic,' I said. 'Five hundred is nearer it.'

'We can have five hundred if we go far enough,' Ben said.

'Whadja mean, far enough?' I said.

'Well, we begin with Adam and Eve,' Ben said. 'Then we have Cain and Abel, but we can have their children and their grandchildren too if you want them.'

'Adam and Eve!' I said. 'What the devil do we want with them?'

'We can't film Genesis without them,' Willie said.

'But they wore fig-leaves,' I said. 'We can't have that. This is a Von Valdron picture. We gotta spend a lotta money on clothes.'

'But they don't wear fig-leaves all the time,' Sammy said. 'They can wear civilised clothes after they get outa the garden of Eden.'

'I gotta swell hunch for that,' Tommy said.

'OK. You can tell me about it later,' I said. 'What I wanta know is – Are there any character parts?'

'One,' Ben said. 'God.'

'But we can't have that,' I said. 'The censors won't pass the picture. Lookit what they did to *The King of Kings* and *Green Pastures*. And even if Will Hays *did* allow it we got all them hick states to think about. What you can get away with in one state you can't get away with in another.'

'That's O.K. chief,' Ben said. 'There ain't no censorship in Hell.'

All the same I had a hunch that some of them string-necked dames with the flat chests who're always tryin' to prevent folk from gettin' a kick outa life would have somethin' to say about it even in Hell. Because I reckon it's in Hell a lotta them old dames oughta be.

However, I had more to worry about than that. First I had to cast the picture. Gee, baby, I never guessed what I was lettin' myself in for.

Every skirt in Hell wanted to be Eve. We had a whale of a time with them, so I said: 'Let's ask Eve to play the part herself.'

'Reckon it would take a million years to look for the original Eve in the monkey's heaven,' Charlie Darwin said.

Well, time was no object, but I didn't aim to wait all that long. Besides, I didn't like to think what Eve would look like by that time. So I said we better have a ballot. All the dames were agreeable, and when Old Nick said he'd draw the winning-ticket hisself there was a queue at his office a mile long.

Cleopatra won. That suited me OK for Cleo's the kinda dame who looks classy in a figleaf. I was quite lookin' forward to directin' her. But it didn't suit everybody. The British Colony was annoyed; they thought a British actress should o got the part. I heard that old Queen Victoria especially was lettin' off a lotta steam, so I wasn't surprised when she invited me to a cocktail party.

She was all over me when I got there and asked me to sit beside her on a sofa. It wasn't a very wide sofa, so I didn't feel very comfortable. But I couldn't help laughin' at the way the old dame went about it. She didn't get on to the subject right away, but handed me a lotta soft-soap about how nice it was to have an intellectual guy like me in Hell. I'll say it takes them classy English actresses to put over a swell highbrow act, especially as the old dame had a copy of *True Stories* pushed behind the cushion.

'Tell me about Hollywood, Mr Von Valdron,' she said. 'I feel so interested in it. I would like very much to go there.'

'Well, Queen,' I said. 'Why don't you? You can get a pass-out, can't you?'

'Affairs of state, Mr Von Valdron,' she said. 'Affairs of state.'

I drank a cocktail and said nothing. I was watchin' a tall guy with a kilt and a beard. I didn't like the look in what I could see of his eyes as he stood over from the sofa watchin' us.

'I always wanted to be a vamp,' Queen Victoria said. 'But the British public wouldn't stand for it.'

'Though they stood for a helluva lot,' King Neddy said, and he winked at the Jersey Lily.

'We are not amused,' Queen Victoria said. 'And neither we are sure is Mr Von Valdron.' She turned to me and said: 'I'm so interested in the film you're gonna make. May I offer a few suggestions?'

'Sure, Queen,' I said.

'Cleopatra's a very charming woman,' the old dame said. 'But she's hardly the type for Eve. Cleo is a vampire. Eve was the maternal type ... the Eternal Mother – '

'Like you, mamma!' King Neddy said, and he and the Jersey Lily started to laugh.

'We are not amused,' Queen Victoria said.

'OK Toots!' King Neddy said, and he and his sweetie vamoosed pronto. The old dame settled herself more comfortable on the sofa and patted my knee. 'Children are such a responsibility,' she said.

'You've said it, sister,' I said, thinking I'd keep her off the subject of films. But it didn't pan out the way I expected.

'Besides, Cleopatra is a foreigner,' Queen Victoria said. 'She isn't eligible. Isn't there something about a quota or equity or something? Why don't you choose a British actress like they're doin' for the film of my life?'

I drank a cocktail and said nothin'. I was busy watchin' the guy with the kilt. I didn't like the dirty looks he was givin' me.

'Say, Queen,' I said. 'Is that your king?'

'No, Albert's in Heaven,' she said. 'That's only John. Don't mind him.'

All the same I didn't like the look of the guy. So I edged along the sofa a bit. I was beginnin' to feel a bit warm anyway. But the further I got along the more the old dame seemed to expand.

'Must Cleopatra play Eve?' she said, lookin' coy at me.

'Sorry, Queen,' I said. 'All due respect to yourself, but I guess you just don't look the part of Eve. Can you picture yourself wearin' a fig-leaf?'

'But it's not for myself,' she said. 'It's for my great-great-great-great-great grandfather.'

I drank a cocktail and said nothin'. I was tryin' to figger how many cocktails the old dame had drunk.

'That's him over there,' she said, pointin' to a sulky-lookin' young fellow standin' beside the door.

'Now, Queenie!' I said.

'That's King James I,' she said. 'I'm so worried about him. He says that if you don't let him play Eve he'll go to Heaven and join the boys in the angels' choir.'

'Don't worry,' I said. 'Maybe they won't let him in.'

'But he can look quite angelic if he wants to,' she said. 'You must stop him, Mr Von Valdron. To please me. I don't want any of my relations to go to a foreign country. I've had so much trouble on account of that in the past.'

'But your husband?' I said. 'Didn't you tell me he was in Heaven?'

'He's not a relation,' she said.

'I'm sorry, Queen,' I said. 'But I just can't do it.'

'I'm sorry, too,' she said. 'Still, I suppose it can't be helped. Dear James is so un-British anyway. Perhaps we'd be better without him. He's such a bad influence on the younger people.'

I drank a cocktail and said nothin'.

'Are your other parts cast?' Queen Victoria said.

'All except God,' I said. 'I dunno who's gonna play him.'

'What about me?' Queen Victoria said.

I drank three cocktails and said nothin', but the old dame talked all the time.

'I'm only a woman, of course,' she said. 'A poor weak woman. And a woman is only a woman while a rich cigar is a smoke as Mr Kipling said – or was it dear Alfred Tennyson? I must ask him the next time he comes to lunch. But I'm a very important woman, Mr Von Valdron. I'm easily the most important person in Hell. Who, I ask you, has a better right to play God? After all, I *was* God to millions of people, the poor blacks and the heathen Hindoos – the Great White Mother!'

'There ain't no blacks or heathen Hindoos here,' I said. And I drank another cocktail and passed out.

The British Colony was so mad at what they called my insult to the majesty of the British throne that they said they wouldn't have nothin' to do with the film, and they started to make a film for themselves with Queen Victoria as God and King James I as Eve. I wished 'em luck and started to get on with the casting of my own film. But God worried me. It seemed that old Vicky wasn't the only dame who wanted to play the part. Every man, woman and child in Hell wanted the part. So I was mighty glad when Old Nick called me into his office and showed me a letter he'd just got by angel-air-mail.

It said:

'Dear Nick me and some of the gang aim to come and see you next week my rheumatics is hurtin' me somethin' cruel so I reckon I need a change it's too darn cold up here and the blankets the Salvation Army give us ain't none too warm so Jesus is gonna run the show for me so I won't need to worry none about that me and the boys aim to make whoopee and look to you to help us hoping this finds you well as it leaves me except for my rheumatics your old pal God.'

The week just couldn't go past quick enough for me, and on the day the boat was to arrive I was down at the landing-stage in my best suit hours before the time. I was so het-up with excitement that the box of candy I was gonna give God melted and I darned near ruined my suit. But I charged both it and the candy up to the company.

Nick arrived just before the boat did, and he stood beside me while they was tying up. There was a big crowd at the top of the gangway and I tried to pick out which one was God. But they all looked pretty much alike to me. They was all big men with floating robes and halos. However, they all stood back and let a big guy with a sword get the start of them down the gangway.

So this was God! I wondered if I should wave to him. Gee, baby, I was so nervous I didn't know what to do. Can you imagine me being nervous? I grabbed a firm hold on my box of candy and started to press forward. But Nick gotta holda me. 'Steady on,' he said. 'That ain't him.' And he cried: 'Howya, Gabe?'

'Fine, Lucy,' Gabe said. 'How're you yourself?'

'Don't call me Lucy,' Nick said. 'Folk'll think I'm a sissy.'

Another big guy with a golden key in his hand was steppin' down the gangway. He was better dressed than Gabe, so I said: 'Is this him?'

But Nick yelled: 'Howya, Pete, you old son of a sea-cook.'

'Not so good,' Pete said. 'I was kinda sick comin' over.'

'Them oysters you took for lunch,' Gabe said.

A regular swarm of them came down the gangway then, each of them more imposin' and better-dressed than the one afore him. They was all full of themselves. And every time I made up my mind that this was God at last Nick would say it was St Paul or St Andrew or St Simon Staly somethin' or other who stood on top of a pole. I sure was lost among them all. I felt like a kid amongst a crowd of Sunday-school teachers, so I kept a firm grip onto Nick's tail.

'But where's God?' I said when I could get breath.

I thought I heard somebody say 'Here I am,' but I wasn't sure; they was all pressin' so much around me. I never knew there were so many saints in existence. They all seemed mighty glad to see Nick and they was all talkin' to him at once, yellin' out and tryin' to get him to answer their questions. I had an awful job tryin' to make myself heard, so pulled Nick's tail and cried:

'Where's God?'

This time there wasn't no mistake about it. A small voice behind me said: 'Here I am,' and I turned round and saw a little guy with an old wrinkled face, not nearly so well-dressed as the rest and so small that I'd thought when I saw him at first in the crowd that he was one of the sailors.

'Whatya say?' I said.

'I said I was God,' he said.

'Good God!' I said.

'I try to be,' he said. 'Come up to Heaven and see sometime for yourself.'

I was that bowled over I could say nothin' but: 'How about givin' me your autograph, God?'

'OK' God said, and he took my book and wrote somethin' in it. 'A poor thing,' he said. 'And unfortunately, not even it is my own.'

I looked at what he had wrote. The writing was pretty poor on account of him havin' no schoolin' I guess.

It was God this and God that
And God the other thing.
Good God, said God,
Where do I come in?

Two, three days passed before we could get started on the picture, because there was a lotta quarrellin' between St Paul and Ben Cellini. Ben had appointed hisself the picture's press-agent, but St Paul said he should be press-agent because he'd been such a successful press-agent in the past.

I'd of given both of them for Hiram, so I left them to fight it out for themselves and got on with the shootin'. We took one or two scenes between Adam and Eve in the Garden of Eden. Cleopatra sure looked swell in a figleaf, but she didn't seem to think so. She wanted to put a fig-leaf on her breast too, so's she could hide the asp's bite. But Rabelais said there was nothin' about it in the script.

'You should of thought about it sooner,' Rabelais said. 'Why didn't you let the asp bite you somewhere else where it wouldn't show?'

Napoleon was playin' Adam and him and Cleo was at each other's throats all the time. Nap would persist in hoggin' the camera and he was annoyed because he had no place to put his left hand.

'I'd show him where to put it,' Rabelais whispered to Tommy Urquhart. 'Only it's not in the script either.'

The first day we shot God we did the scene where he appeared to Adam and Eve in the garden.

'Now, you understand,' I said. 'You don't show yourself completely. You just shove your head out from behind the tree.'

'Yes, Mr Von Valdron,' God said.

'You don't wanta frighten them too much. see?' I said.

'Yes, Mr Von Valdron,' God said.

'OK' I said. 'Shoot.'

The scene was goin' good, but when it came to God's cue he didn't shove his head out like I'd told him. 'Look here,' I cried, goin' towards the tree, 'You gotta obey the director.' But when I looked he wasn't behind the tree. I couldn't see no sign of him. 'Where is he?' I said. Nobody said nothin', but one of the electricians jerked his head to the you know what.

'Nervousness,' I said.

God was just back and we'd got started to shoot again when Napoleon's English butler came and said it was four o'clock, time for Nap to have his afternoon tea. So we had to sit around while Nap drank his tea and repaired his make-up.

'OK now?' I said.

'Yes, Mr Von Valdron,' they all said.

But we'd only been shootin' for about a quarter of an hour when Cleopatra walked off the set.

'I t'ank I go home,' she said.

'Do you want somebody to come with you?' Rabelais said.

'No, I wanta be alone,' she said.

All the same I said we'd call it a day and I took Cleo home myself.

The next day we was scheduled to shoot the Makin' of the World scene. God was the only actor needed and he was called for nine o'clock, but when I came on the set at ten he wasn't there. I went to his dressing-room, but there was nobody there but Tommy Urquhart reading a back-number of

Film Fun and Rabelais squeezing blackheads out of his face in front of the mirror.

'Where's God?' I said.

'How should I know?' Rabelais said. 'Am I my brother's keeper?'

'This ain't no time for wisecracks,' I said.

'That ain't no wisecrack,' Rabelais said. 'It's in the Bible.'

Round about half-past eleven God arrived. 'Sorry to be late,' he said. 'But my auto got caught in a traffic jam.'

'That's an old one,' I said. 'Cut out the excuses and let's get on with the shootin'.'

'Yes, Mr Von Valdron,' God said.

'What does it say in the script?' I said.

'In the beginning God created heaven and the earth,' Rabelais read.

'Well, you better strip,' I said to God.

'Why?' God said. 'We ain't gonna play poker, are we?'

'You gotta strip,' I said. 'We're gonna shoot the beginning of the world.'

'Why not shoot the people in it and be done with it?' God said.

'Cut out the wisecracks,' I said. 'And strip.'

'Why?' God said.

'Because this is the beginning of the world,' I said. 'And if this is the beginning of the world there can't have been anythin' before so you can't have any clothes. So strip.'

'No,' God said.

When I recovered I said: 'Why not?'

'Because that's not the way it happened at all,' God said.

'Listen,' I said. 'Is it you that's makin' this picture, or is it me?'

'You,' God said.

'Well, strip,' I said.

But he wouldn't strip. No, baby, he was a stubborn old cuss. He walked right off the set and broke his contract. In a way I wasn't sorry to see him go. He was a ham actor. He had no appearance, no voice, no personality; he hadn't got what it takes to make the money come rollin' into the box-offices.

But he left us in a fix. We just had to get on with the shootin' because our scouts told us that the British Colony was pretty near finished makin' their version of Genesis and that old Queen Vicky had made a swell job of bein' God.

Well, you know what the British are, always crowin' about bein' there first and wavin' the Union Jack, so I was determined they wasn't gonna get a chance to do that here. 'Anyhow,' I said. 'No woman's gonna beat Gus Von Valdron.'

So I played God myself. And how I played him! Gee, I reckon God had nothin' on me. It was colossal, stupendous, gigantic. And I sure was annoyed when I woke up at the preview and discovered it was all the result of that supper I had at Clark Gable's.

Cleopatra?

Now, baby, don't get sore. Cleopatra had nothin' on, but Cleopatra had nothin' on you.

VIII

Water Water Wallflower

Water water wallflower,
Growing up so high,
We are all maidens,
We must all die
Except –

The sweet voice of Jessie, one of the two Highland servant girls singing the old children's song, rose into a skirl of shock on the last word as somebody pushed her from behind. The shock turned into pain when, throwing out her hands to save herself, they came against the hot front of the big kitchen range.

'What the devil are you playing at, Meta Fraser?' she cried, turning in a whirl of red-haired fury.

There was nobody behind her. She could hear Meta in the pantry singing 'except Jessie Mathieson. For she's the youngest of us all. And she can dance, and she can sing, and soon she'll show her wedding-ring.'

The sunlight streamed on the flagstones of the big kitchen. Jessie looked around in disbelief. There wasn't even a shadow near her. She could see Meta's back through the open pantry door.

'Look you, what kind of pranks are you at?' Jessie shouted.

Meta turned from the shelves where she was arranging jars of the raspberry jam she and Jessie had helped Miss Christine to make the day before.

'Pranks? I'm not playing any pranks whateffer. I'm putting the jars where Miss Chrissie told me.'

'What do you mean by pushing me?' Jessie said.

'Whateffer are you havering about?' Meta said. 'I haf not been within a mile of you for the last ten minutes.'

'Well, somebody did,' Jessie said. 'I felt two hands on my

back and the next minute I fell flat against the range. See my hands!'

Meta came into the kitchen. 'My goodness, but they do look sore. We'd better get some ointment for them. Oh, Miss Chrissie,' she said as a small elderly woman bustled in with a rustle of long silk skirt and petticoats, 'poor Jessie's gone and burned herself badly.'

Miss Christine McGregor-Bothwell clicked her tongue in a mixture of sympathy and exasperation. 'Really, you lassies! How often have I told you to be careful?'

'But I was, Miss,' Jessie protested. 'It wasn't my fault. Somebody pushed me against the range.'

'It wasn't me, Miss,' Meta cried before their mistress could say anything. 'I was in the pantry sorting out the jam and minding my own business.'

'And since when have you ever minded your own business, Meta Fraser?' Miss Christine said. 'If you didn't push her, who else could? There was nobody here but yourselves. Are you sure you didn't trip, Jessie?'

'No, Miss, I swear to God I was standing there when I felt two hands in the middle of my back and then they gave me such a push I just fell forrit. I could not be saving myself at all.'

'Och, it's your imagination, lassie,' Miss Christine said, rummaging in the corner cupboard for a tin of zinc ointment and some bandages. She laughed: 'If I didn't know you better I'd have said you'd been at the Colonel's bottles!'

'Oh, Miss Chrissie!' Jessie was so scandalised that she almost forgot her burnt hands. 'And me a Rechabite!'

'It's funny,' Meta mused. 'Where were you standing, Jessie?'

'Just fornent the range. See there. About a yard from it.'

'I declare to God,' Meta said in an awe-struck tone. 'That is just where I was standing last night when I felt the hand.'

'What hand?' Miss Christine, who was smearing ointment on Jessie's palms, looked up sharply like a pert little robin.

'I was not meaning to say anything about it whateffer,' Meta said. 'I thought you'd all say I was daft, and I was for keeping it to myself. I thought maybe I *was* daft. It was just before I went to bed last night. Jessie had gone upstairs, and I was standing on my lone there with my candle, wondering if I'd locked up everything, when I felt a hand stroking my shoulder. Oh, dear God, but I did jump! I near jumped the height of myself. But there was nobody there. I stood still for a minute, I couldna move for fright, and then I ran like a scadded cat up the stairs.'

'I knew something had upset ye,' Jessie said. 'Your face was like a sheet when you came into our room, but I was thinking it best not to let out a cheep.'

Miss McGregor-Bothwell looked from one girl to the other. 'Humph!' she muttered. She could not make up her mind whether Jessie had actually sensed Meta's terror or whether she was agreeing with the other maid in order to strengthen her own story.

'Och, it's your imagination,' she said, briskly wrapping bandages round Jessie's hands. 'It was probably one of those big French spiders that touched you, Meta. As for you, Jessie, you must just have lost your balalnce. Come on now, we must hurry or the Colonel 'll be ronnying for his tea.'

*

'It's happened.'

Christine had spoken only about mundane matters while they were having tea, but as soon as her brother had lit his pipe and sat back she made the announcement she'd been suppressing for the past half hour.

The Colonel, a tall thin man of sixty-five, looked up from his book. 'What's happened?'

'I don't know,' Christine said. 'But whatever it is, it's what I've been expecting ever since we took this place. It shows why we haven't been able to get any of the local women to come and work here, and it explains why we're getting it so cheap and why it's stood empty for so long.'

'My dear Kirsty!' the Colonel said. 'You're speaking in riddles.'

'Ach, Rory, you make me sick!' his sister cried. 'And stop calling me Kirsty. You know I loathe it.' She took off her pince-nez, breathed on the glass, rubbed them vigorously with the hem of her lilac silk dress, and placed them firmly again on her stubborn little snub nose. 'Use your imagination, man.

Didn't you smell a rat when the agent hedged so much about giving us information about the château? Didn't you think it peculiar? Didn't you sense there was something wrong with the place?'

'I don't know what you're talking about,' he said.

She told him what had happened in the kitchen. 'Mind you,' she ended, 'I know they're Highland lassies and full of imagination and feyness and superstition, but they've got their heads screwed on the right way for all that. It's not as if they were glaikit bits of craturs, afraid of their own shadows. And they're not liars. I know they felt something. And if it's not a ghost, what is it?'

'How do you know they felt something?' the Colonel said.

'Because I felt it, too. Yesterday.' She sat bolt upright, fastened her pince-nez to the lace on her bosom and looked at him steadily. 'I was in the kitchen on my own when I felt two hands on my back and was given a great push. But I didn't fall against the range, like Jessie.'

The Colonel raised his shaggy grey eyebrows.

'I should 've fallen,' she said. 'But I didn't. It was incredible. My hands came up against a wall. A blank wall.'

'Now really, Chrissie!' He laughed. 'You're as bad as these girls. You don't expect me to believe that, surely?'

'You can believe it or not,' she said. 'I'm simply telling you what happened. I came up against a blank wall. I could feel the wall in the air. It was the only thing that kept me from falling on the range. Yet, as soon as I regained my balance and felt for it, the wall wasn't there. I waved my hands about, but there was nothing there but air.'

*

Colonel and Miss McGregor-Bothwell had seen the empty Château d'Houdelines when they were on holiday in Brittany two months ago. It was small, charming, picturesque and compact, situated about a mile from the village of Houdelines, and although it had a park and gardens it was not encumbered with too much land. They liked the look of it; it appealed especially to Christine, a keen painter in water colours. And, hearing that although it was for sale it might be let for a period, they went to see the agent, M. Berthou, and leased it for two years. Berthou told them it had been built in the early 17th century – which the Colonel, who was interested in architecture, had discovered already while making a tour of inspection for dry rot and other discrepancies – and that it had belonged until about 1870 to the ancient family of D'Ancelot. Just before the Franco-Prussian War the last Count D'Ancelot had sold it. In the past thirty years the house had changed hands several times, and the present owners, rich Americans, had shut it up two years ago.

The McGregor-Bothwells asked the agent to hire a cook, a housemaid and two gardeners locally, and then they went back to Scotland to settle their affairs there. They leased their estate in Perthshire to an Indian Maharajah, complete with most of the staff, and then travelled to France, bringing the two Highland maids and Cunningham, their coachman.

They had been now at the Château d'Houdelines for over a week.

When they arrived they were greeted with apologies from Berthou because he'd not been able to engage all the staff they required from among the local people. He had managed to hire one gardener, but he could get no women from the village willing to do cooking or housework, except old Elaine, who would come daily and do rough housework but who refused to live in. These, with the Poulons, the couple who had lived in the lodge at the main gates for years and who had acted as caretakers, were the best he could do. Madame Poulon was agreeable to come and work occasionally, if badly needed, but she refused adamantly to do any cooking. Miss McGregor-Bothwell drove into the village next day to try to hire another couple of women and an under-gardener, but everywhere she was met with evasive, though effusive excuses, and she'd been forced to come back defeated. On the following two days she extended the scope of her enquiries, but again she was received with the same apologetic curtseys and the same murmured, '*Mais non, madame …* '

At the end of these two days, too, they lost the services of Elaine. This was not altogether as bad as it seemed. The old woman was simple and more trouble than she was worth. She was a thin gangling creature with a cleft palate, and she spoke in such a garbled patois that Christine couldn't understand her; nor did she seem to understand Christine's own excellent French that had been gained in a finishing school in Paris. It made the giving and taking of orders difficult, and their exchanges, especially the old woman's leerings and cacklings while she twisted her face and body into all kinds of contortions, sent the two Highland girls into gales of giggles.

By this time, in the intervals of scouring the neighbourhood for servants, Christine, a good cook, was trying to teach Jessie the rudiments of cookery. Jessie had been the kitchenmaid in Perthshire and was supposed to have gone on as such at Houdelines and learned something from a French cook; so the situation of suddenly finding herself cook elect was too much for her. She gaped and giggled enough at being taught pastry-making without having Elaine there to add to the laughter.

So Elaine was banished to do scrubbing and polishing as far from the kitchen as possible. But this did not work out, as intended, for she suddenly took a fancy to the Colonel – 'She evidently thinks another tall thin drink of water like herself is a twin soul,' Christine said maliciously – and dogged his footsteps. She did not even trouble to make excuses, she would sidle into his study and start polishing whatever shiny surface lay nearest, ogling him and cackling.

'That old girl's off her nut, Chrissie,' he said. 'You must forbid her to come into my study. If she does it again I'll go off my rocker myself.'

But before this could happen, Elaine had an accident. She was scrubbing the kitchen floor when she fell and hurt her head on the edge of the bucket. The two maids were upstairs. Christine, who was studying a cookery book at the window, wondering if she could find any pudding simple enough for Jessie to tackle on her own that evening, heard the crash and whirled round to find the old woman on the floor amidst a pool of greyish water. The old woman's screams and lamentations brought the girls running downstairs, and although Christine was glad of their help in trying to quieten Elaine she was thankful they could not understand her frenzied torrent of words. She could scarcely understand them herself, and all she could really make out were '*les mains ... les mains ...* '

The noise brought the Colonel from his study, where he wa

working on a history of his regiment, a book he'd been writing for the past twenty years. And when they had got the hysterical old woman's head bandaged he ordered Cunningham to take her home in the brougham at once. That was the last they had seen of her, and her last coherent words had been '*les mains ... les mains ...* '

*

I suppose it's a poltergeist,' the Colonel said, and very unwillingly he led the way to the kitchen to make his own investigations. His presence and questions embarrassed the maids. They giggled and contradicted each other and repeated their stories with such variations that the Colonel was on the point of exploding with exasperation when suddenly there was a diversion.

Miss Christine was pushed onto the range.

She was standing with her back to it, one hand holding up her long skirts, the other fiddling with her pince-nez, when she received a violent push in the chest. She couldn't prevent herself from staggering back, but she managed to throw her hands forward so that only her bottom came in contact with the range. There was a smell of smouldering silk.

'That,' she said acidly to her brother, 'was done to give you proof. It was quite unnecessary, as far as I'm concerned.'

The Colonel fetched Cunningham to give himself some masculine support, but although the two men hung around the kitchen for the next hour, while Christine superintended the preparations for dinner, neither they nor any of the women received even the hint of a touch. Before he went back to his study the Colonel told Cunningham to keep his eye on the kitchen from now on.

Cunningham was a big fair randy man of about fifty, with a blond tonsure and a blond moustache and beard that were beginning to grey. He fancied himself as a ladies' man, so he welcomed the excuse to come into the kitchen to chaff the lassies. He needed their company, anyway, in this outlandish country, for he could not make himself understood, even by signs and loud roars that he imagined to be French, by the Poulons or Simon, the surly gardener, and he could not spend all his time talking to the horses while grooming them. Neither

Jessie not Meta was partial to Cunningham. They looked on him as a loud-mouthed Lowlander, and when he appeared in the kitchen next morning they gave him short cuttings.

'Well, I've come to find the ghostie,' Cunningham said, taking up his stance in front of the range.

Jessie sniffed. 'I'm thinking it will take a bigger and braver man than yourself to find anything,' she said. 'My auld granny used to be saying that only a bold man full of innocence was able to grapple with the forces of evil. And innocent you are not, Mr Cunningham, though you may be thinking yourself bold in the wrong way.'

'So ye're a bit pert this mornin', are ye?' Cunningham grinned slyly. 'Better behave yersel', my lady, or ye'll suffer for it. It's a pity ye weren't the mare and hitched to the shafts o' the brougham. I'd soon tickle yer backside with the whip.'

Jessie ignored him; she knew that any retort would lead to further words. And she did her best to ignore him for the rest of the morning, although it was difficult. She and Meta disliked Cunningham and, like all the other servants on the Perthshire estate, they called him 'Fly Bacon' behind his back. They were annoyed because he'd been brought to France with them instead of Tom, the good-looking young under-coachman, whom they were always flirting with.

That day Cunningham stood for hour after hour in front of the range, but nothing ever touched him. It was the same the next few days. Hour after hour, day after day, he took up his stance, but nothing happened. It got on Jessie's nerves, and she complained to Miss Christine. 'I ken he's a terrible fine man and all that,' she said, 'but I'm not for having him in my kitchen any longer. I can't be tholing it.'

'Well, the Colonel ordered him to stand there, Jessie,' her mistress said. 'There's nothing we can do about it until this mystery gets cleared up – if it ever gets cleared.'

Christine spoke to the Colonel, who only laughed and said teasingly: 'Now, Kirsty, you're just being a typical old maid and worrying about these lassies' virtue. They're well able to look after themselves – except where ghosts are concerned.'

Then one rainy afternoon when Jessie's temper was ready to boil over she was pushed violently against Cunningham both of them fell against the stove, and Cunningham took the opportunity to kiss her. She slapped his face.

'I was fair mortified, Miss Christine,' she said. 'I will just not be having those big fat lips of his slobbering all over me. What between him and the ghost I'm not biding here any longer. I'm away for home.'

'But Jessie – '

'I'm sorry, Miss, my mind is made up. And so is Meta's. I was thinking this house was evil as soon as I set foot in it, and now I know. There's a presence.'

*

Christine wired the Maharajah's housekeeper to send two of the other servants as replacements immediately: Margery, a placid middle-aged woman from Peebles, who could be relied upon to do a little cooking as well as her usual duties as parlourmaid, and Beanie Donaldson, a scullery-maid from Aberdeen. It required all her tact and patience to keep Jessie and Meta quiet for the next week, and then she took them by train to Dieppe to meet the other maids. And it took all her ingenuity to keep them from telling Margery and Beanie their tale of horror before she got them safely on the boat – not that Jessie and Meta put off much time with their fellow servants, they were in too big a hurry to scurry aboard with their luggage.

Beanie Donaldson was seventeen, a big sonsy lass with black hair, a high colour, and bold brown eyes. She already had a fine set of false teeth that Miss Christine had got for her when she first came into service. Until she went to Perthshire, Beanie had never been outside of Aberdeen, but she accepted the long journey to France in the same way as she would have accepted a day's outing to Crieff or Pitlochry. She gazed stolidly at everything: at the harbour and ships of Dieppe, at the chattering French families in the train, at the curtseying Breton women as the brougham drove through Houdelines, and at the park and the château. But Margery, usually quiet, kept up a flow of exclamations and observations, expressing exaggerated pleasure or surprise at everything. Christine suspected that this was because of nervousness and the long journey from home, but she thought nothing of it; she knew that Margery would settle down placidly as soon as the wonders of the journey had worn off and that she'd be a good, solid standby.

It was Margery, however, who was pushed first by the ghost. And it was Margery who had hysterics that almost outshone those of old Elaine.

She was alone in the kitchen the forenoon after she arrived. Beanie was in the scullery, peeling potatoes and staring out of the barred window at the stable-yard where Cunningham was polishing some harness. Margery was about to lift a pot of boiling soup off the range when she was pushed against it so that her hands came in contact with the back of the chimney.

Her screams brought Christine running from the small drawing-room where she was painting a water colour of the view from the window. But it was several minutes before Beanie moved from the scullery; by the time she appeared in the doorway Christine had got Margery seated on a chair and was trying to pacify her. Beanie stared bovinely at the weeping woman. 'What's ado wi' her, Miss?' she said. 'I nivir heard siccan a turryvee. Ye'd think the De'il himsel' had sent for her.'

'Get me those smelling salts out of the corner cupboard,' Christine said. 'Quick!'

The smelling salts made little change in Margery's condition, and it was not until Christine and Cunningham, who had run in from the yard, led her into the maids' sitting-room that she stopped screaming. 'I'll never go near that range again,' she said when she had quietened down. 'No, not for a million golden sovereigns. I knew there was something funny about that kitchen as soon as I set foot in it, even if he – ' jerking her head at the coachman – 'hadn't told me what riled the other lassies.'

'Really, Cunningham!' Christine said. 'I told you not to say a word.'

'I'm sorry, Miss, it just slippit out,' he said sheepishly. 'I didnie see any harm in warnin' Margery, her bein' a sensible sort of body. I never thocht – '

'Sensible!' Margery cried. 'I'm sensible enough not to go near that range again, anyway.'

And she remained adamant about that. Christine harangued and pleaded with her, and at last she agreed to remain at Houdelines instead of leaving on the first train for Dieppe, as she'd threatened, but she refused to work in the kitchen any longer. 'I'll do the rest of the house,' she said. 'But Beanie 'll have to do the cooking.'

And so Beanie found herself promoted from scullerymaid to cook: a promotion she accepted with the same stolidity as she accepted everything else. And for several days nothing of an uncanny nature happened, so that Christine was prepared to breathe a sigh of relief, believing that perhaps Beanie's phlegmatic nature had routed the ghost.

Then, one afternoon, Beanie opened the door of the small drawing-room, leaned her plump shoulder against the jamb, and said in a matter-of-fact tone: 'It's been after me, Miss. I was just goin' to put a pan on the range when it shoved me.'

Christine lowered her paint-brush and sighed. 'Well, lassie, what did you do?' she said, wondering which of her other Scottish servants she could send for, knowing well that Jessie and Meta would have spread the tale already and that none of them would come.

'Och, I just pushed back,' Beanie said. 'There was nothin' there ava.'

She started to close the door, saying: 'I'd best get back. That pan o' water 'll be boilin' by this time.'

'Just a minute,' Christine said. 'Tell me: weren't you scared?'

'Scared? And what would I be scared at?' Beanie said. 'There was nothin' there. It would take more than a French ghost to frighten a Donaldson. I thought I'd just let ye ken, Miss, in case ye were worryin'.'

*

'It's high time something was done about it,' the Colonel said. 'I'm tired of having hysterical women about the place. I wish to God they were all built like you and Beanie, but as they're not ... I wonder if a spot of exorcism would do the trick? I don't believe in it, any more than I believe in the poltergeist or ghost or whatever it is; I think it's just giving in to superstitious twaddle, but maybe I'd better see the priest.'

Next day Cunningham was sent with the brougham to fetch he village priest. Père Antoine was in his early thirties, a countryman who looked as though he'd be happier with a gun over his shoulder and wearing gaiters and gamekeeper's cap instead of a cassock and shovel hat. He had pale blue eyes that gazed as if into a great distance, both outwardly and inwardly, and his straw-coloured hair appeared to have been cut by his own hand. But he was not as simple as he looked. The Colonel soon found that he was shrewd and intelligent, and that he knew a great deal about the château and the D'Ancelot family.

'I've read all the existing parish records,' Père Antoine said, 'and as many local histories as I could find. They were a rather fascinating family and, like so many of the old regime, of course, they had all kinds of queer incidents in their history. A D'Ancelot was executed in 1652 for necrophilia and performing Black Masses. Several of them were murdered, and several committed suicide. And some who weren't murdered committed murders. Oddly enough, though, none of them was guillotined during the Terror; I expect they were too astute to get caught. Most of them seem to have had a knack for keeping out of that kind of trouble. I can find no record, for instance, of any of them dying in battle – except one. Charles. He and his brother, Count Alain d'Ancelot were the last known members of the family. They were both in their teens during the Revolution of 1848, and Charles was killed in Paris in the Commune. There's a suggestion in one of the histories that Alain helped to organize his death.

'Alain himself married a beautiful young heiress, Gabrielle Fouquet. By that time the D'Ancelots were very poor and had sold most of their land, except the acres that now go with the château. So I expect he married her for her money. Anyway, after they'd been married about ten years she was drowned in the lake in the park. She and the Count were alone in a rowing boat, and it capsized, and although he saved himself he wasn't able to save her. Her body has never been found. That lake is said to be very deep in places. Evidently her death preyed in the Count's mind, and he brooded about it so much that he couldn't live in the château; he travelled a great deal in Africa and America and the East, and he came back here only for short visits.

'Then in 1869 he sold the château and disappeared. Ther

was a rumour that he'd gone to India to become a Buddhist. But he turned up after a few years and hanged himself in the stable out there. I expect it's his poor ghost that is haunting the place and causing your excellent sister and her maids so much trouble. These strange disturbances have been going on in the kitchen for nearly thirty years now, and they have driven every owner out of the place – very often merely because they couldn't get servants to work here. Some of them were not themselves either very imaginative or sensitive, I fear! The villagers won't come near the place if they can help it. You were able to get Elaine only because she is simple, poor soul. Her neighbours did their utmost to prevent her from taking the job.'

'And now they won't let her come back?' Christine said.

'Exactly, *madame*.' Père Antoine sighed. 'Ah well, let us to our exorcism. Perhaps we can give the poor Count's lonely spirit the peace he has been unable to find so far.'

The ceremony of the exorcism was watched by Christine and the Colonel with fascination mingled with scepticism, by Cunningham with a sly smile, by Margery, who peered from a safe distance, with nervous twitchings of the mouth, and by Beanie with her usual bovine stolidity.

Afterwards the priest went round the gardens with the Colonel and gave some sound advice about the nurturing of different plants, then he stayed to dinner and entertained them with more stories of the D'Ancelot family. When he left, he said: 'I hope your troubles will be over now.'

*

Next morning Beanie opened the drawing-room door, leaned her shoulder against the jamb, and said as though she were asking how many guests there would be for lunch: 'Miss Chrissie, there's a woman singin' in the chimney. I canna make out the words right, but it's the tune of *Water Water Wallflower*, and they sound like:

> ' – poor Gabby Dansylow,
> She can't dance and she can't sing,
> But she can *still* show her wedding ring.'

Christine rushed to the kitchen and listened. But there was no sound from the chimney. She was on the point of saying 'Are you sure, Beanie?' when a look at the girl's stolid face and solid figure leaning against the large table made her keep her mouth shut. She braced herself, leaned forward and, looking up the chimney, shouted: 'Are you there?'

There was silence.

Christine turned away and gazed pensively out of the window.

'Dear God!' Beanie cried.

A great gust of black smoke had come down the chimney and was filling the room. Another gust followed, and then another ...

'Rory!' Christine shouted, rushing to the door. 'Rory!'

The chimney continued to smoke, and when the Colonel came in there was such a dense cloud in the room that he said: 'Good God, what's going on in here? It's as black as the Earl of Hell's waistcoat.'

'You and your exorcism!' Christine said.

At intervals all that day and the next the chimney went on smoking. The following day Cunningham and Simon, the gardener, swept it. But the day afterwards it smoked worse than ever. A black pall hovered continually beneath the kitchen ceiling, causing Beanie to remark to Margery: 'Whatever else auld Fly Bacon's good at sweepin' he's nae hand wi' a chimney ava.'

And three times during these days Beanie came to the drawing-room to report that she had heard the woman singing in the chimney.

'This 'll never do,' the Colonel said after a week of it. 'That old range is to blame. I've always thought it should have been taken out when we came in. Well, it's never too late, and if we're going to be here a couple of years we might as well have things comfortable for the maids. We'll get a new one – and damn the expense!'

*

When the builders took out the old range they found that bricked up behind it was what in olden days had been a powder closet, a tiny room used by the French aristocrats for the powdering of their wigs. Inside it was a skeleton that was identified as that of a woman aged about thirty. On the left hand was a wedding ring inscribed *Gaby et Alain, 7th Septembre 1855.*

IX

Proud Lady In A Cage

'Here, hen, are ye sleepin'?'

The voice came from among the women skirling and shouting obscenities around the cage, laughing lewdly and gloating over the prisoner's humiliation. It came from a small wizened-faced witch who had joukit past the English guards and was rattling the iron bars. The prisoner stood erect and looked disdainfully over the harridan's head. But she could not ignore her. The leering face grew larger and larger, blotting out the other women; the rattling got louder and the voice shriller, drowning the screams and the jeers.

'I cannie stand here all day till you come out o' yer daydreams, hen. I asked a civil question, and I want a civil answer.'

Bella Logan came back through the whirling currents of centuries until her eyes focused on the woman's face. She shook her head to clear away the nightmare. She was aware again of the intense cold, and her teeth chattered.

'Are ye all right, hen?' the little woman said, peering inquisitively with bird-bright eyes through the glass and thin gilt bars encircling the enquiry desk. Bella recognised her as Mrs Cessford, who lived in a vennel on the banks of the Tweed with her grandson, Zander, a tall skeleton-thin lad with long carroty hair who did odd jobs in the supermarket.

'Ye look as if ye'd seen a ghost, hen.'

'I'm okay,' Bella whispered. 'I think.'

She closed her eyes for a moment and saw again the crowd of harpies and the great iron bars of the cage. Her neck was still raw from the rope that had been around it.

'Is it yer monthly, hen?' Mrs Cessford leered

sympathetically. 'Oh, I ken what it is!'

Bella nodded. It was a lie. But better to pretend to this old bitch than have her blazoning the truth abroad. Not that anybody would believe what had been happening to her. The cold terror of it drooped over her like a frozen shroud.

'I was wantin' the shredded wheat, hen,' Mrs Cessford said. 'I've been huntin' everywhere but I cannie find it. Where have they put it? Or are ye no' sellin' such simple things as shredded wheat in this braw new place? I cannie see why ye needed to move. The auld store in the Wool Market was guid enough for me and folk like me. I don't think I'll ever get used to this great barn o' a place.'

Bella held her throat with one hand as she directed Mrs Cessford to Aisle Seven where the cereals and their assorted companions were shelved. 'Ta, hen!' Mrs Cessford leered and set off, her shopping bag and the supermarket's wire-basket slapping against her spindly shanks on either side. 'You watch that period now, and I'll dance at yer weddin'.'

Bella shivered. The enquiry desk that stood on a raised dais in the middle of the new supermarket had felt like a refrigerator ever since she set foot in it this morning, just before the store opened for the first time. She was in the cash desk of the old store, and while this new building near the railway station was going up Mr. Stott, the manager, had offered her promotion, asking her to take charge of the enquiry desk the owners thought necessary in the new supermarket's vastness. 'Our public is sure to get lost and need a helping hand, Miss Logan,' Mr Stott had simpered. Bella experienced a pleasant glow of satisfaction, thinking of the rise in salary, when she entered it for the first time. But the glow had been dispelled by the sudden unearthly chill that had crept through her limbs. And then *that* had happened.

Despite the darts of icy cold that still pierced every part of her, her neck burned. It was a great red-hot itch. She closed her eyes and massaged it with her fingertips. Then she felt herself being drawn back into the nightmare. Once again the rope was almost choking her. Once again she could see the great backside of the horse she'd been dragged behind, her hands tied at her back. The soldier on the horse had turned round every now and then, laughing and jeering at her as he jerked the rope to make her stumble. And the watching crowd laughed with him, shouting: 'Come 'n' see the prood leddy bein' draggit through the mire! Come 'n' see braw Bella o' Buchan drinkin' in the reek frae the horse's dock!'

They had come to an iron cage suspended by chains from the castle's battlements. The cage was about six feet high and three feet in diameter. It swung a yard and a half above the ground. The rope was taken from her neck, her hands were untied; then two soldiers lifted her and flung her so violently through the door of the cage that she fell, banging her forehead against the bars. She was raising herself on her knees when the door clanged. A herald started a proclamation, but she could hear nothing until he came to the words: ' ... be incarcerated here in his burgh of Berwick-on-Tweed during His Majesty's pleasure. And may God have mercy on her and cause her to repent and plead for the mercy of His Majesty.'

'Never!' she cried, standing straight in the narrow cage and looking disdainfully over the heads of the crowd.

It was then that the harpies had surged forward, surrounding the cage and cackling obscenely.

Bella lifted her handbag from the floor beside her feet and took out a small mirror. Looking to make sure nobody was watching, she held the mirror to her neck. There was a broad red weal around it.

She shivered with cold and dread. Had she fallen asleep, and was it a nightmare? But she knew she hadn't slept. And the livid weal was not out of a dream.

*

Bella Logan was totally lacking in imagination. She knew nothing of history or tradition; she was prosaic and unromantic. She never read a book. Every week she bought two or three women's magazines but never read anything in them except the knitting patterns. She knitted constantly. In the cash desk in the old store she had always had a partly knitted jumper or pullover, scarf or socks on her knee, knitting needles clicking quickly between customers. A part-finished magenta cardigan was in the pink-and-fawn striped knitting bag lying at her feet this morning, but she hadn't managed to take it out yet. She never made mistakes with her additions on the cash-register, never dropped a stitch or made miscalculations with her knitting. In the Kelpie, the pub seven miles from Berwick that she visited on Saturday nights with Rod Wishart she chalked the scores of the darts team on the blackboard, and never once had anybody found her making a mistake. She did the mental arithmetic easily, automatically, and was usually talking to somebody while doing it.

Bella was twenty-two. She was an only child, lived with her parents and was dominated by her mother. Mrs Logan, in her turn, was dominated by her mother, Mrs Dickie, a formidable eighty-three-years old. Mrs Dickie's name was Isabella, though she'd always been called Bella. She had christened her daughter Isabella too, but Isa Logan had insisted on being called Isa since she was four years old; she would never, on any account, answer to 'Bella'. Yet when she christened her own daughter Isabella, she decreed that the child was to be called 'Bella' from the start. 'After your granny, dear. You love your granny, don't you? So what could be better than being called after her? We can't have two Isas in the house. It would be a fine how-d'ye-do and cause no end of trouble. So Bella you're going to be, my girl. And like it.'

Bella Logan never protested. She accepted the name as phlegmatically as she accepted everything else. When rude boys at school used to shout, 'Let me rub yer belly, Bella!' she had always tossed her head and sniffed. Once, after he had been to Sicily for ten days holiday, Rod Wishart had said: 'Bella! It means beautiful in Italian. Bella bellissima!'

'So what?' Bella said.

She had been walking out with Rod Wishart for three years. They had never had sexual relations, though often Rod's need had been urgent when they were walking over the golf links in the dark or when they'd been coming home in his firm's car after drinking at the Kelpie. But Bella would never do anything to ease him. 'I'm not going to do it till we're married,' she said. 'I respect myself if you don't, Rod Wishart. My mother would have fifty fits if she knew what you keep trying to do.'

'Well, let's get married then,' he always replied. 'What're we waiting for?'

'I'm not going to get married till I'm twenty-five. I don't see why I should tie myself down.'

'What about me?' he said. 'I can't go on like this. I want us to get settled down and ... and, well, I suppose we should have some bairns ... '

'I don't want to be a mother just yet,' she said primly. 'Besides, you keep saying your firm might shift you to another territory. We'd better wait till that gets settled.'

Rod was the representative for a company that sold agricultural foods and seeds to farmers. He spent most of his life in the open, standing in farmyards talking about the prices of cattle cake, grain and fertilisers. At the week-ends he played full-back for a Berwickshire rugby team. He was twenty-nine, a big dark young man with a ruddy complexion and blue eyes. He went out with the boys several nights a week. Bella's father, owner of a good-going small builder's business, kept saying: 'It's high time you stopped playin' rugger, Rod, and did some tackling in your own back yard.'

Rod always said he'd retire from rugger when he was thirty. 'And then it'll be up to Bella.'

This year he was going to Jugoslavia for a holiday with some of his team-mates. 'It'll be my last fling with the boys, Mr Logan.'

Last year Bella had gone abroad for the first time. She and Rod went to Majorca, but what between Rod's amorousness, brought on by the strong sunshine and the Spanish atmosphere, and the food not agreeing with her finicky stomach, she had not enjoyed herself. This year she was going to be a devil, though, and give abroad another chance: she and Peggy Allardyce, her best friend, were going to Venice for a fortnight in September.

*

Peggy Allardyce, who ran one of the cash-desks, had taken over the enquiry desk while Bella was at lunch. 'My, you've got a fine cosy wee corner here, dear,' she said when her friend returned. 'It's real groovy, and I love it. You're a right lucky-bag, Bell.'

Bella made a face, but she said nothing. She started to shrug out of her cardigan while watching Peggy click-clack on high heels towards the exit. But she had scarcely sat down in the desk before she quickly pulled the cardigan back on. It was chillier here than outside. She picked up her bag of knitting. There were few customers in the supermarket at this hour, and it was hardly likely anybody would stop to ask her anything. As she was counting her stitches somebody placed a deadcold finger on her forehead and pressed it into her skull. The pain and the cold were excruciating. Then the finger moved backwards over her skull and down her spine. As it moved, icy waves swept over the rest of her body. She gasped for breath and huddled her cardigan tighter around her.

The rain was coming down in torrents. She clung to the bars of the cage with hands so frozen she was sure the skin would come off if she let go of the iron. Her palms burned. Her saturated gown clung to her body, encasing her like armour. The cage had been pulled up higher; it hung now about ten feet from the ground. The downpour had driven away most of the crowd who came to gloat, but many women had taken refuge from the deluge in doorways and windows, from whence their gimlet-brimstone eyes probed into her humiliation and their frog-gawped mouths opened to shout insults. Among them were the old witch with the dirty white hair who came every day and the red-headed youth who was always with her. The English sentries still stood around the cage. They were almost as soaked as she was, but every now and then they took turns to escape into an embrasure in the castle walls and sheltered there for a while.

She had been in the cage for seven days and seven nights. She was fed and watered like an animal, but the cage was never mucked out. She thought of what they had done to William Wallace at Smithfield last year. Fine handsome Sir William who had endured such degradation and agony before death mercifully came. She remembered Sir William, after the battle of Stirling Bridge, coming to Methven Castle to discuss his campaign against the English with her father, the old Earl of Fife. She had been but a child in that year 1297 but she had fallen in love a little with the handsome knight. She closed her eyes. A quarter of his tortured, dismembered body had been displayed here in Berwick last year. She wondered if her own head might not grace a spike on Berwick's walls, unless Edward, the so-called Hammer of the Scots, God rot him, considered it important enough to flaunt on London Bridge.

She clasped her hands around her neck and shuddered.

'The braw leddy's pee-ed hersel'!' the white-haired witch shrilled. 'See ye! The grand leddy's water is juist like yours and mine.'

After a time the rain slackened. It turned into a drizzle. She wanted to shake her shoulders to ease away the dress clinging to her back, but she would not do this before the rabble. She was gazing upwards, intent on ignoring all the taunts, when there was a creaking of the chains by which the cage was suspended. It began to come down. Its descent was so uneven that she was forced to grip the bars to steady herself. It was about shoulder-high from the ground when a scullion ran from the castle gate carrying a plate of food. He thrust the plate through the bars and emptied its mess of boiled oatmeal and pieces of half-raw meat onto the floor.

'Eat hearty, my lady!' he jeered before running back to the gate.

A big brosy-faced soldier standing in the embrasure laughed. He fumbled with his crotch and shouted: 'Wouldst like a taste of this meat, lady? Put thy hand through the bars and grasp it.'

She turned her back on him, but this made her face the doorway in which the old witch and the red-haired youth were sheltering. The youth put his hand between his legs and imitated the soldier, shouting lewd remarks.

She had such a convulsion of disgust that her entrails seemed to rush in icy globules up to her throat. A great wave of terror coursed through her. Bella did not know whether she screamed or not. She came back to the present, clutching her throat. Someone was making spine-shuddering scratching noises on the glass of the enquiry desk.

A tall thin gangling youth with greasy carroty hair hanging well below his narrow shoulders was leering at her. 'How ye doin', Miss Logan?' he mouthed. The wisps of his straggly moustache and beard could not hide the blackened stumps between his yellowed teeth. 'Gettin' on all right then?'

'I'm managing quaite well, thankew, Zander,' Bella said, giving him a cold nod.

'Well, ye know where to apply if ye want anythin'.' he

leered. 'If ye get into any trouble, Miss Logan – er, Bella, d'ye mind? – juist you give me a wee shout and I'll be here at the toot.'

'I don't think I am likely to have any trouble, thankew, Zander,' she said through pursed lips. 'I am quaite capable of looking after myself, if I may say so.'

Zander gave her a mock salute and, sidling and squirming, said: 'Well, duty calls! I'd better get crackin', Bella, or I'll have auld Stott on my top. See ya, Bella!' He gave a high screeching giggle and wavered away.

*

Though Bella fought against them, trying not to think of them, the nightmares or hallucinations continued. Every day, at different times, sometimes once, sometimes twice, she would be dragged back by a gigantic ice-cold hand into that iron cage with its smell of excrement, and see again those gloating, pitiless faces revelling in her humiliation. And then, wondering if she could endure another minute of the agony, she would be dragged back as suddenly into the present, and with frozen hands and feet and a cold dread at her heart she would tell herself that probably she was sickening for influenza.

Bella told nobody about these experiences for fear of being laughed at. She felt she should tell her mother, but she was afraid Mrs Logan would whisk her off to the doctor. As it was, Mrs Logan said one lunchtime after the uncanny happenings had been going on for about a week: 'You're off your food, dear. I'm wondering if your new job agrees with you. You're looking kind of peakit.'

Bella assured her mother she was all right, and she forced herself to eat what was put in front of her. Ten days after the supermarket opened, she did something she had never done in her life. On her half-day she went to the Public Library. She was there for three hours, looking at books an assistant librarian kept bringing to her. 'What does little Miss Prim want?' asked another assistant, an auburn-haired girl who had been at school with Bella, though they never acknowledged each other when they met.

'She wants something about the history of Berwick.'

The auburn-haired girl sniffed. 'Can she read? It's the first I've ever heard tell of it.'

At last, after looking through a great many volumes, Bella discovered that Berwick's ancient castle stood once where the railway station was built. Many atrocities had taken place in the castle. One was the hanging from its walls in July 1306 of a cage imprisoning Isabella, the beautiful young Countess of Buchan. This punishment had been ordered by King Edward I of England because the Countess, acting as the representative of her brother, the Earl of Fife, who was Edward's prisoner at the time, had crowned Robert the Bruce as King of Scotland at Scone. The Countess had been kept in this cage for four years, then she had been removed to another prison, and her end was not known.

On her way to meet Peggy Allardyce, Bella tried to imagine what the Countess of Buchan must have felt like after four years of being battered by the elements and the even more merciless crowd, but even with what she had experienced in her own supernatural flights, if indeed they were supernatural, she could not picture what state Isabella of Buchan must have been in by the time she was taken to another prison. Before she reached the café in the Scotsgate where Peggy was waiting, Bella had turned her mind to the dress she would wear at the rugger club dance the following Saturday night.

That evening she considered confiding in her mother, but after a lot of deliberation she decided against it. She knew her mother would either laugh and tell her she was daft, or she would insist on taking her to the doctor. One thing Bella was aware of, however. Every time she experienced the terrors of the cage she had noticed that either old Mrs Cessford or her gangling grandson was in contact with her before or after the happening.

Next morning, fighting against the chill creeping up her legs, she saw with a sense of fatality Mrs Cessford approaching the enquiry desk.

'Can I have a word with ye, hen?' The witch stretched her gap-toothed mouth into an ingratiating smirk.

Bella stopped knitting and said: 'I suppose so. It's what I'm here for, isn't it?'

'Ye'll have heard about my misfortune, hen?' Mrs Cessford said. 'I swear to you, it wasnie ma fault. It was a mistake. I had the money in ma purse. It was juist absentmindedness that made me put the stockings in ma bag instead o' into the wire-basket wi' the other things I was buyin'.'

'I'm sorry,' Bella said. 'I don't know what you're talking about.'

'But ye've seen the paper surely, hen? It was front page news in the *Berwick Advertiser*: "Elderly Widow Accused of Shoplifting in Woolworths." Ye must have seen it.'

'I never read the papers,' Bella said.

'Well, I tell ye it was a mistake. As sure as I put up ma hand to the livin' God. I would never dream o' doin' sic a low-down dirty trick. I tellt the magistrates that, but they wouldnie listen. They juist said: "Fined ten pounds. Next case." Oh, it was sic an affront! I'll never be able to hold up ma head in our neighbourhood again. So that's why I've come to you. I was wonderin', hen, if yer faither – him that's so big with the Toon Cooncil – could maybe help a puir auld widow-body. I ken I'm Labour and he's a Scottish Nationalist, but surely he wouldnie let politics stand between him and helpin' a puir body to get a cooncil hoose.'

'But my father has nothing to do with the Town Council,' Bella said. 'He only does contract work for them occasionally.'

'Oh, but he's got their ears all right. And a word in the right direction is all I want. You speir him for me, will ye, hen?' Mrs Cessford whined.

'I'm sorry,' Bella said. 'I know my father couldn't do it, and I'm not going to ask him.'

'Oh, but ye're a prideful wee madam!' Mrs Cessford's small black eyes blazed. 'Ye wouldnie lift a finger to help a puir auld widdy. It's a pity I asked ye. I should ha'e kent better after the way ye've treated my grandson, him that thinks the world o' ye. I've tellt him often enough that ye're a stinkin' wee hoor and that he should look elsewhere for a guid decent lassie.'

'Your grandson is of no interest to me whatever. Now, will you please go or I'll call the manager?'

'You'll regret this, my braw leddy. You'll live to rue the day ye crossed Mercy Cessford. I've seen ye canoodlin' in the back o' his car wi' yon big fitba' player. Ye may think ye're

lucky to be on the pill, but it'll no' aye work. It's nae mair to
be trusted than the french letters we had when I was young. I
just hope ye get caught, ye wee bitch.'

Bella rose and stepped out of the desk. Mrs Cessford skirled
with spleen and flounced away, shouting: 'Ye'll regret it! Just
mark my words. Ye'll regret it!'

Mouth primmed with disapproval, Bella was settling herself
in her chair again when she felt the icy blast sweeping up from
the floor. She stood and held onto the sides of the desk,
fighting against it ...

*

That night the nightmares followed her home. She went to
bed about midnight, after watching television with her
parents, and fell asleep almost at once.

When she opened her eyes it was pitch dark. A fiendish gale
from the North Sea was howling around her. The cage was
swinging so violently that she had to cling to the bars to steady
herself. Sleet and snow enveloped her. Her tattered filthy
clothes were clamped to her soaking body. Her wet hair was
plastered over her face. She gave great sobbing breaths and
pressed against the bars. High above her were wild screams. A
flock of seagulls was circling the cage, drawn to it by the
stench of excrement and the remains of rotten food.

Then, above the screaming of the seagulls, she heard other
unearthly wails. Three figures in snow-encrusted cloaks that
caused them to stand out in ghostly manner in the darkness
were hovering around the cage. The sentries had taken shelter
in the embrasures of the castle walls, knowing nobody would
try to rescue her on such a wild night.

'Are ye there, Leddy Bella? Are ye there? Ye're no' sleepin',
are ye?'

Mercy Cessford, the witch, pressed her ghastly wizened face
against the bars. Her features had a luminous gleam: the long
nose and the high cheekbones stood out, shining grotesquely,
and a wide black gap showed instead of her nearly toothless
mouth.

'We ha'e brocht ye a visitor, hinny,' she cackled. 'A braw
visitor for a braw leddy that's no sae braw now as she aince
was.'

Isabella shuddered and closed her eyes, trying to blot out the three awesome faces. On one side of the witch was her grandson, the red-haired warlock. On Mistress Cessford's other side was another warlock, a tall man wearing a tall black hat. Amber eyes with a reddish glow burned into her under the frown of his thick black brows.

' 'Tis the Master himself come to visit ye, prood leddy,' the witch said. 'He has come with an offer of freedom.'

'Silence, Mercy,' the warlock cried. 'Let me deal direct with the lady. I do not require your offices of mediation.'

'Isabella of Buchan,' he said. 'I can set you free. Only I, Lucifer, can set you free. But in return I wish your allegiance. Will ye swear to give me that in return for my unlocking this door and taking you speedily from hence? Whither wouldst like to go, madam? To your castle at Methven mayhap, to wallow again in silks and fine raiment, to eat once more fine cooked meats and dainty sweetmeats?'

Isabella unclasped her hands from the bars and put them over her ears, trying to deaden the sibilant voice. A violent gust of wind shook the cage and sent her tumbling to the floor. She lay there with her arms over her head.

'All I need, lady, is your word,' the devil whispered. 'Your promise to be my handmaiden sometimes when I need thy help. I will not be a hard taskmaster. Mayhap I might never seek thy services. All I require is your oath of allegiance.'

'No, no!' Isabella cried, but her words were whisked away by the wind.

The Master laughed and whispered: ' 'Tis a small price to pay for thy freedom, lady.'

'Will ye no' join our coven, Leddy Bella?' cackled the crone.

'Hold your tongue, Mercy,' the devil ordered. Then wheedlingly he whispered: 'A silken dress again, a hot perfumed bath, meat served on a silver platter ... What dost say, Lady Buchan?'

'Go away! Go away!' she screamed. 'Leave me in peace, you foul fiends!'

The devil laughed, then he and his minions began to fly around the cage, flapping their arms and making their cloaks fly out so that they looked like gigantic bats. Bella screamed and screamed ...

*

She awoke in her mother's arms. 'There, there, my wee pet,' Mrs Logan soothed. 'It was just a bad dream.'

'Mammy, Mammy,' Bella sobbed. 'I can't take it any longer.'

And it all poured out. Mrs Logan slept with her for the rest of the night. She would not allow her to go to work. And she accompanied her to the doctor at half-past ten, saying: 'Your granny is of the opinion that it must be your nerves. Maybe the doctor'll prescribe Sanatogen or Wincarnis or something like that.'

Dr Nesbitt gave Bella a thorough examination. At her mother's prompting she told him about having nightmares but did not mention their nature. She admitted that her legs and arms and shoulders ached and that she had unnatural spells of icy coldness.

'There's nothing wrong with your heart and lungs,' Dr Nesbitt said. 'You're as healthy a young woman as I've ever come across. A lassie like you should take more exercise. All that's wrong with you is that your muscles are getting cramped with aye sitting in that confined space. Go for long walks on the golf course or along the banks of the Tweed. Go down to the sands and get the sea breezes into your lungs.'

He gave her a prescription for a tonic and told her to take a week off work.

In that week she had no hallucinations during the days, but every night she had visitations from the demon and his witches. She managed not to waken up screaming, and she contrived to hide it from her mother. Mrs Logan noticed, though, that Bella remained pale and nervous, so she had a word with her husband, who, in turn, had a word with Rod Wishart.

'I suggest,' Mr Logan said, 'that you ask your firm for the new territory they keep promising you, then I think you and our Bella had better put up the banns. The quicker she's away from the climate of Berwick, the happier her mother and me 'll be – even if we are going to miss her.'

As soon as Bella returned to the enquiry desk the happenings started again in daylight. She learned, however, to control them a little, making them fainter and farther off, by rising and opening the door of the desk, and she would cling to this while the emanations from the Middle Ages lasted.

One day she was not quick enough. Her mind was so occupied in counting the stitches of a yellow pullover she had started to knit for Rod that the icy waves of terror had swept up from her ankles to her waist before she started to rise. She was forced to sink back into her seat. She clutched her throat and succumbed to the full blast of the chilling, cruel medieval dread ...

The cage swung high above the crowd, but for once the harpies in the crowd were not looking and jeering at her. Most of them had their backs turned. They were watching two great piles of brushwood and logs. In the centre of each pile was a stake. Sagging in her own filth and wretchedness, beaten by the weather, her clothes hanging in sodden tatters, her hair matted and her skin corroded by wind, rain and dirt, Isabella of Buchan saw the old witch, Mercy Cessford, and her grandson being dragged through the crowd by hefty English soldiers. They were tied to the stakes. The old witch screamed imprecations all the time, but the young warlock was able only to gibber. For once, the crowd was silent. There were no jeers and taunts like those usually directed against the Countess. Some women were weeping. Many must have been thinking' 'There but for the grace of God ... '

A herald proclaimed: 'Hear ye! Hear ye, citizens of Berwick! Whereas the perfidious witch, Mistress Mercy Cessford and her demoralised grandson, the warlock, Zander Cessford, have perpetrated divers cantrips and incantations against the person of His Majesty, King Edward the First of England, Scotland and Wales and the territories beyond, His Majesty has decreed that the said witch and the said warlock shall meet their deaths by burning. And may God have mercy on their souls!'

A sigh of despair rose from the crowd, and there were some half-muffled shouts of protest when fiery torches were thrust into the pyres. Isabella leant her forehead against a cold iron bar and sighed with the crowd. As the first thin smoke came through the brushwood, the old witch looked up at the cage and keened: ' 'Tis thy fault, prood Bella, for not doin' what the Master askit. And 'tis thy fault for crownin' the Bruce and bringin' the wrath of King Edward upon us. Ye will regret thy work for centuries to come. My dyin' curse on ye, prood leddy.'

And then the old woman started to scream again. Isabella closed her eyes. The woman's screams turned into throat-strangling retches. The warlock shrieked every few seconds. But gradually the screams became fainter and, finally, ceased. When Isabella opened her eyes she could see nothing but the flames and, above them, great clouds of dark grey and black smoke. Swirls of wind blew the smoke into the cage. Her eyes were stung, her nostrils filled, her throat seared by the salt of strong iron tongues being thrust into them. Isabella started to cough. She clutched her throat and struggled against the billows of smoke …

*

Bella coughed and coughed, her throat scalded by the sour-sweet clutch of wood smoke, until she slumped in a heap in the enquiry desk. She recovered consciousness lying on the floor with her head on a folded rug that had been taken from a pram. The infant in the pram was yelling with temper. Its mother, her back turned to it, was leaning against the pram shoogling it, her mouth half-open, looking at Bella and Mr Stott and the spectators who had gathered.

'I want my mother,' Bella gasped. 'I want – '

'Now now, Miss Logan, take it easy,' Mr Stott murmured in agitation, on his hunkers beside her. 'We'll get you sent home presently. You seem to have had a wee turn, but you'll soon be all right. I would take you home myself, but I can't leave the market. I'll get somebody else to take you in their car in a minute.'

That evening Peggy Allardyce came to see Bella in bed. 'Isn't it awful,' she said when she had finished commiserating with her friend, 'there's been a terrible fire in Percy's Vennel and two folk were burned to death. Auld Mrs Cessford and her grandson Zander. You know him, Bell, don't you? Yon nice laddie with the ginger hair that does odd jobs like filling the shelves and sweeping the floor. Poor soul! What a dreadful death!'

'Yes, isn't it?' Bella said, handing Peggy a knitting pattern. 'D'you like this, Peg? I think it would be smashing in powder blue and white.'

'What's this I hear?' Rod said when Mrs Logan showed him into Bella's bedroom later on. 'I hear you fainted in the street and the Fire Brigade had to be called out. And fancy being brought home in a police car!'

'Funny, aren't you?' Bella said.

'Never mind, dear,' he said. 'Your fainting days are over. I heard this morning that the firm are putting me in charge of their Perth territory, so we'd better get spliced. Okay by you?'

Bella gave a little nod and said: 'I suppose so.'

She made no objection next morning when her mother would not allow her to return to work. She wrote a short note to Mr Stott, giving in her notice.

In the next few weeks, getting ready for her wedding, she did not have time to think about her other-worldly experiences, except one evening when she was approaching the supermarket to meet Peggy and she had a faint emanation of once again standing in the cage with the wind and the witch and the warlocks whirling around her.

But she was aware of much more than a faint emanation on the evening that Rod announced that his firm had got them a house near Perth.

'It's at Methven, about ten miles from Perth,' he said. 'A very nice house I hear, with four bedrooms, a lounge, a kitchen, bathroom and two lavatories, and all the usual. It's built where the ruins of Methven Castle used to stand.'

Bella heard no more. The ice-cold terror swept over her again, and she found herself on the back of a prancing horse while the clash of battle raged all around her. She was watching a tall man in armour on a black horse. He had a circlet of gold on his helmet, and the June sunlight sent sparks from it as he galloped full tilt against some English knights Beyond the battlefield she could see her father's castle of Methven, and she was still gazing toward its towers when the English soldiers surrounded her and took her prisoner.